Praise for Gwyn Cready and her tempting
time-travel novels

ACHING FOR ALWAYS

"Cready builds on her reputation for writing sensuous,
romantic time-travel books. This delightful story is passionate, suspenseful, adventurous, and highly entertaining. Readers will find themselves constantly smiling and
wonder where the time went when they come to the end."

—*Romantic Times* (4½ stars)

"Creative plus delightfully entertaining. . . . The imagina-
tive storytelling leaves the reader totally satisfied."

—SingleTitles

"A fun adventure."

—Fresh Fiction

FLIRTING WITH FOREVER

"Entertaining and lively. . . . A compelling romance that
will leave readers breathless."

—*Publishers Weekly* (starred review)

"Take a wonderful jaunt through time with likable characters and some excellent humor. . . . Thoroughly entertaining."

—*Romantic Times* (4½ stars)

SEDUCING MR. DARCY

**Winner of the 2009 RITA Award for
Best Paranormal Romance**

"Sexy fun."

—*BookPage*

"Hot, adorable, and irresistible. Rip its sexy white shirt off and have your way with it."

—DarcyWars

"Clever and fun."

—*Romantic Times*

TUMBLING THROUGH TIME

"Fun and sexy . . . a reading adventure you don't want to miss."

—Janet Evanovich

"Tackling both time travel and the concept of authorial intent in fresh ways, this romance debut is a joy and its author is worth watching."

—*Publishers Weekly*

Also by Gwyn Cready

Aching for Always
Flirting with Forever
Seducing Mr. Darcy
Tumbling Through Time

Available from Pocket Books

A
Novel
SEDUCTION

GWYN CREADY

POCKET STAR BOOKS
New York London Toronto Sydney New Delhi

Pocket Star Books
A Division of Simon & Schuster, Inc.
1230 Avenue of the Americas
New York, NY 10020

This book is a work of fiction. Names, characters, places, and incidents either are products of the author's imagination or are used fictitiously. Any resemblance to actual events or locales or persons, living or dead, is entirely coincidental.

First Pocket Star Books paperback edition November 2011

POCKET STAR BOOKS and colophon are registered trademarks of Simon & Schuster, Inc.

For information about special discounts for bulk purchases, please contact Simon & Schuster Special Sales at 1-866-506-1949 or business@simonandschuster.com.

The Simon & Schuster Speakers Bureau can bring authors to your live event. For more information or to book an event contact the Simon & Schuster Speakers Bureau at 1-866-248-3049 or visit our website at www.simonspeakers.com.

Cover illustration by Craig White

Manufactured in the United States of America

10 9 8 7 6 5 4 3 2 1

ISBN 978-1-4516-1264-6
ISBN 978-1-4516-1266-0 (ebook)

For Cameron

There is another name that I dare not call you,
but you know what it is. You are the completion of
so many things for me and the beginning
of so many more. I love you.

ACKNOWLEDGMENTS

Special shout-outs to Pam Maifeld, one of my favorite Canadians, for giving me insight into her country's culture, eh?; the folks at St. Paul's, Covent Garden, for quickly scouting up the info I needed; Garen DiBartolomeo for the lowdown on photographers and their equipment; Marie Guerra for being a caring and helpful first reader; Manuel Erviti, my go-to guy and adopted brother, for sharing what it's like to live with diabetes; and Scott Smith of East End Brewing in Pittsburgh, maker of the incomparable Monkey Boy hefeweizen, for showing me what's what in the world of microbrewing, and who described the explosive Bugs Bunny event that takes place in this book.

Thank you to David Chesanow for his fine copyediting and for admiring my Whopper analogy. As always, I am grateful to the wonderful team at Pocket Books, who make my books come to life and reach an audience, especially Ayelet Gruenspecht, Jean Anne Rose, Laura Litwack, and the all-powerful Megan McKeever. The cover is whoopworthy. Thank you. Thanks, as well, to Claudia Cross for keeping this journey both fun and forward moving.

Lester Pyle helps me in ways I can't even begin to enumerate. Love you, pal.

Almost every reader has a book that made them fall in love with romance novels. *A Novel Seduction* was inspired by mine. Thank you, Diana.

Chapter One

Offices of *Vanity Place* magazine, Manhattan

"Cripes, Axel," Kate, the photography editor, said. "You look like you slept in the street."

Sleep? Now, there was a novel prospect. Axel Mackenzie scratched the bristle on his cheek, then stretched his aching neck. Did the floor of an abandoned warehouse count? He was getting too old for this kind of life. What would really hit the spot was an ice-cold Hard Hat beer. For a number of reasons, including the fact that even the most liberal-minded New York City bar didn't open for a good three hours, the idea was a nonstarter. He took a sip of the magazine's thick, strong coffee and made a noncommittal noise.

Kate shook her head, frowned at a missing button on his thoroughly wrinkled shirt and looked down at her own scuffed Nikes. "And it's not exactly like we set the bar real high around here, either." She scanned his proofs as he stuffed his shirt into his jeans. "Lucky for you, you're good."

"Ah, if I had a dollar for every time an editor's said that to me."

"I notice you didn't say 'woman.'"

"I notice you didn't say 'great.'"

Buhl Martin Black, *Vanity Place*'s Humpty Dumpty–esque publisher, burst into view at the far end of the office-lined hallway, gripping the latest issue of his magazine, cheeks puffed in fury. With his body angled toward his destination like some sort of fleshy road sign and his short legs pumping furiously to keep up with his head, he looked like a character in some cartoon.

Axel instinctively tucked himself out of sight against the cubicle wall. On the other hand, Kate, whose desk was directly in the line of fire, clutched the corners like a spectator in one of those fifties atomic bomb films, waiting for the blast.

But Black roared by without a word. He passed his admin, flew into his office and slammed the door.

Two long, terrified beats later, Axel watched as one head after another rose slowly along the wall of cubicles and gazed wordlessly at the others. *Yeesh.* There were many reasons he preferred freelancing to full-time employment, but avoiding intraoffice hissy fits was definitely one of them.

He had worked with Kate for years, and if there was one thing he knew, it was she was always the professional. She buzzed her wheelchair to life and swung it around her desk. "If you don't mind, I think I'd better see what's going on."

"Yeah, yeah, go ahead." She disappeared, and Axel grabbed the current issue of *Vanity Place*. A moment later his phone vibrated. He flipped it open and stood, like the others, to take in the battlefield beyond the low wall.

"Mackenzie here."

"Dammit, where's my money?"

Axel kicked himself for not checking the caller ID before he answered. His buddy Brendan was selling his microbrewery, and Axel wanted it. Unfortunately, Axel's bank account didn't seem nearly as supportive of the idea as Axel.

"C'mon." Axel lowered his voice. "You know I'm good for it. I've sent you almost all of it." Kate wheeled not into Black's office but into the office of Phil Peck, the managing editor and the man most likely to have some insight into his publisher's dark mood. Phil jumped up to close the door behind her.

" 'Almost,' Axel. 'Almost,' " Brendan said. "I got a guy here who's got the whole thing. He's waving a check at me."

Brendan had run the microbrewery in Pittsburgh as a hobby. Sadly, the beer had tasted that way. Now Brendan's ten-year marriage was going bust, and he needed every spare dollar. Axel had liquidated everything he owned to buy his pal out. Microbrewing was his dream.

"C'mon, Brendan. I'm what? Ten short?"

"Ten? Try twenty-three."

Twenty-three? Axel winced. "Look. Give me another month—"

"A week. I'll give you a week."

The sound of something hitting the wall in Black's office—something large and made of glass—blasted the quiet of the office. Then the lever on the publisher's door jiggled, and every head, including Axel's, ducked. But the door remained closed.

"A *week?*" Axel said under his breath. "This is your college roommate here. Gimme two at least."

"Not sure you want to harken back to those days, my friend. You wrecked my car, stiffed me on two months' rent, and I'm still not entirely sure if you made a pass at Tracy the night of our engagement dinner."

"In retrospect, you'll admit, probably not a bad thing—"

"A week, Axel."

The line went dead and so did most of Axel's hopes. But before he could consider next steps, the greatest set of legs he'd ever seen—as familiar to him as his favorite camera—emerged from a conference room. Ellery Sharpe, the owner of the legs, was talking to some overwhelmed junior editor. Axel could tell the poor schmuck was an underling by the Martha Stewart finger she wagged in his direction as she spoke.

The pair parted, and Ellery bent to get a drink at a fountain. Her dark ponytail shone against the softness of the pale blue sweater, picking up the ebony of her pumps, and he found himself entranced with the way her cream-colored fringed wool skirt made it look as if she were wrapped in a Hudson's Bay blanket, a situation in which she had been in his bed on more than one occasion. She straightened, unaware he was watching, and started down an adjacent hallway.

"*Pssst.* Pittsburgh."

She swung around as if she'd been hit with a spitball.

His doctor would have called it an unconscious death wish—which is what he had called a lot of Axel's former habits—but God, he'd forgotten the fire that could blaze in those eyes, the same stunning violet as what had once been his favorite recreational drug.

She marched toward him, looking left and right to see if anyone had overheard. "I told you never to call me that."

"You told me a lot of things. A friendly heads-up: If I were you, I'd consider a long walk to the cafeteria."

Her gaze narrowed. "Why?"

"Black," he said. "Something's up with him. Something bad."

She shrugged, the thick sable hair flipping over her shoulder like the tail of an irritated cat. "Not my problem. I'm heading to the Art Department to look at layouts. Now, if you'll excuse me . . ."

He gave a theatrical bow and waved her on, but after two steps, perhaps feeling the prickle of something she didn't like, she stopped and turned. He dropped his eyes, but it was too late. She'd caught him gazing dreamily at the swaying fringe.

"Hudson's Bay," he explained, heat rushing up his neck.

She rolled her eyes. "Canadians."

With a sigh, he dropped into the chair, returning to the more prosaic parts of his day. A week, Brenden had said, though he might as well have said an hour. Axel had already short-leased his apartment for the month to a visiting couple from Osaka to try to scrape up more cash and was crashing on friends' couches when he could and warehouse floors when he couldn't. His leg bounced anxiously. All he had left to hock was his camera, and he wasn't quite ready for that.

Damn. He would have given his left eye for a smoke, a Seconal and about three quick beers, but he settled for a hard rub through his hair. He picked up the magazine and, as always, flipped immediately to the book review section and scanned the lead story. *Vanity Place* won the award for the most pretentious thing going. He felt like he needed to apologize for dropping out of grad school whenever he read something in it, and that was often no more than the table of contents. But this review—a beautifully constructed Stinger missile aimed at the recent memoir of Bettina Moore, head of Pierrot Enterprises, the world's most successful romance novel publishing company, and the darling of the publishing world— carried razor-edged pomposity about as far as it could go.

> *Moore's estimation of her impact on American culture is as overstated as her dress on the book's cover. If romance novels are, as Moore says, "candy conversation hearts that speak to the soul of a woman," let's hope future instructive aphorisms include "There's more plot in the phone book," "Romance Novels: Publishing's Answer to Farmville" and "Get a Library Card!"*

Axel shook his head. Incisive prose was one of Ellery Sharpe's gifts. But he hated to see her use it as a weapon of mass destruction. What had happened to that starry-eyed twenty-two-year-old who was going to revolutionize journalism with her own biweekly rag; who had convinced him to work for her for free when he had national offers pouring in; and whose fierce pride in her hometown had caused him in a semidrunken glow to nickname her "Pittsburgh"?

Kate wheeled in behind him. "Sorry, Axel. Bit of a firestorm. Where were we? Oh, right, the photo proofs." She pulled up to the monitor and hit PAGE DOWN a couple times. "These are fantastic."

She'd upgraded them from "good." About time. "Right. What's next?"

"Hmmm." She punched up the project list.

"I'm looking for something fast," he said. "Fast and lucrative."

She lifted a brow. "How about a shot of Sasquatch?"

"Will it pay twenty-three grand?"

She snorted. "Sure. If you get him having a beer with Jimmy Hoffa. Seriously, though. I've got a John Irving shoot I'd love you for."

"Is it soon? Is there travel?" He thought of the per diems he could pocket in addition to his fee.

"Yes to both. It was supposed to be next month, but his schedule changed and he wants to do it this week. Ellery's finalizing the date."

Axel's dreams of a quick payoff sputtered like a rapidly deflating balloon. "Ellery's writing the article?"

"She is the head of the literary section here."

"Yeah, um . . ." He gave Kate a polite but regretful shake.

She angled her head. "What? You two don't click?"

He remembered when his relationship with Ellery imploded five years ago, after which he had given up and split for New York, and imagined himself as Sylvester the cat, listening to the *click, click, click* of the bomb Tweety has slipped into his catnip canary. "Oh, no, we definitely click. It's like a freakin' click fest when we're together. We just, um . . . do our best work with others."

"Is that so?"

Kate gave him a piercing look, but he hadn't spent thirty-six years with four older sisters without developing strong self-preservation strategies. He kept his face blank.

Kate went back to her screen. "Well, other than that I've got—"

Black's muffled voice shook the room. "Yes, Phil," he shouted, "I mean *now*! Find her and get her in here!" This was followed by the sound of a phone being slammed into its cradle and perhaps through the desktop.

"I take it," Axel said, "there's a problem."

"Sixth sense of yours?"

"What can I say? Years of experience."

"Yeah, well, Black's not too happy about the article Ellery wrote on Bettina Moore," Katie said.

Axel cast a quick, concerned glance down the corridor, where he'd spotted the legs. Pittsburgh's grand ambitions would be imperiled. Technically, he should have no interest in what happened to her one way or another, but even after all these years he hated to see her get into trouble. "Why not? Does Black's wife love romance novels or something?"

"I don't think Black's wife loves anything about Bettina Moore."

"The article was a little harsh, I suppose, but nothing out of the ordinary for this place." He gave Kate a "Gimme a break" look.

She met his eyes. " 'Publishing's answer to Farmville'?"

"Okay, okay, it was cruel. But you guys don't exactly encourage writers to use kid gloves."

Kate sighed. "Black doesn't see it that way. Not on this one."

So Pittsburgh would get a slap on the wrist. She'd live. Black could be quite vindictive if he chose, but it didn't seem like he had a real beef here.

"Why didn't he quash the article?" Axel had had more than one project end up dumped in the circular file for no better reason that some suit upstairs didn't like the story.

"He was out of town when it was turned in."

Axel scratched his ribs. "You snooze, you lose."

"Only he wasn't snoozing."

Axel stopped. "Oh?"

Kate looked to see if anyone was close and lowered her voice. "Black was supposed to be at a publishing summit in London."

"'Plugged In: The Future of Publishing'?" Everyone who was anyone was supposed to be going to that. An old colleague, Barry, had mentioned it to him when they'd run into each other a few weeks ago.

"Nope, that's later this week. This was a magazine editor summit, but the point is, Phil has it from a very well-placed source that Black was actually spending a long weekend with someone he shouldn't have been."

"And this makes our most reverend publisher suddenly sensitive to condescending writing?" Hell, if that's all it took to get this place to pull its head out of its ass, Axel wished Black had discovered the delights of adultery a long time ago.

"That someone was Bettina Moore."

Axel leapt to his feet to see if he could stop Ellery, only to spot her waving a cheery hello to Phil Peck as she joined him outside Black's office, unaware she was waltzing into certain annihilation. "Oh, *shit*."

"A conversation heart for the ages."

CHAPTER TWO

"Well, actually, yes." Ellery allowed an ironic smile to rise at the corner of her mouth and gazed curiously at the shards of what she hoped was imitation eighteenth-century French porcelain scattered across the floor. "I thought parts of it were *quite* funny."

She knew Black shared her wicked sense of humor. In fact, there were even some parts of the article—the line about romantic novels doing for adverbs what Lady Gaga did for hat wear popped to mind—she'd written specifically for him. She leaned forward to give him a broad collegial smile, though why it looked as if he were choking on his tie, she didn't know. She hoped he hadn't taken to ordering the salami breakfast burritos in the cafeteria again.

"You have to admit, you took some cheap shots," Phil said carefully from his perch on the edge of the adjacent visitor's chair.

"Yeah," she said, laughing, "I did. I especially liked 'the literary equivalent of word-search puzzles' line." Her phone vibrated and she stole a quick glance at the screen. A text from Axel? EMERGENCY! TRUST ME ON THIS, it began, and she clicked the phone off automatically. The last time he used that line, she'd ended up with sixteen tubs of something that looked like rabbit pellets and smelled like the floor of a bar stacked in her entry hall for six months. Life with a Canadian had not been easy. They seem to have beer in their blood.

"But it isn't the books themselves," she went on, "it's that woman and the way—"

Phil cleared his throat.

"—she insists on seeing her achievement as something more than having figured out how to build the biggest crap-shoveling machine in the history of publishing."

Phil made an even louder noise and began waving his hand back and forth below the edge of Black's desk.

"It would be like the head of BP writing a book on harnessing the power of the ocean," she said, "or the owner of the Pittsburgh Pirates on squeezing profits out of a sports team. I mean, they have the credentials, but who would want to read it? And, my God, the outfits she wears—"

Black slammed his fist so hard on his desk, Ellery jumped. "I think," he said slowly, "it's time for a little fair balance."

Ellery looked at Phil. He looked as if he'd been laid out sitting up. All he needed was coins over his eyes and a bugler playing "Taps."

"Fair balance?" she repeated.

"Yes," Black said. "I'm curious as to why so many women love those books, aren't you?"

She flicked her eyes to Phil, like a runner looking for a sign, but got nothing but the faint whiff of embalming fluid. This was like some weird, otherworldly experience. Buhl Martin Black wondering why women liked romance novels? The man who could give you the name and theme of every short story that had been published in the *New Yorker* since 1972 and who had cried when John Updike died? "Well, I mean, I guess."

"Good," Black said. "Because I want you to write a piece on it."

"Me?" She felt the world shifting under her feet. "I don't know the slightest thing about them."

His eyes shone like round, hard nuggets of coal. "Really? You seemed to have formed quite a clear opinion."

"But—"

"I want three thousand words," he said. "A real ode to the subject. Why don't we try for the upcoming issue?"

She blinked. They had moved from the absurd to the impossible. "The issue being put to bed next Monday, as in 'one week from today'?"

"That's the one."

Three thousand words? On a topic she neither understood nor could tolerate? "In *Vanity Place*?"

"Are you under the impression, Miss Sharpe, that understanding what makes women tick is somehow beneath our notice? As far as I know, they still make up half our readers, though I am only the publisher, so perhaps I've been misinformed."

This from a man who had nearly drummed her out of the editorial room for once professing a small liking for *Bridget Jones's Diary*? "But—"

"But nothing. I want the article to be in essay form. Your personal journey, discovering the marvelous world of romance novels."

"I—"

"You will be the literary critic who convinces the non-romance-reading public they've been wrong all along. You will be credited with the Great Awakening. You will go down in history as the Pied Piper of Romance."

She supposed it wasn't the best time to remind Black that, at least in the story she read, the people the piper cast his spell over followed him into a river and drowned. She cleared her throat. "You know I was supposed to be doing the John Irving interview."

"Does John Irving have something to do with why women like romance novels?"

She shook her head slowly. "Not as far as I know."

"Then Irving can roll up his wrestling mat and pound salt."

At this, Phil emerged from the dead and hopped to his feet. "We'll make it happen."

CHAPTER THREE

"He said 'an ode,' Phil—an effing ode!" Ellery rubbed her temples and wondered whether a jump from her managing editor's third-story window would be enough to kill her.

"I know it seems like a challenge—"

"A *challenge*! An undercover piece on Colombian drug trafficking would be a challenge. A first-person report on sexual discrimination aboard the Space Station would be a challenge. This is . . ."

"A chance to really show your range?"

"An intellectual impossibility. What the hell was going on in there?"

Phil made a slightly embarrassed cough. "I'm not definitively sure, but a good guess is that Black is bedding Bettina Moore."

"Oh, *crap*." Now her head really started to ring. Why did sex have to get in the way of good writing? "Really? Bettina Moore?" A vision of Jack Sprat and his wife sprang into her head and—thankfully—raced out again. "I can't think of two people less suited for one another."

Peck shrugged.

Eight years of increasingly challenging roles in the magazine world. Two years of strong work as literary editor at *Vanity Place*. Ellery's goal, to run her own literary-themed monthly by age thirty, was within reach, and in fact she knew she was one of two candidates being considered for just such a role with Lark & Ives Publishing, one of Buhl Martin Black's biggest competitors—big in the bottom-line sense, for of course no one could outdo Black in the girth department. Lark & Ives was the most literary-minded magazine publisher around, and all that remained was for them to review each candidate's body of work and get final approval from the board, an effort they said they would finish in a matter of weeks—just long enough for an article on romance novels to sink her helium-fueled dreams like a shot from Cupid's BB gun.

"My reputation's on the line here."

Peck inclined his head sadly toward Black's office. "So might your job."

She weighed her choices: potential unemployment versus a potential job offer. Peck had been a great boss and had taught her a lot. She owed him the truth. She got up, closed the door, and turned to face him. "There's something I should tell you."

He gazed at her over his reading glasses. "You're in line to launch your own magazine at Lark & Ives?" He smiled.

"But—"

"Don't be surprised. Who do you think they called after you interviewed. You'll be great, and you're ready."

"Thank you." His approval meant everything to her. "Who are you up against?"

"Barry Steinberg."

Peck made a quiet whistle. "Tough one."

"Tell me about it."

"But you're better."

"Phil, this article will sink me. John Irving was going to be my blaze of glory."

"I know. It's a bad time to have gotten your foot caught in a clandestine affair."

Getting any part of her body caught in a clandestine affair would have been a nice change of pace, had the affair been hers. Too bad the only spank she'd be getting out of this one was to her professional ego. The whole thing was infuriating. She bit her lip. "I'm not sure I can write that article, Phil—at least, not the way Black wants me to. The last thing I want to do is go down in history as the Pied Piper of Romance."

He nodded. "I know. Write it the best way you can. I'll fight for you."

She hoped she wouldn't be congratulating herself on her impeccable principles in the unemployment line.

CHAPTER FOUR

Bettina answered after the first ring. "Buhl," she said in her pouty British voice, setting his heart to race, "your Wittle Sprout is very unhappy. I hope you have some good news for her."

Bettina had christened herself Wittle Sprout after their first fevered dinner—as she'd said, the natural complement to the delightful giant she'd found nestled in his green boxers after she'd unzipped his trousers during the raspberry flan.

"Yes," he said under his breath, not trusting his locked office door or the disposable cell phone. It was hard keeping a lover happy. Especially one an ocean away. "I've taken care of it."

"Taken care of it? How? Your Wittle Sprout wants to know."

Black switched the phone to his other ear and daubed his forehead. He sometimes wished his Wittle Sprout were more "ho-ho-ho" and less poisonous nightshade.

"She'll be writing an article."

"An *article*? That's not much of a punishment."

Moisture poured down his back like condensation down the side of a Palm Beach gin and tonic. What had she expected? That he'd have Ellery put before a firing squad?

"Yes, an article. For next month's issue."

"On what?"

He could hear the disapproval seeping into her voice. Disapproval would mean no more of that glorious hand wrenching him into a nirvana so profound, it made his thirty-year-old marital bed look like a bowl of off-brand cornflakes. "On romance novels, of course. Their impact on women."

"Oh, for God's sake!" she cried, all horticultural tendencies gone. "She'll eviscerate us!"

"She won't," he said firmly. "She has her marching orders. She doesn't like them, but she knows it's either fall in line or fall out—permanently."

Bettina made a sprouty sniff. "I'm not sure I like it. How will it fix what she's done to me? She was very mean about my memoir."

"By building awareness of the inspiration romance novels bring to women's lives, *Vanity Place* will open the flood gates." He thought of the inspiration those warm, confident fingers had brought him under the table that night, and—like a bear roused from a long winter's hibernation—his pecker slowly stretched to life.

"What are you saying? That every woman will want to get their hands on one?"

"God, I hope so," he said, closing his eyes and remembering. "It would certainly make American men happy."

"Hm."

She was softening, unlike Martin, who would now have to cancel his nine o'clock meeting with the women's health editor or risk another HR complaint.

"The only problem is," Bettina said, "a story like that would help every romance novel publisher."

"You're sixty percent of the market, my dear. It might help every publisher, but you'll be carrying the biggest bag of money to the bank. Just think of what it could do for *Vamp*." He held his breath. *Vamp,* the love story of a vampirette who worked in a Pittsburgh steel mill during the day but danced at night to win the heart of an ancient vampire, had been the biggest book by far ever put out by Pierrot. The book had been a huge crossover hit, drawing in women readers of all ages and reading preferences, and had been sitting atop the best-seller list for months.

"She'll write about *Vamp*?" Bettina said in a small, hopeful voice.

"Of course. Highlight of the story."

"Will there be pictures?"

Black had been thinking more of a puff piece than a photo spread, but what the hell? "You bet."

"And are you absolutely certain she doesn't want to do it?"

"Yes, but you don't need to worry. I'm *making* her."

Bettina made an "Mmm-mmm" of such length and satisfaction, Martin felt his balls begin to tingle.

"Then it sounds *perfect*," she said.

CHAPTER FIVE

Ellery walked into her cube and threw her notebook against the wall, furious. "Shit."

"You okay?" Kate called lightly over the divider.

"If you call writing a story about something you hate okay, then yes," Ellery said, sinking into her chair.

"There's a reason they call it work, right? Say, I didn't know you knew Axel Mackenzie."

Ellery's heart leapt into her throat. "Oh, jeez, what did he tell you? I made him promise he'd never tell anyone—"

"About the threesome?" Axel appeared over Kate's divider, and Ellery winced. She'd thought he had left.

"Blame Brad Pitt, not me," he said. "That man does not know how to keep a secret." He gave her a sympathetic look. "Tough meeting?"

She growled.

"What do you have to write about?" he asked.

She wished she hadn't said anything. "Romance."

"That shouldn't be hard. I'm sure you know a lot about it."

The sound of Kate's laughter floated up from her cube, and Ellery stuck out her tongue so that only Axel could see. She also moved closer to the divider because it was clear he wasn't going to end the conversation and she was sensitive to the fact that Kate would be at a conversational disadvantage if she couldn't see Ellery's face. Unfortunately, Kate could sniff out a story better than any reporter when it came to Ellery's love life, and since she was coming over to dinner, Ellery had better play it cool or the questions would be as thick as gunpowder smoke at the Civil War reenactments Kate participated in. Ellery thought she made a striking war widow, with her black dress, neatly pinned red hair and period-perfect wheelchair.

The faint apple scent of Axel's hair sparked memories that hit Ellery like a wallop. His clothes might be rumpled, but the man himself had always looked and smelled great.

"I have to write an ode to romance novels and get it into the next issue," Ellery said. "It appears our fearless leader is having a little something on the side with Pierrot's Bettina Moore and has decided that romance novels are our new favorite literary genre here at *Vanity Place*."

"Sex does funny things to people," Axel said, the corners of his mouth curving, and Ellery pretended she hadn't heard.

Kate, however, *had* heard, and moved her wheelchair forward and back, eliciting the faint *buzz-buzz* that had become a signal between her and Ellery: "Wake up" if your lids were drooping in a meeting, "Do it" if she caught Ellery gazing at the box of doughnuts, "Woohoo" if the guy from the mailroom with the ass like Colin

Farrell walked by—a sort of private double-exclamation point. Nothing like a demure Civil War widow.

"Romance novels, eh?" Kate shook her head. "We're not in Kansas anymore."

"Or perhaps the problem is we *are* in Kansas."

Ellery's phone chimed, reminding her she had an unread text. She slid the bar automatically and remembered it was from Axel. EMERGENCY! TRUST ME ON THIS. BE SORRY ABOUT MOORE STORY. BUHL BOFFING BETTINA.

She banged her head with her palm and looked at her erstwhile white knight, who shrugged regretfully.

"It could be worse," Kate said.

She gazed at Axel's thick brown locks and ropey arms and thought of those shirtless men on romance covers with their bulging thighs and the way they always seemed to be pressing the heroine into a particularly complicated sexual position. Axel turned toward her, and she jumped. "Worse? How?" she asked, finding her place in the conversation again.

"I thought you were going to get fired," Kate said. "And just so you know, I happened to be quite a romance reader in my younger days."

"So were my sisters," Axel said. "Still are, as a matter of fact."

Axel was the youngest of five children, and the only boy. His sisters had once hung him upside down in a toilet until he promised to carry their books to school on his bike. Ellery wondered if they'd learned that in a romance.

"Romances taught me everything I needed to know about men," Kate said happily.

"Gee, and I thought that was *Lord of the Flies*." Ellery sniffed.

"Ignore your colleague," Axel said to Kate. "She hasn't had a nonliterary book teach her anything since *Dick and Jane*."

Ellery said, "Well, if you're trying to get a handle on the driving male personality trait, Dick would certainly be the place to start."

Axel waved away Ellery's cynicism and returned to Kate. "So, what did romances teach you?"

She fiddled with the accelerator knob on her wheelchair, smiling nostalgically. "First, forget money. Forget looks. Without honor, there's nothing."

Axel nodded appreciatively. *Oh, that's rich,* Ellery thought.

"Second, the only heroine of any worth is one who makes things happen for herself."

"No argument there." Axel tipped his coffee in a toast to Kate and Ellery, ignoring Ellery's rolling eyes. "And?"

"And there's nothing more fun than an unruly hard-on."

Ellery whooped. Kate had always been able to make her laugh. Axel unfolded himself and stood. "On that note, I believe I'll excuse myself."

"No excuses necessary," Kate said, cheeks pink with amusement. "We know all about hero envy."

He pointed to Kate. "Call when you find something, okay?"

"I always do."

And when he'd sauntered off, Kate turned her sights on Ellery like a double-barreled shotgun. "So, what's the poop with you and Axel?"

"Poop?" Ellery said innocently. "No poop here. I'm entirely poop-free."

"So good to hear it. Health Department rules and all. And yet, I'm still getting that funky smell from your side of the divider."

Ellery arched a brow and returned to her chair, effectively blocking Kate's view of her face. Undaunted, Kate revved her wheelchair to life, peeled into the corridor and turned into Ellery's cubicle.

"You're kidding, right?" Ellery said. "I'm facing the most horrific assignment of my life, and you're here looking for details?"

Kate flicked the handbrake and laid her BlackBerry neatly on her lap.

"I'm not saying anything."

"You slept with him?"

Ellery pressed her lips together.

"And exactly how unruly is he?"

"Kate!"

"Cough, sister."

Ellery sighed. "It was a dark chapter that ended right before I came to New York."

Kate chewed her lip. "Dark?"

"Dark."

"Okay, I can see he's a little edgy for you."

"I beg your pardon." Ellery realigned her narrow, hammered Tiffany bangles.

"But he's so damned charming."

Ellery threw up her hands. "Oh, *Christ*. You and everybody else. Of course you think he is. Instead of dependability, he offers charm. Instead of honesty, he offers fun.

Instead of trustworthiness, he offers . . ." She groped for the word.

"Unruly hard-ons?"

"Gah!"

"Not a bad trade."

"It was for me. You know how you reach into a box of Whoppers and you think, *Oh my God, I can't wait to eat this perfect round, crunchy ball,* and then you bite it and you discover it's one of those horrible chewy Whopper mistakes? That was Axel: a chewy Whopper mistake. He failed me when I really needed him."

Kate observed her friend thoughtfully. "You know what you need?"

"What?"

"The opportunity to console yourself for a week with about thirty romance novels."

"I hate you."

"I know."

CHAPTER SIX

Axel hopped into the lift just as the doors were closing and found himself face-to-face with Buhl Martin Black, who twisted his torso like a strand of top-heavy DNA and adjusted something in his trouser pocket.

"Mackenzie." He nodded a greeting.

"Mr. Black."

The last time Axel had an interaction with Black, he'd been shooting an exposé of the lawyers who defend the cigarette industry. He hoped Black had long forgotten the lawsuit for trespassing. And the one for assault and battery. And the room service bill.

"So, what are you working on?" Black asked.

No need to appear anything less than indispensable. "Well, I'm working on the John Irving shoot and—"

"Forget it. It's been canceled."

"Oh."

"Didn't you work with Ellery on that James Frey piece?"

That story had happened years ago, right after things

had gone south between him and Pittsburgh, and it had been done for a magazine other than *Vanity Place*. It had been after Frey's memoir, *A Million Little Pieces,* had come out, but before anyone knew he'd lied about nearly every relevant fact in the book.

"I did," Axel said.

"You thought the approach should be interested skepticism? She wanted to paint him with wings and a halo?"

Christ, what a memory. Black knew the literary landscape as well as he knew the back of the menu at Alain Ducasse. "That's the one." Interested skepticism had prevailed with the editor in charge, and Ellery promptly changed her cell phone number and listed everything Axel had left at her apartment on Craigslist.

"I liked how the piece turned out."

Axel preened. Black had perhaps the industry's finest feel for this sort of thing. Nice of him to remember.

"How well do you know her?"

The question juked Axel so badly, he nearly lost his train of thought. "Ellery? You know, about what you'd expect."

Black gave him an assessing look. "That bad, huh? I believe the two of you used to be an item."

Wow, he *did* know the landscape. "It was pretty bad."

"I can imagine there might have been some clashes."

"Leonidas at Thermopylae, sir."

A bike messenger got on at eight and Black had to step back to give him room. "I'm sorry to hear that, Mackenzie. I was rather hoping you could help me."

"Help you?" Then it struck Axel. "Hang on. Do you mean the romance novel piece?"

The bike guy smirked. Christ, even the messengers were snobs here.

Black said, "Ellery's talked to you about it?"

"Well, I heard her mention it." As she whipped her notebook across her cubicle.

"She's excited about the assignment?"

"I imagine she is."

"You're not a very good liar, Mackenzie."

"Certainly explains why the poker invitations keep rolling in."

Black chuckled. "Well, I'm going to need a good photographer on the assignment."

"I really don't think that's a good idea." A vision of Leonidas butchered on the battlefield filled his head.

"The story's going to feature *Vamp*."

"*Vamp*?"

Axel's confusion must have been obvious for the messenger snickered. Then he got it. *Vamp*, Bettina Moore's pride and joy. "Oh, of course. That makes sense."

"And there's going to be international stuff as well— you know, all those assembly hall dances and strolls along the seawall at Lyme Regis, that sort of thing. Lots of pictures. Lots of color. Lots of reader engagement."

And lots of money. Hell, the overseas per diems alone would be twice as high. Axel groaned, thinking of the brewery. "I don't know . . ."

"Mackenzie, I need a person who carries some persuasive power with Ellery."

"Wow, you just couldn't have picked a worse person."

"The James Frey piece was great. And I want her to write a piece that really makes romance shine."

Axel held up his palms. "Whoa. That's where I'm going to have to stop you. I have never had and most certainly never will have any effect on what Ellery Sharpe writes. It's like trying to derail a locomotive."

"I thought all that would take is a few pennies."

"But who wants to get close enough to find out? No, I absolutely do not possess such otherworldly powers."

"Unless . . ."

"Unless what?"

The elevator jerked to a stop in the lobby and the door opened, and the messenger hurried out. Like Axel, the knot of employees queued there waited for Black to step forward. But he didn't, and when the man in front—a guy Axel recognized from the production department—made a move to enter, Black glared so hard, the guy stumbled backward and nearly fell.

Black punched the UP button, and when the door closed he said, "Unless you find your persuasive abilities improved by some extra cash."

Axel blinked.

"I'd be willing to double your fee for the story I want."

It was as if the answer to Axel's prayers had just floated to earth and landed on the other side of a buzzing high-voltage substation fence. "Mr. Black, I'd love to help you. I would. But there's absolutely nothing I can guarantee about Ellery Sharpe's writing except that it will be excellent."

"You know what, Mackenzie? I'm willing to take my chances. You sign on for your regular fee, and if the story just happens to be as positive as I'd like, I'll double it."

The answer to his problem just beyond the reach of his fingers. Did he dare?

"I can't promise you anything."

"Understood. But you'll try?"

Axel sighed. "I'll try."

"Remember, I want a story no woman can resist."

Oh, there'd be at least one woman who'd resist it.

CHAPTER SEVEN

**The Andy Warhol Museum, Pittsburgh,
Six Years Earlier**

"How long you two gonna be here?" the guard said, jingling the coins in his pocket and observing them with curiosity.

The museum was closing in ten minutes, and once they got the place to themselves, Axel knew he could nail the six or eight shots Ellery wanted for her article and still have time to hit Mullen's Bar & Grill down the street.

"An hour," Axel replied, unzipping his equipment bag.

"All night," Ellery said firmly.

Axel allowed himself a private smile. Ellery was a ball of fire, and he could think of a lot worse things than basking in her determined glow for the rest of the night, even if it meant giving up Mullen's fine dark ale. He gave the guard an affable shrug. "Gotta listen to the lady."

"That's fine," the man said. "I lock up in fifteen, when the place empties out, and don't come back till eleven. If you leave before then, you'll trip the alarm."

"Okay," she said abstractedly, gazing around the gallery. Axel could tell she was already in that Zen place where writers found their muse—an impressive skill for a twenty-two-year-old. It had taken him years to develop that sort of focus, and even now—he slipped one of those magic uppers into his mouth—he was known to use some help.

"Will we need to let you back in?" Axel said.

"No. I have a key. You'll hear me. The system makes a beep. Say, didn't I see you in the paper?" the guard asked, narrowing his eyes.

"May have." Axel knew what was coming. "I do a lot of photography."

"No, no. I mean you yourself. Didn't you just win a prize or something?"

"I was nominated," he said carefully, pulling out his Canon. "Didn't win."

"It was the *Pulitzer*," Ellery said, and smiled.

"My dad was a steelworker," the guard said. "He said that picture really captured it."

"Thanks." News and editorial offers had been flooding in since the nomination. He knew it would make sense to relocate to New York, and had actually been planning to, but for some reason forward motion on the effort to leave his adopted hometown had stalled. He couldn't say why, but he thought he had an idea.

Ellery swung her long black hair over her shoulder and scanned the room. This was their third job together. The first, the job on which they'd met, had been for an article in the local newspaper. The second had been at her invitation, a story in a regional history magazine. And now, at twenty-two, she was breaking out to launch her own literary and arts paper and had convinced him by sheer force of will to donate his work for her launch issue.

She wasn't classically beautiful, he considered objectively, used as he was to tousled blondes of more classical proportion. But she had ebony hair and bright blue eyes and transformed a pair of jeans into something way more sexy than a string bikini. Occasionally, though, there was a flash of disconcerting wariness on that open face, as if there were a fortress underneath perennially ready to stave off a battalion. It was no doubt the result of losing both parents before she'd finished college. Fortunately, the flashes were rare, and her usual joie de vivre more than made up for it. He watched her eyes shine as she took in each new work of art in the gallery and widen in delight at two circles of blinking neon words. Reflexively, he lifted the camera, clicking off half a dozen frames before she turned.

"This stuff's amazing," she said, unleashing a grin enthusiastic enough to have cracked even Warhol's ironic stare. "I didn't think it would be my style, but the underlying sense of humor in some of this stuff really surprises me. I know just what I'm going to write and exactly how it's going to be laid out."

Axel cocked an impressed brow. "Nice to be in charge of your own paper."

"In charge?" She laughed. "With only me on staff? I don't exactly call that 'in charge.'"

"Hey, don't forget your trusty photographer."

"I'm not in charge of you. First, I'm not even paying you. Second, 'in charge'? Ha! Remember, I'm the one who thought a landscape shot was better."

He grinned. "You can't blame yourself for not knowing as much about photography as I do."

She made a noise reflecting her long suffering and shook her head. Then something caught her eye and her face filled with pleasure. "Oh, Axel! Look!" She hurried toward a smaller room at the end of the main gallery.

He grabbed his bag and caught up with her. He knew what she'd seen. He'd been there before. The high-ceilinged room was filled with silver Mylar balloons the size of king-size pillows that tumbled slowly through the air, fueled by fans attached high on the walls, like some pop-art slumber party. The pillows floated up and down, between guests, twisting and turning, their mirror-like surfaces reflecting the faces of the room's enchanted observers. One could hardly help but inter-act, and a little girl of two or three clapped her hands as one of the balloons floated over her head. "Look, Mama! Look!"

Ellery giggled, a stream of tinkling semiquavers, and a plump, gray-haired woman in a lavender pantsuit and what his sister, Annie, would have called "good Winnipe-gian walking shoes" looked over and smiled.

"Hold on," the little girl's mother said wearily, and pulled the girl's crying baby brother out of a stroller.

Ellery crouched beside the girl and pointed to an on-coming balloon. Axel felt an electric charge go up his arm. Without thinking, he raised the camera to his eye. He didn't know what was going to happen and he hoped the angle was right, but he knew he wanted to capture it. A balloon floated into the corner of the frame, and he made three deliberate clicks of the shutter.

He wheeled around, out of the light, and with the girl's laughter rising behind him he pulled up the shots, shading the screen from the room's lights with his body. In the first, the little girl eyed Ellery nervously. In the second, she grew more intent. In the third, eyes wider, she watched her reach to bop the incoming balloon. Axel let out his breath. Ellery's smile lit the frame, and the joy on the little girl's face was magical. Axel stood transfixed, lost in that instant of shared happiness, but even more so in the breathtaking beauty of Ellery's face.

He had seen this three or four times in his career—the way a camera could transform a subject, bringing out an allure unapparent to the naked eye—but he had never felt the same incapacitating throb of desire and affection upon seeing it. He felt a schoolboy's adolescent crush descend over him like a clap of thunder, and tried to shake it away, but couldn't.

"Axel?"

Ellery touched his arm and he swung around, flushing painfully. He extended the display automatically, hoping she would see it as just another of his shots, not the cause of the bottle rocket that was sending reverberations through his gut. She laughed, too busy swinging the girl now in her arms to notice anything.

"I *love* this place," she said.

"Yeah." He nodded. "Me too."

CHAPTER EIGHT

Offices of *Vanity Place* magazine, Present Day

"The way I'd describe it," Phil Peck said carefully, "is a partnership."

"A partnership?" Ellery felt her irritation grow. She had already begun to plan her strategy on this piece, and she didn't need any upstart partner wasting her time. Partnerships were unwieldy. Partnerships were filled with time-wasting arguments. Partnerships were the reason she had left the world of staff writing and worked hard to become the head of literary criticism. Authoritarianism was efficient.

"According to Black, you and the photographer are to treat this like a photo essay."

"Oh, God," Kate whispered under her breath and closed her eyes.

"A photo essay!" Ellery cried. "You might as well tell a writer 'Just use the stuff the last writer did' or 'The thing that sells books is the cover.' So Black needs the head of literary criticism to write *captions*?"

"First, it's not just captions. The key phrase was 'like a

photo essay.' He's giving this four extra pages, but it's still an essay. Second, Black doesn't need the head of literary criticism to do it. He needs the person who trashed his mistress's memoir to do it. The fact that you're the head of literary criticism here is irrelevant."

"No need to sugarcoat it, Phil. Tell me what you really think."

"In any case, the photographer you'll be working with is great," he said. "I'm sure everything will be fine. And it's going to involve some travel. Black's okayed ten grand of travel money."

"Ten grand of travel money *and* four extra pages?" Kate shook her head. "Jeez, I think the last time that happened here was to cover Lincoln's funeral."

Travel, huh? Ellery had to admit she liked the travel part. Paris, she thought. Or maybe St. Kitts. "Who's the photographer?"

"You may have already worked with him. He's done great stuff for us and every other mag in town. I know you know his work. Axel Mackenzie?"

Kate whooped, and Ellery dropped her head in her hands.

"Oh, yeah," Ellery said. "I know his work. Say, what are the chances of us choosing a different—"

"None. Black's personal choice."

"Super. When do we start?"

CHAPTER NINE

Axel slouched against the front of the *Vanity Place* building, chewing a tasteless oat bar and letting the fresh air sharpen his thinking. Corralling Ellery wasn't easy on the best of days, and this was far from her best. He personally didn't know a thing about romance novels. The closest he'd gotten was claiming to have read one in high school, and that had been mostly to get his college girlfriend, Flip, into the backseat of his '91 Subaru and out of her cutoffs. Unlike Ellery, however, he had nothing against romance novels. He'd gotten enough pleasure from writers like Ian Rankin, Dennis Lehane, Larry Niven and Ray Bradbury to have great appreciation for genre fiction.

He had promised Black he would try to get Ellery to write the article just the way Black wanted it. This presented a few obstacles. Obstacle one: handling Ellery. He figured he had only two weapons in his arsenal that might carry any weight in this battle: his natural charm and a driving desire on her part not to be fired. God, he hoped that driving desire was pretty driving.

Obstacle two: content. Ellery was a writer who could make words sing, but only as long as she was passionate about the topic. He remembered one time she'd picked up an extra assignment for a local newspaper as a way to cover the cost of some camp for her little sister. The topic had been straightforward enough—municipal strategic planning—and the municipal manager had been both loquacious and interesting, rare in a municipal anything. In short, a softball had been lobbed her way, and a writer a tenth as good as she was should have been able to knock it out of the entire strategic planning zone, let alone the ballpark. Not Ellery. He'd come in before dawn one night to find her stringy-haired and pale-faced, staring at the laptop screen like some zoned-out Call of Duty refugee. And the little bit of writing she actually had completed—good God! It sounded like a set of instructions for building an IKEA computer desk without the page-turning plot developments.

She'd been smart to start her own arts paper as early as she did. It was a move that had elevated her quickly in the writing world and kept this glaring inability from being discovered.

Thus, even if she did agree to write the story for Black in the hopes of saving her job, what would she write about? His fingers started itching for a cigarette, even though that, too, had been one of the joys his doctor had insisted he give up.

He wished he could remember the name of that damned romance he'd told Flip he'd read. He could see the cover: a bare-chested Scottish guy with red hair, protecting his sultry heroine with a massively phallic sword.

In Canada, it would have been a guy with a mouth guard holding a hockey stick, but Axel got the general idea. Big man plus big tool equals happy woman. Pretty true to life, actually. In fact, his sister used to say—

Axel smacked his forehead. His sister. She's the one who'd had the book, which is how Axel had known about it in the first place.

He slipped his cell out of his pocket and dialed.

"Annie!" he cried when she answered. "Thank God."

"How's my favorite photographer? By the way, we still haven't gotten the pictures from Christmas and—"

"Hey, do you remember that romance with the red-haired guy on the cover?"

"Interesting segue. You always did have a gift for the fine art of conversation."

"So, do you? I need to know the title."

"You've taken to reading romances?"

"I've taken to recommending them," he said. "I seem to recall you had a special fondness for that one."

" 'Special fondness'? You call locking myself in my bedroom for three days and vowing to get the Forster family coat of arms tattooed on my hip a 'special fondness'? Yes, I remember the book. I'm not likely to forget it, either. No woman who's ever read it has."

Axel chuckled. He loved that his psychotherapist older sister, normally so pensive and deliberate, sounded like a headbanger describing a Slipknot concert when talking about romance novels.

"So it's a good one, eh?"

"Oh, yes," she said, sighing dreamily. "Jemmie is the most romantic hero ever created: tall, brave, handsome and true. He's willing to sacrifice everything to uphold the vow he's made to Cara, and because of it, he's a man torn—between his clan and his heart. Oh, and that red hair . . . !"

Axel thought of his own mop of hair that in certain lights shone a coppery-red—a fact that, combined with his perennial summer sunburn as a child, had earned him the appalling childhood nickname his sisters had bestowed upon him.

"Does your husband know you feel this way?" Axel asked.

"Richard understands his place. He's a great guy and all, but he knows all bets are off if I ever get a crack at Jemmie."

"Good to hear you have your priorities in order. So what is the name of this book again?"

"*Kiltlander*. But what exactly is this sudden interest in romance? Ooh, does it involve a woman? I really liked that Flip. Why don't you date nice girls anymore? You know, you're a great guy. There should be a lot of nice girls interested in you."

Ah, the joy of older sisters. "What? You didn't like the TV reporter?"

"Ugh. Suede boots and shorts? At a Canada Day cookout?"

"The boots were red."

"Maybe you should've dated the boots, then."

"Always appreciate the helpful input."

She laughed. "And the reason for the book?"

Axel sighed. "It involves Ellery."

He could feel the heavy pause and immediately wished

he hadn't said anything. His sisters—Annie, especially—had loved Ellery, and they hadn't liked what happened to Axel after she left.

"Are you and she—"

"No. It's an assignment at *Vanity Place*. It was bound to happen eventually. It's a small town, especially in the magazine biz."

"Axel, I just never understood why the two of you broke up. She used to make you laugh so hard, I thought you'd need heart paddles."

He'd needed heart paddles a lot around Ellery. When she made him laugh, when she outfoxed him in a debate, and when she unhooked the front of her bra and let it slide slowly over her breasts.

"Oh, you know," he said, pushing away the familiar rush of emotion. "Just your typical Axel behavior."

There was a longer pause, and he was glad he and Annie weren't having this conversation in person, where he'd be feeling that appraising gaze on him.

"*Hm*. Well, tell her I said hello. And what's the story about? *Vanity Place* doesn't seem like a romance novel kind of place."

"You can say that again, sister. I am so ready to ditch this town."

"You know I'm all for people chasing their dreams. I just think you need to think about whether you're running after your dream or running away from something."

Oh boy.

"Sorry, I don't have the co-pay to cover this. My new plan kicks in in January. Let's pick this up then."

"I'm just saying—"

"I think I'm losing you." He tapped the phone against the wall and made a grinding noise like an espresso machine.

When he returned the phone to his ear, she was laughing. "Got it," she said.

"So, *Kiltlander*. Do you need a copy?"

"Why?" he asked, eyes cutting to the bookstore across the street. "You gonna send me yours?"

"The one I keep in a shrine in my bookcase? The one that taught me it's possible to have an orgasm with no more than—"

"Ack! I don't care to know how that sentence ends. No brother should have to hear it."

She chuckled again, then sighed. "Oh, Axel, there's so much you need to learn about women. Think you'll try to start something with her?"

"Who? Ellery?"

"Yes."

"For heaven's sake, I'm not going to jump her bones just because it would please you. There are many good reasons to jump her bones, believe me, but pleasing my sister isn't one of—"

"Axel?"

He nearly dropped the phone. He wheeled around and found Ellery's younger sister. "Jill," he cried, throwing his arms around her. "Oh my God. What a surprise!"

He hadn't seen her in years, and she wasn't so little anymore. Getting to spend time with Jill had been one of his favorite things about dating Ellery, and he looked in amazement at Jill's transformation from gangly, braces-wearing young teen who had clashed constantly with her older sister-slash-guardian to a young lady who shared her sister's astonishing beauty.

"My God," he said with honest pride. "You've grown up."

She beamed. "I'm twenty."

"Of course, you are. Jeez."

"So what's with jumping Ellery's bones?"

Axel felt his face burst into spontaneous flames. "I-I-" He could hear Annie's tinny laughter through the phone's earpiece. As so often happened with Axel, he'd reached his limit with sisters.

He held up a finger to Jill and put the phone back to his ear. "Appreciate your help. Gotta run."

"Yeah, have fun with that one, Boner."

Axel stood in front of the cashier, copies of *Kiltlander* and *Vamp* in his hand; the only thing keeping him from Jill's promised interrogation in the adjoining coffee shop was the prospect of a new graphic novel by Marjane Satrapi, which had sent her running to the back of the store. He prayed the book would be so engrossing, she'd forget he was here.

The cashier took *Vamp* and ran it across the scanner. She was blond, twentyish and wore an "X" of red bobby pins in her hair. Her name tag read *Sierra*. "You Team Britta or Team Ynez?" she asked.

"Pardon?"

"You look like a Team Ynez guy. You know"—she grinned wickedly—"sorta scruffy."

"Er, thank you. I guess."

"Personally, I think Ynez is wrong for Harold."

There was a romance hero named Harold?

"Don't you just love that he took the name of the Danish kings for the cadet branch of his vampire line? Like, they even had vampires in Denmark." She laughed.

"Good point."

"Ynez knows his soul, but Britta knows his heart."

"So you like Britta?" he said.

"Nah. Way too wet-spaghetti for me. But the bigger question is: Will Harold break the cadet branch oath to marry her?"

"That *is* the question, isn't it?"

"Unfortunately," Sierra said with an audible sigh, "we'll have to wait till *Pyre* comes in November to get the answer."

"*Pyre?*"

"The sequel. Get it? *Vamp-Pyre.*"

"Shouldn't that be *Vamp-Ire?*"

She giggled. "You're so funny. Who'd buy a book called *Ire?*"

Sierra took the other romance from him, and Axel looked around. Were two books going to be enough? Ellery would need at least a sense of the whole landscape, and Scotland and vampires didn't exactly add up to a survey course in romance. There was a display next to the checkout line, to tempt shoppers into last-minute purchases. He scanned the titles, bypassing the usual thrillers, Oprah authors, and mysteries to concentrate on the love-story end of the rack. A shirtless cowboy was on one, a lake house on the next, and a woman in a long pink gown on the third. He grabbed the last and added it to the others on the counter, then handed the woman his credit card.

"Oh, you like that too?" Sierra raised an amused brow.

Before he could ask what "that" was, another clerk interrupted, on the hunt for a copy of the latest Stephen King novel being held behind the counter. By the time that was sorted out, Sierra had slid his credit card back to him and was putting his purchases in a bag.

He pointed to *Kiltlander*. "Any thoughts on that one?"

She put a hand on his chest and closed her eyes dreamily. "It's a classic. It's the first romance I ever read."

"And, em, Jamie . . . how does he stack up to Harold?"

"Jemmie," she corrected. "Well, it's hard to compare a Highland warrior to a vampire, and Jemmie's pretty old-school."

" 'Old-school'?"

She flushed. "You know."

He didn't, but nodded.

"Jemmie's the man you wish every man was like," she said. "He's a slow burn. Harold's a case of Roman candles viewed on your back from the flatbed of a pickup truck."

He couldn't quite tell her preference. Both seemed to delight her. "So . . . Jemmie, then?"

"Oh, believe me, there's a place for the Harolds of this world." She handed him the bag and he noticed a piece of paper stapled to the side. Jill was in the coffee shop, waving him over. Only she wasn't alone: Ellery was seated at the table beside her, arms crossed, staring at him.

"Have a great day," Sierra said.

"Not likely."

Chapter Ten

"So nice to see you, ladies," Axel said quickly, trying to finesse the conversation in a friendly direction. "I ran into Jill outside, and, may I add, what a shock. You're in college, of course, at . . . ?"

"Penn."

"Oh, yes, I do think I'd heard that." He hadn't dared ask Ellery, but Kate, who apparently enjoyed some sort of aunt-like status, had had a picture of Jill wearing a Penn sweatshirt pinned over her desk a year or so ago.

"Did you hear?" Ellery looked like a baby seal about to be clubbed.

Axel blew out a quiet whistle of relief. Someone else had broken the news. That had saved him an hour's worth of torture at least. "Yes. We can make it work. Don't worry." He wondered if baby seal fur could compare to that dark, gleaming mass of hair.

She dropped her forehead in her hands. "I know why Black picked me," she moaned into her latte, "but why, oh, why did he pick you?"

Jill bit her lip to keep from smiling

"You may recall I'm actually pretty good at what I do," he said politely.

Ellery groaned.

"Relax, Pittsburgh. I have—" He was about to say "a plan," but caught himself. Ellery liked her own plans. "Em, some ideas."

Her head snapped up.

"But I'd love to hear yours first."

Her shoulders relaxed. "Well, I've pulled some articles on romance in popular culture. There's a sociologist in Edinburgh I definitely want to talk to. The head of the Jane Austen Society teaches at London College, and there's a historian at the University of Reading with some interesting things to say about Fielding.

Axel did his best to keep his eyes from glazing over as she went on. The story she was describing had none of the joy Black was looking for. More important, it had none of the joy he'd heard in the voices of his sister and the cashier when they talked about *Vamp* and *Kiltlander*. If he had any shot at all at rerouting this locomotive, he needed to infuse Ellery with some divine inspiration.

". . . and then I thought a visit to Hardy's Wessex, perhaps to the hanging site of Tess—"

"My goodness, that does sound like a lark." He rubbed his palms together. "Is anyone as hungry as I am? I hear they make great Greek salads here." He had no idea whether the Greek salads were good, bad or indifferent, but given the look brewing on Ellery's face, an exit strategy was in order. Besides he knew from his time with the Sharpe girls, feta had magical calming powers.

To his relief they both wanted one, and he jogged to the counter. "Three Greeks," he said, "and please take as long as possible."

Jill appeared at his side. "El wants extra feta."

"Of course she does." The counter attendant had heard and he nodded.

"And a Sprite." Axel turned to Jill. "You're still a Sprite girl, aren't you?"

"You bet."

"And two Diet Cokes." He turned to look at Ellery, who was scribbling furiously on a notepad. "Em, make that one Diet Coke and a really tall Beck's."

The counter guy looked at the clock, which barely showed eleven, shrugged his shoulders and angled his head toward the cooler with drinks behind them.

Jill lingered, gazing at the different offerings. "It's really good to see you again."

"You too. I was just so surprised to see you."

"I came into town for Grandma Marion's annual 'Birthday with the Granddaughters' luncheon."

"Oh, God." Axel remembered the woman distinctly. "Did she go into her avocado tirade?"

"Yes. Also, salt, the New York Lottery, gabardine and people who don't read newspapers. Do you remember the time she asked you if photographers made enough money to earn a living, and you said you got paid by the inch which is why you always tried to volunteer for assignments about skyscrapers and giraffes? God, I laughed so hard I thought I was going to die."

"Yeah, well, you're an easy laugh."

"No, I'm very particular."

She paused, tracing a finger on the display case, and he wondered if something was bothering her. Then he realized a question was coming.

"So I hear you and Ellery are going to be working together again."

There was more there than the words would suggest. "You know your sister," he said lightly. "Can't stay away."

She smiled. She knew how angry Ellery had been with him. "And what exactly do you have planned?"

"Nothing," he said flatly. "I have nothing planned."

"Jumping her bones counts as nothing?"

He winced. With all the Team Ynez and Jemmie stuff, he'd forgotten Jill had heard that. "To hear Ellery tell of it, yes."

She giggled, and Axel remembered with a rush of guilt how sad she'd been when he and Ellery split.

"I don't mind if you jump her bones," Jill said with a glint far more knowing than he would have thought possible, "just don't hurt her."

"Thank you for the clarification." He felt distinctly off balance at having such a conversation with someone who'd been reading *The Princess Diaries* last time he looked. He wished he hadn't told the attendant to take his time. "You may recall, hurt can be a two-way street."

Her eyes widened. Oh, God. She hadn't known. He'd said too much.

"Look, our salads are ready." He took the tray out of the counter guy's hand and headed toward the table. Pittsburgh was staring at him with the same X-ray gaze as her sister. He pressed his way forward, buffeted by the debilitating pulse of roentgens. Out of the frying pan into the real firepower.

"And I have a tone for the piece," Ellery said as he distributed the salads.

"Excellent." He slid the tomatoes off his plate and onto Jill's. "Let's hear it."

"Docu-style. Pulling no punches. The good, the bad, the ugly. You'll do a Diane Arbus sort of thing with the shots."

Axel ran a hand across his stubble, groaning silently. Diane Arbus had photographed oddballs and outsiders—the circus folk of life. The piece sounded like it would be about as uplifting as a Centers for Disease Control report. He supposed he should be glad at least Ellery thought there might actually be a good to go along with the bad and the ugly.

"I had a slightly different take," he said.

Ellery, who had been transferring the cucumbers from her plate to his, paused. "Oh?"

"More . . . magical."

"'Magical'?"

"I'm pretty sure that's how women look at romances." He slipped the books out of his bag and spread them across the table. Ellery looked at them as if he had just dissected a kitten and was offering her the remains.

"The covers." She moved a horrified finger closer, but not close enough to come into actual contact. "Look at them."

"Pretty, isn't it?" Jill said, picking up *Vamp*. "Don't you like the apple? Very Garden of Eden. You know, of course, this is set in Pittsburgh."

Axel's head snapped around. "It is?"

"Oh, yeah. Metaphor for hell. The old steel town image. The vampires hang out at the Monkey Bar on Carson Street. It's supposed to be at the gates to their underworld."

Axel gazed down, chagrined. The Monkey Bar had been a sticking point with him and Ellery. He'd hung out there frequently, enjoying the wide selection of European beers, watching hockey and closing the place down as often as he could. Since Ellery devoted evenings to writing, he'd felt justified giving her the quiet she needed. Of course, he thought with a kick from his conscience, it probably wouldn't have mattered whether he'd felt justified or not.

He ran a finger down the moisture that had condensed on the side of the Beck's. When he looked up, Ellery looked away.

"I, em, have to hit the head." He dug a small leather case out of his bag and headed to the back, feeling Ellery's eyes on him the whole way.

Ellery felt the familiar icicles of anger form in her gut.

"Why are you looking at him that way?" Jill demanded.

Reluctant to expose Jill to the sort of man Axel had been and apparently still was, Ellery shook off the feeling. "It's nothing."

Jill looked from her sister's face to the men's room to Axel's bag. "You think he's taking drugs."

"It's not out of the question," Ellery said after weighing the options. "I've seen him do it before."

"So have I."

Ellery's jaw fell, but she pulled it up quickly. She hadn't realized how much her young sister had seen and understood. "Then you can see why I'd be suspicious."

"Axel never hid what he did. Why would he hide it now?"

"Maybe it's worse."

"Maybe you're paranoid. Weed and some uppers do not exactly enshrine him in the John Belushi Hall of Fame."

"He may have done coke too."

"*May* have. Hmm. You know, your little sister *may* have done coke too."

Ellery's heart seized. "Have you?"

"Can't remember. The lacrosse team left before the roofies wore off." She flashed a bright smile.

Ellery forked a large hunk of feta. "I hate you."

"No you don't. You just hate that I'm right. Speaking of that, are you going to go to the Monkey Bar for this story?"

"Er . . ." Ellery gazed at the shot of a shirtless vampire holding a bloody apple on the cover and growled. Pittsburgh, of all places? She had loved the town growing up, but now it represented all the things that had gone wrong for her. Spending a day reliving any of it, especially with Axel at her side, would be like ripping open a scar. "I doubt it."

"You should. I want a picture. Is it really like, well, like what they say?"

Ellery frowned. "I don't know. What do they say?"

Jill leaned forward and lowered her voice. "In the book, Ynez owns the place. Her vampires are almost all women.

The way they earn her trust is by crossing the bars."

"The bars?"

"The monkey bars."

Ellery almost snorted a kalamata olive up her nose. She hadn't thought about monkey bars since the third grade. She had been the girls' champion at Howe Elementary School. "You're telling me that vampires earn their stripes in this hell-with-the-lid-off vampire headquarters by crossing a set of *monkey bars*?"

"It's not just that. The bars are high and they lead to a platform. If the vamps want to wear Ynez's coat of arms, they have to take off their outer skins and throw them in the fire there."

"There's a fire at the end of the monkey bars, like a pot of gold at the end of a rainbow?"

"A fire pit," Jill said. "It symbolizes the casting off of their old life."

"Uh-huh. And then what? Navigate a corn maze to find their new one? Or is it a game of hide-and-seek to the death?"

"You're making fun."

"Damn right I am."

"It's pretty cool when you read about it. Very feminist. Very empowering. Makes you want to join Ynez's army yourself."

Feminist? Empowering? Ellery looked at her sister. "I thought you were majoring in economics?"

Jill grinned proudly. "Ynez *is* an economist. She works for the State Department."

Which no doubt explained why Ellery's passport had taken so long to arrive.

"Try it," Jill said, pushing the book toward her. "And definitely go to the Monkey Bar."

Ellery didn't know what she would do. Once she'd determined her preferred strategy of running wasn't going to work out, she had figured out a way to get her arms around the topic. But she was perfectly aware that the way she'd chosen was not in keeping with the way Black wanted it to be written. Every assignment had an ebb and flow, and as one did research and interviewed sources and responded to changing internal or external requirements, the whole nature of a piece could change. Ellery prayed this was going to be one of those times. She knew she couldn't write the article the way Black wanted. She was too close to another job—the job of her dreams—to have even the hint of romance novels wafting through her résumé.

Axel ambled back, looking pleased with himself. It was profoundly irritating to Ellery that his tattered insouciance still made her breath catch. Why, when she had her pick of grown-up men with custom-made suits, investment portfolios and nicely creased trousers, did the sight of those muscular forearms extending from their rolled-up sleeves and the perennially scuffed Nikes make her shift in her seat like a college coed?

She speared a wedge of tomato and growled into her salad.

Axel settled back into his chair. He swore he could feel the liquid coursing through his veins, settling into the tips of his fingers and toes.

"Feeling better?" Ellery said.

"Much." He slipped the case into his bag. "Where were we? Oh, right. The books. These are the ones I think you might want to . . ." He considered "read" and settled on ". . . examine. I have it on good authority that these are, em, highly representational." As long as he kept the discussion in graduate seminar territory, he figured he was on safe ground.

The word seemed to disarm her. "Of course. You're right. They're artifacts, after all—an indication of how women in certain socioeconomic circumstances interact with the world."

Axel rubbed his chin, flicking his gaze for an instant to Jill, who gave him an amused look. Not what Black had in mind, but far better than the dreadful outcasts-of-society angle she had proposed earlier. Baby steps, he reminded himself. Baby steps that would lead right to a lovely little microbrewery, if he was lucky.

"Yes," he said. "Absolutely. And do you think it makes sense to cover some of the key locations in the books: Pittsburgh, and, em"—he picked up *Kiltlander* and gazed at the kilted man on the cover—"someplace in Scotland, I presume, and, well"—he picked up the last book, the one with the woman in a shimmering pink gown, flipped through the pages until the words "Covent Garden" popped off the page—"London?"

He held his breath, waiting for her response.

Ellery's knife and fork hovered over the plate. "I guess."

Axel tipped the Beck's and drank. *Step number one.*

CHAPTER ELEVEN

"How's that John Irving thing going?" Carlton Purdy, Ellery's potential new employer asked.

Ellery banged the phone's headset against her head like a mallet. Why did she insist on answering outside calls?

"Great. Just great. How are things at Lark & Ives?"

"Super-duper. You know, we're getting to the final paces in our search process."

She could just see him, vibrating with Carlton Purdy pleasure in his seersucker suit and Dartmouth "Big Green" bow tie. She prayed he was about to offer her the job so she could quit the one she had and put this horrible day behind her. "Glad to hear it."

"And things are looking quite good for you, missy."

"Also good to hear."

"Listen, the board is eating up—I mean, just devouring—everything you've written. Your criticism is great, and you really know how to get the big guns to open up to you."

He probably meant the interview she'd done with Don

DeLillo, which had graced the front of *Vanity Place*'s December issue. She sighed, thinking of that happy accomplishment, then noticed the copy of *Vamp* sitting on her desk and coughed. "I have to admit," she said, turning the book over, "I've gotten a few coups."

"With Irving in your sights."

Technically true, though some vampire named Harold, not John Irving, appeared to qualify for the slot marked NEXT.

"Tell me, what's he like?"

"John Irving? Fantastic."

"Oh, I bet it's going to be a killer profile."

Well, the *topic* of John Irving had certainly achieved a lethalness around here. "I hope so."

"When can I see it?"

She jerked. "Um, well, it's sort of in process."

"Next issue?"

"Actually—" She stopped. If she told him it had been tabled for a future issue, he'd want to know what she was working on for the upcoming one. "Probably."

"Excellent. I'd love to read your take. The *board* would love to read it. Send over what you have. I wanna love me some of that John Irving."

"You know I will. As soon as it's ready."

"Super-duper-ola."

Ellery hung up and looked at the books, disconsolate. *John Irving would be so much easier to write,* she thought.

"Irving's fantastic, huh?" Kate had maneuvered herself into Ellery's office. "You must be something of a telepath, since I know you haven't sat down with him yet."

"Gimme a break. I'm doing an examination of romance novels, for God's sake."

"An 'examination.' My goodness, the issues are going to be flying off the shelves."

"Hey, it's the best way to approach a difficult subject. Strip it to the bones and make it beg for mercy."

"Which difficult subject are we talking about?"

Ellery gave her a piercing look.

"So, exactly what sort of relationship did you and our Mr. Mackenzie share? Holiday party gone awry? Deadline fever? I checked the database: You haven't worked with him in the last five years."

"You should have checked back a little further. We worked on a number of pieces together. In Pittsburgh," she added quickly, as if the mere setting made the notion of it being anything more than a regrettable fling unimaginable. "Before he came here to do his thing and I came to do mine."

"Ah. And when you two were doing your mutual things," she paused, giving the last two words as lascivious a sound as possible, "what was that like? I mean, is he the sexiest guy who ever coaxed his zoom into close-up mode or what?"

Ellery shook her head. "The zoom work was fine. I told you, it was the depth of field that was lacking."

Kate considered this. "Yeah, I guess it sort of makes a difference if you're in it for more than a few shots."

"Yeah, it does."

"But here you are, working together again?"

"Yep."

"And you say the zoom work was fine?"

Ellery gave her a haughty *hm*.

"What?" Kate lifted up her palms. "It's not like you're slapping away the offers. I'm just saying a little tight-in stuff can do wonders for a girl's portfolio."

"Who's working on their portfolio?" Axel draped his forearms over the cubicle wall and smiled amiably.

"Ellery," Kate said. "I told her she needs to tighten her prose—you know, focus on the really big stuff."

"You've already started writing?" he said to Ellery, surprise on his face.

"No, not yet." Why did the copper hairs dusting his forearms have to sparkle like a daytime meteor shower?

"Well, perhaps you'll have some time on the plane. I've looked into flights. We kind of have to hightail it around, given the Monday deadline. I thought we'd head to Pittsburgh tomorrow. According to Jill, the Monkey Bar's the best place to connect with *Vamp* fans."

"I have an interview to do in London."

"And I have a friend at a hotel with a connection to a romance readers' group there. So we'll head to London the day after tomorrow. Will a day there be enough? I figured we could catch the train to Edinburgh for the sociologist you found, and if there's anywhere else we need to go for *Kiltlander,* we can head out from there with a rental car. By the way, Kate," he said, gazing at the novel on Ellery's desk, "are all vampires cut like a Spartan in *300*?"

"All the ones worthy of my notice."

"Makes a man feel rather humble."

Kate smiled. "Probably a novel feeling for you."

Ellery arched her brows in agreement, though she had seen Axel's abs and he had no reason to hang his head.

"I think for efficiency's sake we'd be better off splitting up. You go to Pittsburgh, get the shots you need of the Monkey Bar and whatever else." She growled internally, thinking of the stupid Monkey Bar. "I'll head off to London tonight, which would give me an extra day there. We can meet up once you arrive and go on to Scotland from there."

A flicker of something crossed his face, enough like disappointment to make her heart contract for a second.

"There's stuff to write about in Pittsburgh," he said. "You should come there too."

She knew he was right. Only a lazy writer missed an opportunity to add depth to her story, and Ellery was not a lazy writer. "I-I- I just think if we want to get this done by the deadline—"

The *buzz-buzz* of Kate's wheelchair interrupted her thoughts.

"—it would be easier if we split up and—"

Buzz-buzz. Buzz-buzz. Ellery put a hand behind her back, giving Kate a signal of a different nature.

"Ellery," he said, his eyes turning a fathomless green, "come with me. Please."

She could feel the familiar pull and felt herself weakening. His earnestness was a trick. She knew that. He was a dating iceberg—the sort of boyfriend who looks great on the surface but has the power to sink any relationship with the dangerously bad behaviors hidden underneath. And she remembered all too clearly that, unlike the *Titanic,* she hadn't even bothered to try to turn.

CHAPTER TWELVE

The Andy Warhol Museum, Pittsburgh, Six Years Earlier

Ellery watched as Axel adjusted the lens on his camera, the muscles in his forearms rippling as he moved. He'd grown quieter after he'd shown her the picture he'd taken of her and the little girl, his usual sly humor replaced with a sort of tremulousness, and Ellery wondered if it was something she'd said. They had the museum to themselves for another two hours, and this was the time she should have been banging out a first draft of what was to be her paper's first cover story so she could work on the paid stuff tomorrow, but there was something about the way he set up a shot that made it easy to lose track of her work.

"You need help with that?" she called as he moved the light he was setting up.

He snorted. "If I said yes, would you actually get up?"

"Hey, I'm the one who got you the beer."

She had dragged an upholstered visitors' bench from the hall into the center of the room and was lying on her stomach on it, typing on her laptop while the balloons gamboled around her. There was a way someone moved when they were expert at their craft, with a sort of undivided intensity that was fascinating. It was like watching a very practical ballet. Axel crouched to adjust a cord, his shoulders flexing under his shirt, then stood again and withdrew a light meter from his pocket. She was very lucky he had agreed to do the photos for her. Besides the fact that he was working for free and had arranged to get them in after hours to shoot—the mere fact of having his name associated with her paper—gave it instant credibility.

He lifted the beer to his mouth and drank, the long muscles of his neck moving up and down. He was on his third bottle, and she'd picked up the six-pack only half an hour ago. She'd found herself more and more attracted to him with each assignment, but he inhabited a world far different than hers. He was a grown-up, for one, eight years older than she was, with a real job and a real income and a list of credentials as long as her arm. More important, though, he had a street edge to him that seemed completely out of reach to a girl whose most serious excess was miniature Kit Kat bars.

"I can't believe you thought this would take an hour," she said, pulling her eyes back to the screen.

"I can't believe you thought it would take all night."

"Typical male point of view." She gave him an innuendo-filled smile. "Always trying to shortchange the rightful process."

He didn't reply. "Did you hear what I said?" she asked.

"If an hour's not enough to do the job," he said, turning to meet her eyes, "perhaps you need more competent partners."

She felt a boom, as if a mortar had just gone off, completely altering the landscape between them, and she was both thrilled and petrified.

"You have a high opinion of your work," she said drymouthed, turning back to the keyboard to hide her unsteadiness.

"I have an impressive résumé."

And he did. She knew of at least a TV reporter and local artist whom Axel could number among his conquests, although he himself never mentioned them. Her own list was considerably shorter. Two. Her high school boyfriend, even though they had done it so badly it could hardly count, and the French grad student who'd done a full-court press during her junior year in Paris. Ellery's parents had had a rocky marriage, even before her father cut out entirely, and Ellery had learned to expect, well, if not the worst from men, then at least not the best, which meant she did not give her heart willingly. This had kept her safe—and focused on her writing—but it had also kept her circling the same emotional ground. Although she dated a lot, each relationship always ended up stalling, like a car with a bad fuel pump. She was starting to be afraid she would never feel the thrill of full-on acceleration.

"What are you doing?" Even without looking, she could feel him turn the camera in her direction, and she was relieved to change the course of the conversation.

"I'm setting it on auto timer," he said without pulling his eye from the viewfinder. "Don't worry, you're not in the frame."

Like rugged climbing vines, his legs were woven into

those of the tripod, and there was an enthralling intensity to the way his hands made minute adjustments to the lens and dials. For some reason she was instantly jealous.

"Can I look?"

He gave her an amused smile. "Are you art-directing me now?"

"I *am* the editor, right?"

He bowed, and she made her way to the tripod. She didn't know what she was looking for, but the idea of inserting herself into his milieu was irresistible.

An electric charge shook her as she peered through the viewfinder. She could smell the piquant beer malt that had become his signature scent to her and feel the fading warmth of his hands on the camera body.

"What do you see?"

The shot was amazing. The pillows of silver drifted slowly in and out of the shadow-dappled frame, but she was finding it hard to formulate a reason, given the immediacy of his arms and the fact she could feel his breath brushing over her shoulders.

A sheen appeared on her palms. "Shouldn't there be something playing in the background to channel your concentration? You know: Anne Murray, Celine Dion, a Maple Leafs game?"

"Don't worry. I have my muse."

She pulled away from the viewfinder, fingertips tingling. "Looks good."

"I'm glad you approve." He stuffed his hands in his pockets. "I think I'm going to shoot the Brillo boxes now."

"No," she said automatically, visualizing the layout she had in her head. "Too Warhol specific," she said. "The cover story is about art as a reflection of self." She might not know photography, but when she thought of her cover story, she knew exactly how the narrative should flow both verbally and visually, and the Brillo boxes just didn't fit.

A flinty look flared in those green eyes. He wasn't used to having his choices questioned, but the spark was hard to read. Did he like it or not?

"I'm the photographer." He drew shoulders higher. She was close enough to feel his heat.

"I'm the editor."

A small growl. "Then what would you like me to do?"

"Kiss me." She didn't know where the courage to say this had come from, but he complied instantly, finding a home for his hands on the small of her back.

The yeasty bouquet of beer blossomed in her mouth and filled her head, moving the buzz-o-meter on her nerve endings into the red zone.

"Oh," she said, pulling away in a dizzying rush of emotions. "That was nice." Thoroughly flustered, she bent for his bag. "Let's try the self-portraits," she said. "They're upstairs, I think."

He fished the bag out of her hand and followed. When she reached the stairs, he caught her arm and turned her.

The kiss, in his hands, was more demanding, and her knees began to tremble. As always, she knew what she wanted but was afraid she couldn't get it.

She ducked again and took refuge on a step, rocking where she sat. "This is fast."

He dropped the bag. "You'll like it fast."

"I don't even know if you're seeing someone."

"I'm not."

He ran a finger across her collarbone and she leaned back on her elbows without thinking. She wanted to feel those capable hands on her body. He was three steps below her, looking at her with those emerald eyes.

"Do you like me or do you want to sleep with me?" she said.

"*That* is a trick question." He flicked her top button open, put his hands on her knees and kissed her again.

Reason was leaving the arena. If there was something she needed to know, she'd better find out while she still had brain cells left to process the information.

"So, why do you like me?"

She moved up a step, and so did he, opening another of her buttons in the process.

"Are you kidding?" he said. "Because you're a bloody amazing writer, because you have the stones to ask me to work for free and because it's like you have fireworks going off inside you *all* the time."

He slid deeper between her legs and their mouths met hungrily.

When she caught her breath, she moved up another stair. "So you're saying you don't think I'm pretty?"

"Is this the obstacle course you put every boyfriend through?" he said, loosening another button. "If so, I can see why your track record is spotty. For the record, you're beautiful—alarmingly so—but I was given to understand that it is ungentlemanly to focus on the superficial."

One more step. "It is. It was a test. You passed."

He took two buttons as his wreath of laurels. Then he took her blouse.

She could feel her heart beating but was afraid to look down. He slipped his finger under the clasp that rested between her breasts, and she could see the turbulence in those eyes and feel it in his fingers.

She undid his buckle, and he undid her bra.

"Good God," he whispered.

Her breasts were high and full, and she was used to men admiring them, but the look on his face went beyond admiration or even desire, and she knew it would be seared into her memory forever. She took his hands, which had fallen useless to his sides, and brought them to the warm flesh. He made a noise deep in his throat, and she found her own hands quaking.

He cupped her reverentially, then brushed her nipples, igniting her instantly. They fell into a kiss deep and hard enough to remind her that this had the potential to be an epic mistake. A deep-bellied fear shook her, launching hot arrows of doubt through her veins.

"I want to be your friend," she said, slipping an arm back into her blouse. "Not this."

The weight of her statement was reflected in his eyes, which turned an abrupt emerald green. But a curve rose at the corner of his mouth as well. "Do you think at this point we can go back?"

The answer, of course, was no. She damned herself for lifting her mouth to his at that bottom stair and thought of what Hemingway had said: "Always do sober what you said you'd do drunk. That will teach you to keep your mouth shut." She'd been drunk with giddy lust, and it was a lesson she needed to learn. In the course of a single reckless instant, she had ended the heady, laughter- and debate-filled friendship that had roared to a start like a drag race two months ago, fueled by an explosive mixture of admiration, attraction, clashing creative egos, cheap chardonnay and a lot of expensive beer, and launched them, one literal step at a time, into God knew what. If she was lucky, it would be everything they'd had before and more. But she wasn't lucky, and the only thing she knew for certain was that whatever tomorrow would be like between them, it wouldn't be like yesterday.

She gave him a fierce look. "If we're not friends after this, I'm going to be really pissed at you."

"Fair warning."

He leaned between her legs and bent to kiss her.

"I mean," she said, stopping him with a hand, "if you had to pick between our friendship and this"—she fluttered her hand vaguely between his midsection and hers—"which would you pick?"

He laughed. "This," he said, and lifted her to standing.

"That doesn't sound very committed to friendship."

"Doesn't it? Which would *you* pick?" He unzipped her jeans and buried his hands in them.

"Ooh, this." She thrust her head back.

"There you go. We'll sort the rest out later."

In another moment, her panties and jeans were in a heap on the floor and her legs were wrapped around his hips tighter than Warhol's labels on a can of soup.

He carried her back into the darkened gallery and pressed her against the nearest wall.

"I've wanted this since the first day we met," he said, "well, since the first time we argued. Same day, come to think of it."

"That shot should have been in landscape, I'm telling you."

He gave her a long, deep kiss and squeezed her hips. The neon beside them blinked rhythmically, rendering his profile in *Alice in Wonderland* colors.

He dug something out of his back pocket and handed it to her. It was his wallet.

"You're paying for this?" she asked.

"Condom," he said, and unzipped his fly.

He carried her to the adjoining wall, kicking off his running shoes, briefs and jeans as he went, and kissed her with a fire that made thinking seem like an Olympic feat. Her hands were out of sight, crossed behind his neck, and she tore blindly through credit cards, business cards, receipts, pills and cash, which rained down on the gallery floor, coming up at last with the familiar foil-wrapped square.

"Got it," she said, and he looked.

"No, no, no. That's the good one."

She giggled, and he let her slide to the floor. Muscular and tan, his forearms stood out against his pale, lightly haired thighs, and her breath caught as he suited up, handling the long, thick length as skillfully as he did his camera lens, with much the same heart-pounding effect on her.

"Where is best?" he asked.

Her face must have betrayed her shock, and he laughed and said, "I meant here, in the museum," then added in a low voice, "though if you stand with your mouth like that for much longer, I'll have no choice."

His fingers were already exploring the soft triangle of

hair below her belly. She knew she was wet, and he found her bud and rolled it. She curled into him, groaning, and tasted the salty skin of his neck. He turned her gently and pressed her toward the wall. She laid her forehead on her arms and rocked as he plucked her nipples, crying in pleasure.

She wanted him inside her. She could feel his desire, and her imagination was far more wicked than his fingers. His hands trailed down her body, setting off a charge in every cell, before he palmed the curves of her hips.

"God, you're beautiful."

Gooseflesh popped out on her skin, and he made a deep, satisfied noise when his returning fingers found the taut flesh of her aureoles. He lifted her hair and kissed her nape, and she turned, meeting his mouth hungrily. Then she bent her arms around his neck and lifted herself off the ground. He responded automatically to her invitation, spreading her thighs and entering her slowly.

"Oh, oh," she whispered.

He was thicker than she'd ever known, and she locked her ankles behind his back, amazed to discover how much he made her burn without even moving.

He bumped her gently against the wall—once—and the friction nearly lifted her out of her skin.

"Oh, no."

"Oh, yes."

Cupping her buttocks, he coaxed her open further with a second bump.

She dug her fingers into his back, taking in the musky scent of his skin. He thrust a third and fourth time.

A phone buzzed to life. Instantly she patted the pocket

of her shirt, which still hung loosely on one shoulder, and found the object in question, nearly bobbling it as she did.

"What is it?" she asked breathlessly. *My little sister,* she mouthed.

He nodded, his eyes glittering. "Hang up."

"I can't," she said, hand over the mouthpiece. "She's home alone."

"Hang up."

"What, Jill? No, that was the photographer. He's, ah, asking me about a shot."

Axel snorted. He pressed Ellery carefully against the wall and began a more determined beat, lifting her a few inches skyward with each thrust.

"What? No. Where?" Ellery crushed her eyes closed, trying to listen *and* ride this bucking wave. "I don't know what you're talking about. I-I-" The phone slipped from her ear.

Axel grabbed it. "Jill, hi. It's Axel." He listened for a moment and gave Ellery an interested look. "Yes, *that* Axel. Sorry, your sister's looking at a shot. She thought it looked better in landscape, but she's realizing she was completely wrong. Where are you going?" He nodded. "All right. Call with their home number when you arrive." He paused, listening. "Hard to say. Depends on your sister, really. We could be done fast, or it could take all night."

He closed the phone, dropped it on his discarded jeans and slipped his hand between her legs.

"Is she . . . ?" Ellery asked, disoriented

"Probably."

"I should—"

"Yes, you should, but tonight just doesn't seem to be the night for it."

He lifted her from the wall and began a slow procession toward the balloon room, each step punctuated with a deep pump that fanned the flames licking at her belly.

She wanted to ride him, to rake her sensitive flesh along his burning length, heedless of anything but her own desire while he groaned beneath her.

When they reached the room, he lowered her to the bench, and she rolled him to his back.

His eyes widened in surprise, and she grinned, rocking her hips forward and back, putting that fine iron thickness to use. A smattering of bronze hair edged the outlines of his chest. He was more muscular than she'd expected, and he rested his head on an arm as he watched the undulations and the crisp bounce of her breasts. She'd heard someone whisper once that Axel liked to snort coke off of that TV reporter's breasts. Ellery had never seen him do anything more than pills and a lot of beer, and she wondered how reliable a rumor it was. But if it was true, she wondered if that was what he had been thinking about when he looked at her.

"Would you like to try my tongue instead?"

He didn't wait for an answer. He pulled her toward him and began a practiced exploration that made her cry out, back arched hard. He was nothing like the boys she'd bedded before, and when he added his thumbs in a swirling, heat-inducing complement to his mouth, she felt she would die.

She braced her knees, pressing her palms against her

forehead, too dizzy to think. Those twinkling eyes were as potent as any drug, and trying to ignore the danger they represented was impossible. She was falling over the edge, for him and for this. The quake began in her thighs, rising through her belly and chest, and he plied her until she called out, shamefaced, for him to stop.

He gave a rumbling laugh that tickled her skin, then rolled her over.

"Now I can proceed at my pace," he said, kissing his way up her stomach and pausing to suckle each nipple.

He lowered himself between her thighs and entered. The smell of their joining hung on him, making her woozy with desire. He moved with care, pleasing himself with each stroke. He gazed into her eyes as he moved, and she found she had no barrier to raise.

"Would you like this each night?"

"Yes," she whispered.

"I would too."

He worked slowly, moving when she did and smiling at her throaty gurgles. The aftershocks were quickening, and she could feel her still-tingling flesh tighten around him. She stretched her arms as far as they would go, wiggling her fingers as he plucked her nipples. The earth was moving again, and, sensing the shift, he lifted her knee and changed his gentle thrusts to a hammering.

Lava bubbled deep within her, and she flung her head back. The silvery clouds wheeled and turned in the private heaven they'd created, and her fingers stretched along the bench's length to reach them, as if the magic they'd conjured would allow her to command the sky. Then his measured blows unleashed her. He bucked hard, driving the liquid fire from her belly to the top of her head, and she jerked wildly under his shuddering weight.

"Oh, Axel."

He settled against her and held out his hand. "Friends?"

She laughed. "Better."

Looking into her eyes, he made a low, contented noise. "Indeed."

CHAPTER THIRTEEN

Offices of *Vanity Place* magazine, Present Day

Axel sat in an empty cube, gazing at the LCD of his camera and fast-forwarding through the shots still carefully preserved even after all these years. The edge of the bench just protruded into the lower left of the frame, and the first four hundred or so shots were nothing but a montage of slowly tumbling flashes of Mylar, beautiful in themselves but nothing compared to the last thirty. He'd set the automatic repeat on the shutter for ten seconds that night and forgotten it. It wasn't until they finished the shoot and retired to his place that he'd even thought to look at what he'd gotten. He still remembered sitting at his desk, listening to the sound of her soft, sleepy exhalations and gasping when he'd realized what he had.

He looked at the shot numbers. Three ninety-three, three ninety-four, three ninety-five. This is where it began, though the sequence ran for hundreds of pictures. He let the memory slip over him like an old sweater. There they were. Her hands. Stretching into view, palms up, fingers flexing and curling as the clouds of silver danced overhead.

He watched the shots roll by, thinking about that wonderful joining and the time that followed. He'd felt like a vampire himself, his veins infused with this heady new life force. God, he and Ellery had barely left the bed the first few months. It was a wonder *City Sill,* the name she'd given her paper, had ever launched at all. But it had. In fact, it had sold quite well its rookie year—that is, until the end, when everything that had been magic between them died.

He opened another album in his camera's memory, the one entitled "Ellery Before." It held only a dozen pictures, random shots of her those last couple of months they were together. In one she held her hair up in a knot, vogueing for the camera; in another, taken in the stands at a hockey game, she frowned as one of the Penguins missed a shot; in a third she gazed into a mirror, unaware he'd had the camera pointed at her.

As he always did when he looked at these pictures, he examined her face for signs of a change. How had she hidden it from him? And why? Had there been another man? How had Axel—who, after photographing it thousands of times, knew her face far better than he knew his own—missed it? He'd been a fool, and in his foolishness he'd failed her at a time when she'd needed him most. But why, why, why hadn't she told him?

He shook off the regret and smiled instead, thinking of the lunch. There was something thrilling about being on assignment with her again, even if, knowing Ellery, it was going to be equal parts adventure and agitation.

She wheeled into the cube, and he nearly dropped the camera.

Ellery shook her head. "Always lost in the shots, aren't you?"

Axel powered the camera down surreptitiously. "You know me."

"Good stuff?"

"Very."

"My admin dropped off the trip information." She slid a copy in his direction. "Everything is set."

He kept his face neutral as he scanned the arrangements. Looked like she was traveling with him to Pittsburgh. "Great. Thanks. Are you looking at those books?"

She gave him a dubious look. "Not often you get to see the word 'lave' in the back cover copy."

"Pittsburgh, you've been hanging with the wrong crowd."

CHAPTER FOURTEEN

Chelsea, Manhattan

Ellery gazed at the contents of her dresser drawer. Exactly what sort of clothes did one wear to the gates of vampire hell? She held up a pale pink twin set. Jill, who was sprawled on the bed with a textbook, shook her head violently. Kate, who had offered to keep Jill company in Ellery's absence, stopped paging through *Vamp* long enough to say, "Honestly, have you ever been to a bar?"

Jill gave her sister a sympathetic smile. "Think edgier."

Ellery frowned. There was that black turtleneck. Black was always edgy. She dug down to the bottom of the drawer and pulled it out.

Kate sighed. She wheeled over to the chest, dug around and drew out a length of lace-edged silk.

"That's a *slip*," Ellery said.

"A slip *dress*," Kate corrected. "Very cutting-edge."

"Yes," Jill agreed. "Exactly right."

Ellery held it up. The silk was the color of coffee au lait, with a see-through black lace panel running down the seam on both sides. She had purchased it before her third date with a slightly self-centered corporate attorney, who'd given her a potted Meyer lemon tree to mark the occasion. She'd dumped the attorney and kept the tree. When life gives you lemons . . .

"It seems to be a tad, er, air-conditioned for public consumption."

"Nonsense," Jill said. "Nothing a little thong won't fix. Guys love 'em."

Ellery winced. Did her sister have to grow up so loudly? Would it have killed her to pretend she still liked *Dora the Explorer* and *That's So Raven*?

"I know this is going to surprise you, but I'm actually not that comfortable having my underthings show through my clothes."

"Gosh, I didn't think about going with no panties, but I guess that's an option too."

Ellery opened her mouth, but her sister forestalled her. "Jeggings," she said calmly. "I can lend you a pair."

Ellery *hmm*ed, throwing the slip into the suitcase and tossing in a nice pair of sweatpants to counterbalance the blow to her psyche.

"Ahem." Kate fished them out.

"I'm not trying to impress anyone," Ellery said pointedly. "Just hoping to bury myself in my piece."

"Sounds like romance novels are going to be the perfect inspiration, then," Kate said. Jill laughed.

If Ellery was going to wear a slip dress, she was going to need a strapless bra. She threw in her wonderful Slapz brand "Hands of God" convertible bra, lingerie's equivalent of a Swiss Army knife, a bra that boosted, padded, anchored and smoothed, while adjusting its straps for up to nine kinds of top styles. It had cost her almost a hundred dollars, but it had never failed her. Control for her breasts was critical, and she bet she could clear a dozen half twists on a trampoline in it and those babies would move less than a glacier.

Her cell rang, and the number was from out of state. Since she thought it might relate to the rescheduling of the Irving interview, she dashed into the hallway for some privacy, but it was only an exceedingly long-winded recorded call telling her the scheduled departure time of her flight had been changed from 8:18 p.m. to 8:21 p.m. When she hung up, she could hear Kate and Jill talking and paused.

"Gosh, I hope she has fun," Kate said.

"Ellery? Isn't that sort of wishing zebras had TiVo? I mean, what's the point?"

They both laughed, and Ellery felt like she'd had the wind knocked out of her. She knew she was more serious than most people, but surely she didn't give the impression she didn't have fun?

"Sometimes I wonder if the fun gene was flushed out of her after our mom died," Jill said quietly. "Actually, what I wonder is, was it me—taking care of me, you know?"

"I'm not surprised. You guys went through a lot."

"I know," Jill said. "I just worry."

"Well, she'll certainly have fun on this assignment, right? I mean, it's practically a requirement."

"Yeah, nothing like getting paid for one-handed reading— Oh my God, speaking of that, did you love that scene with Harold and Ynez on the platform or what?"

Their conversation turned into a giggling exchange of favorite moments in the book. Ellery collapsed against the hallway wall. Part of her mourned for the fun she had let go of in her life. Part of her was upset that Jill was worried about her. And part of her longed for the easy connection Jill and Kate had formed over *Vamp*. What did Ellery lack that made a sisterhood on such a topic so hard for her? But she could no more crack open a romance than she could a chest for bypass surgery. It just wasn't in her.

She was just about to reenter the room when another snippet floated out: ". . . the whole Axel thing is very curious," Kate was saying with obvious interest. "What exactly happened there, do you know?"

Ellery froze.

"He, ah . . . he lived with us, you know. That was after Mom died. I really liked him, but he was out most nights, photographing, I guess, or with his friends. I'm sure it was trying for Ellery. She was working so hard to get her career off the ground. She . . . she doesn't know I know this, but she went to the hospital once in the middle of the night. I saw her doubled over, but she straightened up and told me Aunt Janet was coming over to watch me so she could go to work. Later that night, though, I overheard Aunt Janet talking to her on the phone, asking her if everything was okay and if she should come to visit the next day."

Ellery put a hand on her chest, feeling her heart pounding, remembering the night vividly and despairing for the tumult she'd caused her sister.

"What happened?" Kate asked.

"I don't know. I don't know if it was stress or something else. Ellery never told me. She was back at home when I woke up, and I asked if she was okay. She said yes. She looked fine, I guess. But that afternoon when Axel came home they had a huge fight. She told him she wanted him to leave, and she told me their breakup had been brewing a long time. Which might be true," Jill added softly, "but she closed herself in her room and cried the rest of the night."

Kate tsked sadly. "Poor Jill. Poor Ellery."

Ellery cleared her throat loudly and walked down the hall into the bedroom. "Just a call from work," she said. "Where were we?"

Kate and Jill had been packing for her while they chatted, and while Ellery couldn't determine everything they'd put into her suitcase, two lacy bras and a handful of thong underwear were scattered across the top, which gave her a general feel for the rest.

"Hmm." She picked up the flimsiest thong—a red-sequined one she'd gotten as a joke at a bachelorette party—and twirled it on her finger. "This will keep me nice and toasty in the Scottish Highlands."

"I thought that's what the sweatpants were for," Kate said.

Jill grinned. "I believe you can use them to signal for help if there's an avalanche."

"If you don't mind, I think I may pack just a few black cotton briefs." She bent to reach into the drawer and heard the sound of the zipper closing on the suitcase and the click of the little travel lock.

"All ready for tomorrow," Jill said with an air of finality. "Honestly, Ellery, I don't know why you have all these wonderful sexy things if you don't wear them."

"I *do* wear them!" she cried. "Just not on assignments! Now, please. How about just a couple of nice, comfortable work outfits?"

Jill looked at her sister.

"You're going to the gates of hell," she said. "You need to make an impression."

"But one little sweater and a skirt can't hurt, right?" Ellery said plaintively. "And a pair of nice cotton briefs?"

The gatekeepers narrowed their eyes.

Kate shook her head firmly. "C'mon, Ellery. You know as well as I do: Nobody goes to hell in a pair of nice cotton briefs."

CHAPTER FIFTEEN

Flight from New York City to Pittsburgh

Axel stopped fiddling with the locking device on the plane's tray table long enough to say, "I know it's ungentlemanly for me to have even noticed, but if I apologize for that up front, can I ask why you're wearing three pairs of underpants?"

Ellery, who had managed to get her bag out of the stuffed-to-the-gills overhead bin and onto the floor of the aisle and was now trying to extract the laptop from it, looked at him over her shoulder. "It's a long story."

The plane hit a bump and Axel grabbed her belt to keep her from falling. She could feel the warmth of his hand on her back.

"Thanks," she said, flushing. She squeezed by his legs, dropped into the window seat and began to boot up.

"Already working on a draft?" he said.

"I'm thinking about one."

"Great. So you've started reading *Vamp*?"

"Gonna look at it on the plane."

He glanced at his watch. "It's a forty-minute flight."

"How hard can it be? It's a romance, for God's sake. When we land, are we going directly to the bar?" He had no hotel listed on his itinerary, and she was curious about where he was planning to stay, but she'd be damned if she'd ask.

"I will. I've got to set up the shots."

No answer there. She pulled the book out of her bag and settled back with the laptop.

He inclined his seat. "Looking forward to seeing the old town again?"

"Not really."

"C'mon, Ellery, you used to love it."

"Pittsburgh is no Manhattan."

"I'll drink to that."

She almost said he'd drink to anything, but he'd limited himself to black coffee so far, so she held her tongue. "Not a fan of the Big Apple anymore?"

He made a noncommittal noise, adding after a moment, "I've always loved Pittsburgh. Great sports. Great food. Great neighborhoods. It actually reminds me of Toronto, but on a smaller scale. And the vision of that skyline when you first emerge from the Fort Pitt tunnel . . ." He smiled, remembering. "It's the only city I know that actually makes an entrance."

She knew he was trying to be companionable and taking a risk doing it, since it would be easy for her to make a biting comment about why she'd felt like she needed to leave, so she dug into her arsenal of polite responses, coming up with the fairly benign and entirely honest, "I feel like I've left Pittsburgh behind."

He gazed at her, his eyes unreadable. "Funny," he said, "I feel like I'm still stuck there."

She waited for a barb, but none came. He settled back into his seat, rolled his jacket into a ball on his shoulder and closed his eyes.

Ellery reviewed the stuff she'd printed out before she left, though she'd already read through it once. She hoped going through the motions of preparation would eventually help her find a way to get the story on paper without destroying her credibility. Axel had said he had a friend in London with access to a romance book club. She wasn't quite sure what that meant, and she generally was nervous about anything that began with a friend of Axel, but they were going to attend a meeting of the club after the London College visit. Now, if she could only get through Pittsburgh and the damn Monkey Bar. . . .

She looked at Axel, who was sleeping blissfully. If ever there was a man whose conscience should bother him, it was Axel Mackenzie, but his chest rose and fell like a baby's.

That was an image she wished she hadn't conjured up, she thought, and reluctantly reached for *Vamp*.

She opened it with care, as if the flames of hell—or, more likely, the stink of mass-market prose—might start rising from the pages, and began to read.

Harold, it seemed, had been recruited into the vampire world because he carried the mark of Odelon, rare in humans, which gave him the occasional power to see what might be. He was weaker than most vampires because his transformation had been incomplete, and he had to battle his way to Romgar, the guardian of the underworld and head of the elite Vampturi organization, to either be returned to his human state or become a full-fledged vampire. Because of his vampy disadvantage, he had to rely on his wits and the help of a rogue she-devil, Ynez—she of the Monkey Bar and Ellery's passport delay—to help him along the way. Complicating his journey was the appearance of Britta, the young woman he had loved from afar in the human world.

Well, Ellery thought, pausing at the end of the third chapter and gazing at Axel's long fingers laced over his buckle as he slept, *if he had told me we were dealing with Joseph Campbell's monomyth here—a hero on an Odysseus-slash-Skywalker-slash-Potter–esque journey—I would have certainly been a bit more understanding. There's nothing like a hero on a quest to engage one's interest.*

On the other hand, she could definitely do without the glowing eyes, iridescent skin and biting as a metaphor for sex. As far as Ellery was concerned, literature had pretty much done all it needed to do with vampires after Bram Stoker's *Dracula,* and even with that book, one needed to read with one's eyes partly averted to keep from straining one's credulity.

Far worse, however, was the amateurish dialogue and characterization, especially those of the teenage Britta, who seemed to spend most of her time yearning for Harold and running her hands wistfully through her "chestnut tresses" and who was potentially the most passive woman in literature since Snow White during her poisoned-apple phase.

Ellery was grateful Jill had aligned herself with Team Ynez, for Ynez at least seemed capable of kicking some cold-blooded ass when she had to.

Which reminded Ellery: She'd better read whatever she

could about the Monkey Bar, for that seemed to be where most of this part of the article would be focused.

She paged through the book, stopping at the first reference to the Monkey Bar she spotted, and found herself in the middle of Ynez's flashback retelling of her first visit to the place. It seemed Romgar presided over it, and it was crawling with criminal he-devils who drank and caroused and pillaged—a pretty spot-on description if she recalled Axel's time there correctly—and who imprisoned the souls of the dead in a cauldron of fire high on a ledge above the bar.

Ynez, determined to free the soul of her beloved grandmother, had wrestled her way across the monkey bars one-armed while fighting off the he-devils with a sword and a killer pair of heels. No woman had made it to the ledge before, and the whores who serviced the he-devils watched in amazement as Ynez, who had been told only a complete sacrifice would free the souls, stripped to her skin and threw her clothes into the cauldron to renounce her human life.

With the help of the now-inspired whores, the souls, finally free of their torment, flew around the bar before driving out the he-devils. Ynez donned Romgar's leather duster and, with tears in her eyes, announced that the gates of hell would be guarded by her army of she-devil whores from that time forward.

Ellery gazed out the window, thinking about what it would be like to kick all the lame-ass men out of *Vanity Place,* starting with Buhl Martin Black and ending with the jerk in Finance who kicked her expense report back every time she submitted one. Then she smiled, remembering how she had led her first set of summer interns through the grueling paces of putting together a magazine like *Vanity Place*. She had felt pretty empowered, especially when they began to master the timelines and the internal politics and the tightening of prose. In a fit of good-natured fun at the end of the summer they'd given her a hat like the one Napoleon wore, but now that she thought about it, she could definitely see herself in Ynez's floor-length leather duster.

Axel made a contented baby coo, and Ellery returned to the book.

Harold, who had been a medic in the Iraqi War, and who had witnessed Ynez's triumph from the cell in which he'd been imprisoned by the he-devils, ran to Ynez. He knew that, despite her victory, the wound on her thigh was grave. She refused the painkiller he offered for fear that if her vigilance waned for even a moment, the he-devils would return.

Harold promised to keep her safe, but she was adamant, growing more frantic as the wound on her thigh worsened. They began to wrestle, and Ynez, with the fierceness of recent battle still coursing through her veins, pinned him beneath her. Harold told her he knew she held his life in her hands, but said that not even a tyrant can rule without trusting someone, and that she needed to trust him or she would die.

Ynez looked into his eyes, determined to find a lie, but could not. She rolled onto her back, opened her mouth and accepted the painkiller he placed there.

The ball of heat that flared in Ellery's belly at this intimate act so surprised her, she jerked and dropped the book.

"Whoa, there," Axel said, stretching. "Horse balk?"

"No." Her cheeks began to burn.

He looked at the novel and his eyes narrowed. "Were you asleep? Honestly, Ellery, you might not like it, but it's an assignment. Can you at least attempt to take it seriously?"

"I'm *reading* it." She fished it off the floor.

"Oh." He shrugged. "In that case, wake me when we land." He balled up his jacket again and settled himself in the other direction.

Men. How had Axel caught her at the one moment she'd been swept into the silly story? Yeesh! Ridiculous twaddle. Nonetheless, she found herself reveling in the moment when Ynez relented and accepted Harold's help. She wondered how long Ynez had struggled on her own and how hard it must have been for her to let down her guard even for a moment.

Gah!

What was she doing? She closed the book and dropped it into her bag. She had spent all the time she intended with Harold and Ynez. She-devils? Seriously? This was not an article that was going to be built on heaving hips and breathless bosoms.

Chapter Sixteen

Monkey Bar, Pittsburgh

Axel had taken all the setup shots he needed: the crowd, the neon, the all-female bartenders and the infamous monkey bars. Now he had to wait until Ellery arrived. For the rest of the shots, he wanted the camera to "see" the place as she saw it.

He settled onto a stool at the bar and ordered a Hard Hat. He was glad to see they carried Brendan's beer here. He hoped that meant distribution was strong enough that he'd have at least a crack of making a go of it if he bought the place.

The bar had changed so much since he'd first frequented the place, he hardly recognized it. Sure, the monkey bars had been there, traversed mainly by drunk college students trying to impress each other; but before *Vamp*, the Monkey Bar had been a proper drinking establishment, filled with muted TVs showing hockey.

Now the place was abuzz with music and littered with *Vamp* memorabilia, and fully eighty percent of the clientele were women—not that he was complaining, mind you, but it was sort of a shock to his system.

His phone rang and he answered without looking, assuming it was Ellery.

"Hey, Boner," Annie said. "How'd you talk your way out of this morning's misstep?"

He flushed to his ears. She meant, of course, the "jumping Ellery's bones" comment.

"A little soft-shoe. Jill hardly noticed."

"Jill!" she cried, disappointed. "I thought it had been Ellery."

Axel smiled. "Oh, that would have been a treat to explain."

"Did you get the books?"

"I did. *Kiltlander, Vamp* and a third." He extracted the bag with the remaining two books from his pack, and when he did, he saw the paper stapled there, which he'd forgotten.

"Only three?"

"Annie, if I can get Ellery to read any one of them, I'll consider it a major victory." He unfolded the paper and found a phone number scribbled there and the name, Sierra. He laughed and crumpled it.

"What?" his sister said.

The bartender dropped off the beer, and Axel fished his wallet out of his pocket and handed him a ten. "I don't get women."

His sister laughed. "That's a fact. But how does it relate to what we're talking about?"

"The clerk at the bookstore today," he said. "I mean, I was asking her questions about the books when I bought them, but I swear to you, we were not connecting on any level."

"So?"

"So she slipped me her phone number. I just found it attached to the bag. I know my charms are irresistible, but this woman was fifteen years younger than me, easily."

"Axel, Axel, Axel . . ."

He could almost see her shaking her head. "What?"

"First, women are stupid. Second, they get considerably stupider when a man of any sort engages them in conversation about a romance novel. Which book were you talking about?"

He gazed into the thick white head of the beer, trying to remember. "*Vamp*, for a while. She was definitely not a Team Ynez supporter. But she really lit up when I mentioned *Kiltlander*."

Annie made a noise somewhere between seeing a basket of puppies and having an orgasm. "See," she cried. "It's *magic*! Honest to God, I don't understand why more men don't read it. Don't they understand they could get any woman they wanted into bed if they just acted like Jemmie in *Kiltlander*?"

Before Axel could fully ponder this pronouncement, his phone buzzed with a blocked number. "Hang on. I've got another call coming in. I think it's Ellery." He pressed the screen and said, "Ellery?"

"Brendan. Sorry to disappoint you, bud. Jeez, are you seeing her again?"

Axel winced. "No. What's up?"

"I hear you're in Pittsburgh."

Axel swallowed a long draft, savoring the up-front

wheat followed by the mid-palate clove. A true Hefeweizen. He thought about what he might do with it if he were in charge. "Word travels fast."

"I know the bartender there. Axel, the guy upped his bid."

Axel jumped off the barstool. "What? We have a deal."

"We got no deal, man. He's willing to kick in an extra ten grand."

Axel groaned. He could barely meet the price before. He'd never be able to meet it if it was ten thousand more. "Look, I want the brewery, okay? This is my dream. We've gotta be able to work this out. C'mon, man."

Brendan sighed. "If only the guy weren't such a jerk."

"He's a jerk?"

"Oh, yeah. He's an investor. No love for beer. He's planning to sell the brand name to some conglomerate, who will promptly kill it; then the guy's going to sell the place off piece by piece."

"You know me," Axel said after drinking most of what was left in his glass. "I love beer."

"Oh, I know you love beer. Everyone who knows you knows you love beer. But I need the money."

"But who's going to keep your baby alive, eh? Who's going to invest the brewery with the same love you do?" Axel was dissembling a bit. Hard Hat was great, but Brendan hadn't taken enough care in years to produce any other beers that rose above the ordinary.

Brendan growled—the unhappy growl of a man about to say good-bye to an extra ten grand—and Axel began to relax.

"If I tell this guy no, I'm going to need something in return, Axel."

"What?"

"Help, for one."

"Sure. Anytime."

"Tonight."

"Tonight?" Axel looked at his watch. He and Ellery wouldn't be done here until two or three a.m. The flight to Philly, where they'd catch the flight to London, left the next day at two in the afternoon. It depended on how fluid Brendan's definition of "tonight" was. "What's up?"

"Dumping the yeast," Brendan said, and Axel grimaced. Ninety percent of brewing was cleaning, but dumping the yeast was one of the dirtiest jobs in the brewing world. "Sure, I can help."

"Help?" Brendan laughed. "I'm cashing in my chips for the night, friend. You're it."

Axel agreed, wrapped up the call and returned to Annie. What had she been saying before Brendan called that had peaked Axel's interest? "Sorry. A beer thing."

"Are you supposed to be having beer things with the diabetes?"

Axel smacked his forehead. He hadn't taken his evening injection. He'd only been diagnosed a couple months before, and the routine still got away from him sometimes. "Yes, Mother. I'm allowed to have a couple beers a day. In fact, it's encouraged. It reduces insulin resistance—in moderation, of course."

"Moderation, huh?"

"Moderation is my middle name."

"Only if your first name is 'im—.' "

Axel's phone buzzed again. "Another call," he said. "Hang on." He hit the ANSWER button.

"Brendan, again. Sorry. I forgot to tell you the key is over the door."

"Got it." He returned to his sister. "I'm back."

"Popular guy. That's okay. I was just calling to razz you."

"Much appreciated, as always." His phone buzzed again. "Oh, for God's *sake*. Gotta run. Love you." He clicked to the other call. "Jesus, can you possibly get everything you need to say into one call?"

"I'll try, Mackenzie," Buhl Martin Black said flatly, "but I pay you enough to listen no matter how many calls it takes."

Axel felt his heart drop to his shoes. "Oh, God, sir, I'm sorry. I thought it was my friend."

"Some friend. How's the article coming?"

"We've only just begun."

"Very catchy. Have you considered putting that to music? Anything else?"

"Well, I've given her some books to read—"

"*Vamp*?"

"Yes. That's the primary one. There are a couple of others. We're in Pittsburgh now to shoot at the Monkey Bar."

"What the hell is the Monkey Bar?"

Axel was moderately relieved to hear that Black hadn't read the book, either.

"Gateway to hell, sir. Very popular with *Vamp*'s female readers." An *ooga-ooga* siren went off, accompanied by a flashing red light, and Axel turned to see a woman mount the stand at the start of the monkey bars and, cheered on by her friends, twist and turn her way across to the platform at the other end as the patrons parted like the Red Sea beneath her. There she squirmed her way out of her bra, slipping it out from under her blouse to the hoots and hollers of the crowd, and threw it into the cauldron. The cauldron, which looked to Axel like a hastily repainted garbage can, served as the repository of cast-off souls. It was also the source of the annoying flashing lights. The barkeep immediately filled a mug with Budweiser and slapped it on the starting platform: the woman's reward for divesting herself of what was undoubtedly a forty-dollar piece of lingerie. She was not able to claim the far more prestigious prize—one of the free Monkey Bar T-shirts pinned on hooks above the cauldron—as that required the blouse to go as well. Nonetheless, the place went nuts. Women whistled, her friends yelled, "Ynez, Ynez!" and the few men in the place gazed at their shoes, unsure whether to cheer or simply hope they weren't asked to leave.

"What's going on there, Mackenzie?"

"Another soul thrown in with Team Ynez, sir. Happens every fifteen minutes or so. Very exciting. They love the book here."

"Glad to hear it. What exactly has Ellery written so far?"

"What's that? I think I'm losing the call." Axel held the phone at arm's length and signaled the bartender for a refill. "We'll have to try to talk tomorrow. I can't hear any—" He hit the END button and turned his phone off.

He hoped Ellery would start writing something soon. There were only so many times that trick was going to fly.

"Team Ynez?" the bartender asked, dropping another mug in front of him.

"Oh, you know it, pal."

Chapter Seventeen

Airport Marriott, Pittsburgh

Ellery rolled the hotel desk chair back and forth, gazing at the empty page on her laptop screen.

It seemed silly to try to write something in the twenty minutes before she had to dress and head to the Monkey Bar, but she thought if she could produce at least a single, stunning sentence on the subject of romance novels, she'd feel like she had some momentum going.

She held her finger over the keys, waiting as all writers do for that kernel of insight to wriggle itself loose from the recesses of her brain and land with a sizzle on the page, accompanied by a crescendo of harp sweeps marking the prose's incomparable beauty.

Unfortunately, the only kernel that wriggled loose was the one she'd already known: Romances were drivel. Yes, Ynez could stir something primitive in her, and Harold could send a shiver down her spine, but it was a trick, nothing more than pandering to a sex-hungry reader.

Oh, God, if she were only writing about John Irving . . .

She loved Irving, loved his muscular prose and the

wrestling and New England characters who filled the pages of his books. She even loved the bizarre tragicomic events that fueled his plots, like Duncan losing an eye in *Garp* and the TV reporter losing his hand to a lion in *The Fourth Hand*. His stories struck her deeply and lived on in her head years after she had finished reading them.

She hit a few keys.

Why do critics wrestle with John Irving?

She loved it. A perfect first line.

> *Literary critics try to take Irving to the mat for his navel-examining plots, character arcs littered with body parts and scenes approaching slapstick, but Irving always manages an escape.*

God, she was on a roll. This was the sort of writing she could do twenty-four hours a day with hardly a conscious thought. Her hands flew over the keyboard until she had a paragraph and then two. She was in the middle of the third, kernels popping like dried Iowa corn in her head, when her eyes came to rest on the copy of *Vamp*. Her fingers slowed as the thought of Harold demanding Ynez's submission to his care crept sultrily through her mind. It was a trick, yes, but tricks were worthy of some investigation, weren't they? For example, if she wanted to take a quick look just to find out whether Harold and Ynez ended up having sex, that certainly didn't mean she had raised the story in her head to the level of, well, literature.

Her fingers had slowed and stopped. She looked at the screen.

> *In his later novels, Irving does just the opposite,*
> *using Harold and other metaphors to demonstrate sex*
> *sex sex Ynez on top?*

She gasped, looking both ways to see if anyone else had seen this, and pushed the chair slowly away from the desk.

Now, *that* was weird.

She supposed it wouldn't hurt just to check to see where they'd netted out. She'd have to know the answer in order to write the article, after all, right?

She grabbed the book and stretched out on the bed. Where had she been? The third chapter? She found the page, reread the scene with the struggle and the pill, feeling the same lurch in her belly, then scanned ahead. Chapter Four, Chapter Five, Chapter Six—bingo!

"Kiss," "caress," and the all-important "iron length." This was the spot!

> *He laid her out on the velvet-covered bench,*
> *heedless of the floor-to-ceiling windows whose*
> *diaphanous silk drapes billowed in the cool summer*
> *breeze. She would be his at last.*

In an instant Ellery was right there with Ynez, laid out on the bench like some Egyptian queen on a palanquin, gazing out the museum windows, feeling the heavy press of Axel between her—

Axel?

Harold, she thought firmly, though the scene certainly called to mind that summer night she and Axel had first succumbed.

> *Her breasts quivered with the beating of her heart.*
>
> *"You will be my first," she said in a small voice.*

"My first"? There's no way this is Ynez's first time, Ellery thought. Not a she-devil who can fight her way to victory! *Please.* Ellery scanned the next paragraph and leapt to her feet, horrified.

"This is *Britta*?" she cried. "You're bedding *Britta* after saving *Ynez's* life? How did that little upstart worm her way into your bed?"

She paged furiously back to the start of Chapter Four and started to read.

The blare of her cell phone lifted her out of a place so deep in the story, she thought for a moment Romgar had returned with the he-devils.

"Hello?" she said, heart pounding from the shock.

"I thought you were coming over after you checked in?" Axel said.

She looked at the clock. An hour had passed! "I was . . . working."

"On the story?"

"Yes!" She hopped to her feet.

"Good to hear. I'm going to have my cell turned off. Long story, but call the bar if you need me."

"Fine. Whatever. See you soon." She lifted the suitcase onto the bed and unzipped it. Harold had thankfully been diverted before he succumbed to Britta's questionable charms, though it was clear he was going to be making some very bad decisions about her soon.

Ellery tossed the phone on the bed and pulled out the first thing she could grab. The red-spangled thong. Perfect. Just what one needs for a long night sitting at the bar. She could almost feel the rash starting. She threw the thong aside and dug deeper. A V-neck sweater cut halfway to the navel, a halter dress, a see-through blouse meant to be worn over a camisole without a camisole, a leather miniskirt, a purple bustier, three lacy satin bras, a handful of barely-there underwear, a pair of jeans so skinny she wondered if they needed to be torn in to pieces and shellacked onto her buttocks, a foot of condoms and the aforementioned slip dress. *This for Scotland, London and Pittsburgh? In November?* Had they left none of the clothes she'd started with? She considered wearing the neatly creased slacks she'd arrived in, but with her sister's "You can give a zebra a TiVo, but what's the point?" still ringing in her ears, she didn't dare.

Ellery kicked off the slacks and all three pairs of underpants and went for the most conservative panty: a lipstick-red retro bikini that managed to evoke both a sixties Maidenform ad and *Playboy* magazine. She unfolded the jeans and considered. She and Jill were theoretically the same size, though Jill had hung on to those coltish teenager legs and sported an ass that looked like it rode on helium. Ellery's own posterior had settled into a more earthy upside-down heart shape—"earthy" being code for "Hello, gravity"—but she was determined to be an appropriately attired bar patron this evening. With an exhalation calculated to reduce both her weight and volume, she herself eased into the jeans, though "eased" didn't quite cover the combination of hopscotch and yoga necessary to get them over her hips, and zipped them closed.

She looked at herself in the mirror. She had to admit, the jeans made her look fantastic. It reminded her of a pair she'd had in college, though those hadn't ridden quite so low on her hips. It was probably good she'd be wearing a slip dress with them and not a camisole.

She took off her top and no-nonsense T-shirt bra and fastened the "Hands of God" around her chest. She felt a little like Chuck Yeager strapping himself into a cockpit, but once all the buckles had been snapped and the safety checklist reviewed, she felt ready for even the bumpiest flight.

Then she pulled the light-as-air slip over her head and let it flutter over her body. Jill was right: She was going to rock in this outfit. She pulled the elastic from around her ponytail and let her hair fall. She was just strapping on her heels when her cell rang.

"On my way," she said, breathless.

"You certainly are, missy," an ebullient Carlton Purdy said. "And I have some very good news."

Ellery's heart made a joyful lurch. *The job!* "You do?"

"I do. I've convinced the board to wait on their decision until the John Irving article comes out. We have two Irving fanatics in the group, and I know they're going to be thrilled."

Ellery felt her test flight careening toward the ground. "Oh."

"I'll be waiting in line at the corner newsstand the day the magazine drops."

Ka-boom. She collapsed on her back on the bed. "That's great. Are you sure you can afford to wait?"

"Missy, we can't afford *not* to wait. You can thank me later."

"You know I will."

Ellery hung up and stared at the ceiling. Then she turned off her cell phone, rolled to her feet and broke the seal on the honor bar.

CHAPTER EIGHTEEN

Monkey Bar, Pittsburgh

Axel put down his club soda. There she was at last. His calls had been going straight to voice mail for the last half hour.

He watched her make her way across the crowded floor. Irritated as he was, he had to admit she looked great. Nor was he the only man in the room with his eyes on her.

She was wearing something bare and silky on top that fluttered over her curves like the delicate wings of a butterfly. The lights of the room lit her hair like a fiery halo, and her cheeks were aglow. He was reminded with sudden sadness of what he'd lost five years ago, and the pain in his back, which had been gone since the day before, returned.

She spotted him, took a step and went over like a sequoia, arms flailing as she fell.

He ran to her side and pulled her up. "Are you okay?"

"I am very fine," she said, catching his shoulder with an air of companionability that surprised him. "Very fine."

"You sure?" He looked her over, curious. "I've been trying to reach you."

"There was a slight, er, development after you called. It took me a while to work my way through it." She hiccoughed and covered her mouth. "Pardon *me*."

Oh *boy*. Dress slightly askew, lipstick drawn beyond the lip on one side, telltale scent of Tanqueray in the air. "Please tell me you took a cab here."

"I did. Came right to the front of the hotel for me." She tried without success to snap her fingers. "So, are we gonna get this party started or what?"

"I wonder if we should get you a spot of dinner first, eh?" He led her back to the bar.

"That's a fine idea." She waved the bartender down. "Martini, please."

"I was thinking food."

"Loads of olives," she amended.

"And a burger," he said firmly. "Tell me about this development."

"I am writing a piece about romance novels." She picked up his beer and frowned when she discovered it was empty. "*Not* John Irving." She waved a finger at him. "No, no, no. Even though Mr. Irving has had more than a few things to say about romance."

"Yes, I know those happily-ever-after endings are one of his trademarks." Axel pried her fingers from the bottle, which she was now holding over her head and staring into like a spyglass.

"You know, just because it ends unhappily doesn't mean it's not romantic. Look at us."

He felt another back twinge and pulled out his Baggie of pills. "I guess I should be honored you remember it as romantic."

"Even you," she said, swaying a bit, "wouldn't have slept with Britta."

"Britta?"

"I'm not saying Harold did, either, by the way. But I think he's going to."

"Oh, *that* Britta." Axel dropped a muscle relaxant on his tongue and swallowed it dry. "A little too wet-spaghetti for me."

"That's what I'm saying!"

The bartender put down the martini, and Ellery reached for the glass, but Axel put his hand on the base.

"Olives first."

"You know," she said, lifting the toothpick and giving him a pouty look, "you never asked me if I wanted any. Never, ever, ever. Not as long as we were together."

"Wanted any what?" He narrowed his eyes.

She leaned toward him, whispering, "Harold unwrapped it and put it directly into her mouth."

"I beg your pardon."

"Those," she said, waving in the direction of his Baggie. "Your . . . stash."

Axel wanted to laugh. It was like hearing his aunt Gloria say it. "My 'stash'?"

She looked around as if she were checking for a cop. "I can take them too."

"You're telling me you want one."

"I'm a big girl, Axel."

He looked in the bag. It held pink Sweet'N Low packets, yellow caffeine tabs, white muscle relaxants and round brown ibuprofens.

"The brown ones are spectacular," he said, pulling one out.

She gazed at it as if it might sprout wings and fly. "Really?"

"Oh, yeah. Major buzz."

"Like Ecstasy?"

"Better. Pop one of these and fifteen minutes later you'll feel like a million bucks."

She reached for it, hand trembling. "Are you going to take one?"

"I told you, I don't take recreational drugs anymore."

With a snort, she placed the pill on her tongue. Axel offered his club soda. She took a gulp from the martini.

She wiped her mouth on the back of her fist. "Did you ever do coke?"

It was the first time she'd ever asked. They'd argued about his "behavior," as she'd called it, and his late nights, but she'd never actually asked him directly. It was almost as if she hadn't really wanted to know.

"Yes."

She gazed at him, fascinated, as if he were an animal in a zoo . . . a friendly one, mind you—maybe a chimp or a llama—but still an animal.

"Did you . . ." Her voice trailed off and she stirred her drink. "I mean, when I first met you, there was this story about you and that TV reporter . . ."

He waited. He didn't know what she meant, and he certainly wasn't going to offer to try to fill in the blank.

"Forget it." She shook her head, then lifted a hand to her temple. "Ooh, I think I just felt something."

He hoped it was the olives hitting her stomach.

"Axel, can I ask you a question?"

"I doubt I could stop you."

"Do you think of me as a fun person?"

It was his turn to snort, but the look of comic sorrow that came over her face made him regret it instantly.

"You're fun," he assured her. "Look, you're drinking a martini and, um, wearing party shoes."

"That's not fun," she said glumly, draining the rest of her glass. "Anyone with feet could do that."

"Your fun's more internalized." Where the bloody hell was that hamburger?

"Great. Like salmonella . . . or an ulcer." She dropped her head on the bar. "You know, I *have* a TiVo. And I am perfectly aware of how to run it."

"See?" He reached for his club soda. "And what says 'fun' more than time-shifted TV watching?"

"Speaking of that, where the hell are you staying tonight?"

He laughed. "Is that an offer? I was going to be staying with a friend, but now I'm . . . doing something else."

The *ooga-ooga* siren went off again, and another young lady began her precipitous journey of renewal.

Axel preferred the view of Ellery's eyes, which glowed a fantastic blue as she watched. The blue turned cloudy, though, when the bartender put the woman's beer on the platform.

"She didn't get a T-shirt," Ellery said, distraught.

"No, for that you have to give up more than your soul," Axel said. "The shirt goes, too, I'm afraid. Not for the faint of heart."

He caught the bartender's eye, surreptitiously pointed to Ellery and made the motion of a pot pouring coffee. "Now, can I ask you something?"

Ellery lifted a brow. "Mm?"

"Why do you have a red thong sticking to your back?"

She straightened so fast she nearly fell off the stool. "I do not," she said, trying to feel over her shoulder.

He plucked it off her dress and handed it to her. He'd never seen her wear a thong before, and between that, the cut-down-to-there dress and the drinking, he was starting to wonder exactly what she'd been up to at the hotel.

Instead of coffee, the bartender arrived with a pitcher of frozen margaritas and a glass the size of a soup tureen filled to the brim. Axel tried to wave the confused woman away, but the smile that burst across Ellery's face made the attempt futile.

"Yum," Ellery said after taking a long slurp.

"You're going to want to slow down a little," he said. "That pill's pretty powerful."

"I know," she said, rolling her head around her shoulders liquidly. "I can feel it already."

"Hello." A guy in a suit, maybe twenty-five, wearing a gold TAG Heuer and about a liter of Obsession for Men, sidled up to Ellery. "I like your moves."

She giggled. Axel bit hard on his straw.

"Wanna dance?"

"Thank you," Ellery said, giving him a much bigger smile than he deserved. "But I can't. We're working."

The kid looked at Axel, who said nothing.

"He's a photographer," Ellery said.

"I guess that makes you a model."

She giggled again. "You're cute. Blind, but cute."

He shrugged. "Okay. If you change your mind, just let me know." He gave her a little wave and Ellery returned it.

"Speaking of work," Axel said, watching the guy walk away, "should we consider taking a crack at the assignment?"

"It's pictures, right?" she said, dismissing the suggestion.

"Yes, but I think Black feels pretty strongly there should be words to go along with them."

She giggled again, though in this case he felt it to be entirely appropriate.

"You're funny," she said. "You might be a lot of things, but no one could ever say you're not funny."

"How you flatter."

She laid her head on the bar and closed her eyes, grinning happily. "I don't know, Axel. I'm feeling it now, and it's feeling waaaaay too good for me to work."

Great.

Then her eyes flew open and she grabbed his arm. "I'm not going to think I can jump off the building and fly, am I?"

"Nope. The flying pills are green."

She snuggled back into the bar, sighing happily.

"I'd let you relax," he said, "but I know you'd never forgive yourself for missing your Jack Kerouac opportunity."

"Jack Kerouac?"

"You know he wrote *On the Road* in three weeks using the same pills you are."

She sat up and blinked. "Really?"

"It's true."

"Oh my God, I'll be like . . . like . . . the Billie Holiday of journalists."

"There you go. So, why don't you do your thing"—

which was to talk to enough people to develop the narrative for this part of the assignment—"while I set up for some portraits?"

A singular determination seemed to come over her face—admittedly a little hard to make out behind the smear of margarita salt curling up from each side of her mouth—and she threw her shoulders back. "My thing! You're right, Axel. That's exactly what I should do."

He didn't quite know how to respond. "Well, um, great. I'm glad we agree. So I'll get the camera set up and then just find you?"

She nodded like she hadn't been listening and hopped off the stool.

Axel dug into his bag, looking for his Tamron AF 28–75. It was the best lens for portraits, though he knew he'd have to bump up the ISO to accommodate the room's darkness.

The *ooga-ooga* siren went off again. He rolled his eyes and hoped Ellery was in position to catch a couple of good quotes.

Ellery stepped into position on the platform, feeling her heart pound.

No fun am I?

At this moment, with Axel's wonder drug tripping through her brain, Ellery knew she was in the midst of a profound change. She was a butterfly emerging from her cocoon. She was a peacock about to spread her feathers. She was Sarah Connor kicking the Terminator's ass. She was a— Wait, butterflies came from a cocoon, right? Or was it a chrysalis? It didn't matter. Buhl Martin Black might hate her. Carlton Purdy might disavow her. Axel might look at her like he couldn't remember they ever dated. But Ynez would understand. Ynez never faltered. She'd faced the impossible and survived. More than survived: She'd conquered.

No fun? Kate and Jill would eat their words. Oh, they would eat their words. Ellery was a zebra with a TiVo, and she would watch whatever show she wanted!

She grabbed the closest rung and swung off the platform, feeling her third-grade muscle memory returning. These weren't even as hard as the ones at Howe Elementary School. The ones at Howe were free-swinging. These were fixed.

She grunted, using the momentum of her body to propel herself. She kicked a leg and her shoe flew off, hitting a spectator in the forehead. Didn't matter. Could apologize later. She could feel the friction on her palms as they rubbed the metal and the buds of blisters, just like in third grade. She should've rubbed her hands in dirt before she began. The bars were set on a rising incline, making the approach a matter of more than just distance. She wondered if she still had the shoulder strength. She wondered if she'd shaved her underarms. In between the sounds of the sirens, she could hear the *thump-thump-thump* of a Donna Summer remix. Or was that just her head?

Each movement jerked her breasts a little higher out of her bra. Was wishing for God's hands to squeeze tighter sacrilegious? She stole a glance at the people below. The world was jiggly. Drunken jiggly. And she was being carried on the glorious slow wave of imbibed substances like a rock star surfing the crowd. The women were cheering. The man who'd wanted to dance flashed her a thumbs-up. She was glad she'd gone for pants under the slip.

She reached the opposite platform, breathless but exhilarated, and a wonderful happiness uncurled into her fingers and toes. She didn't know what was in the stuff Axel had given her, but she knew she could count on him to have the best. It was probably the one and only thing she could count on him for. The garbage can—wasn't it supposed to be a cauldron?—flashed red lights, making it hard to see. She felt more than a little dizzy, but it was a dizzy mixed with thrill and exquisite satisfaction, like one of those Side by Side shakes at Steak 'n Shake. She squeezed her eyes tight to keep the world from spinning. She wished she'd had something to eat.

Axel clicked the lens into place and rejected the light meter for a more hands-on approach. He scanned the heads of the cheering crowd as "Bad Girls" played, looking for the telltale raven hair and ivory shoulders, but didn't spot them anywhere. After another moment of searching, he wondered with a flicker of guilt if she was in the ladies' room, divesting herself of the alcohol she'd consumed. Then he remembered the TAG Heuer guy and with a flicker of something far different hoped she hadn't done something foolish.

"Va-va-voom," muttered a man with a Tweety Bird tattoo. "Look at the lungs on that one. Snow White with titties."

Axel adjusted his f-stop and shook his head. *Effing asshole— Oh, shit!* He jerked his gaze up. Ellery was teetering on the platform next to the makeshift cauldron, her back to the room. To the chants of "Off! Off! Off for Ynez!" she slipped her hands up her dress and came out with something that looked like a cross between his grandmother's girdle and a Madonna throwback. Ellery tossed it into the can. Grinning like a kid, she turned to the crowd and began pumping her fists—and by default everything else under that thin silk—in victory.

Mr. Tweety made a kissing noise and said, "Niiiiice."

Axel stepped directly into the asshole's line of sight. "That's my coworker. Knock it off."

The guy was about to say something stupid and Axel felt his fists tightening, when the room erupted into a roar. Ellery had turned her back to the crowd and whisked off her dress.

It had been a long time since Axel had seen her half naked, but the spectacle hadn't lost any of its power. Catching only a flash of that pale skin in profile, his heart cramped and his balls contracted—the one-two punch of what he'd lost and still desired.

The roar was deafening, and Mr. Tweety, who had caught the look on Axel's face, snickered in amusement. "Thought that was your colleague, jerk-off."

Ellery grabbed the prize T-shirt off the hook, slipped it on and turned to rake in the adulation, her cheeks pink with pleasure.

Axel lifted the camera automatically and clicked off

half a dozen shots. On the sixth shot, however, he saw her take a step backward, which brought her unknowingly close to the edge of the platform. She lifted her foot again. He dropped the camera and ran.

It was as if she were slipping in slow motion, her foot questing and flexing before her arms instinctively went up to balance her. He was flying, his heart working in overdrive. In five paces he was almost beneath her—just in time to see the guy with the TAG Heuer catch her neatly.

CHAPTER NINETEEN

Axel sat at the bar, frowning into his club soda.

At least she was safe, he thought—and finally interviewing someone. In any case, that's what he hoped was happening on that couch in the corner, though he'd never seen an interview conducted with the interviewer's feet in the interviewee's lap. Fucking TAG Heuer. He'd never hated a watch so much.

He glowered into the carbonation, damning his luck. With a wave, he caught the bartender's eye and asked her to take a cup of coffee to Ellery.

"Put some maraschino cherry juice in it," he added. "And tell her it's spiked."

He pulled out his phone and checked it. Two missed calls, both from Black. He rolled his eyes and opened his e-mail. Black hadn't stopped at calling. "Send me what she's written so far. And I want a daily update. Eleven a.m., my time."

Oh, for Christ's sake.

Axel doubted she'd written anything so far—that is,

unless she'd done her writing rolling around on her back. And he knew she'd be in no condition to write after this.

He sighed and looked at the time. Midnight. He had been hoping to get some candids of the people Ellery talked to, but he'd be damned if he'd take a picture of the guy on the couch.

The bartender returned from across the room with the cup of coffee still in her hand. "No luck," she said.

"She didn't want it?"

"Didn't get a chance to ask. The guy's been pouring Dom Pérignon."

"What? No." Axel jumped off the stool. After martinis, margaritas and who knows what at the hotel, the last thing Ellery needed was to turbocharge it all with champagne.

He fought his way through the crowd, but the couch was empty—and so was the bottle of Dom Pérignon, which sat upside down in a champagne bucket.

After a fruitless survey of the crowd, he stopped a waitress. "Did you see the woman sitting here?"

"The couple?"

He winced. "Yes."

"She said something about a zebra, and they went that way." She pointed toward the hallway that led to the restrooms.

Axel trotted down the hallway. When he made the turn, his blood began to boil. Ellery's T-shirt was up to her neck, and the guy had his face buried in her breasts, snorting coke off them.

In two steps he was at the guy's side. He grabbed him by the shirt and shoved him into the wall hard enough to rattle a picture loose. "She's drunk," Axel said. "There's a line."

The guy had no interest in a face-off with Axel and ran off. Axel turned back to Ellery, who had pulled her T-shirt down. She was old enough to take care of herself—Jesus, she was old enough to do whatever she wanted—and she looked at him with no apology. What she hid could fill a book, but in that moment he could smell her skin, taste the salty sweetness of her flesh and feel the coke charging like tiny thunderbolts through his lungs and into his heart. *This must be what an alcoholic feels when he sees a drink,* he thought. It was if he'd done the snorting himself, so alive was his sense of it in this dark corner.

And he had done it, though not with her. He remembered her question earlier and felt a rush of shame, wondering if that was what she'd meant.

Did you . . . I mean, when I first met you, there was this story about you and this woman.

Ellery's look hadn't changed, but her eyes had grown bolder. There was an offer in them, no question. To kiss her? To roll up a bill and finish what TAG Heuer had started? He wished she'd believe he was done with that stuff. He wanted his word to mean that much to her. But he also wanted to lift up that T-shirt, loosen those jeans and plow her thighs.

She touched his wrist. It was too much, as if all his sorrow and longing had been concentrated into a vial and released into his vein with the jab of a needle. He pulled her against him and brought his mouth to hers. She kissed him eagerly, the pungent mix of liquors on her tongue filling his head. She leaned into him, just like the old days, skimming his ear with her fingers and nipping his lips. The aching pleasure of holding her again was more than he could bear, and when he moaned, she bit him.

He wrenched himself free, surprised at the willpower he'd had to marshal to stop.

"Axel," she said sadly, curled into his chest, "why did you have to disappoint me so?" Then her body went limp and he caught her before she fell.

"Oh, there you are," the bartender said, turning down the hall. "Your hamburger's at the bar."

CHAPTER TWENTY

Ellery's head hurt, but that was nothing compared to the horrible sensation in her mouth. It was like she'd been chewing the lining of a litter box. She moved a little. Nope. Wrong about the head. It was definitely as bad as the mouth.

She slitted an eye.

Holy Christ, she'd been moved to the inside of a steam engine. Large silver vats topped with tubes and dials surrounded her. She could feel the *glug-glug-glug* of the pistons and smell the smoky scent of something cooking. She wondered for an instant if she'd been shrunk to the size of a cell and injected into the engine block of her mother's '71 Olds Cutlass.

She heard a scraping noise and shifted her head. It was Axel on a ladder at the top of one of the vats, and he seemed to be scrubbing the inside with something at the end of a pole. He was stripped to his khakis with his shirt tied around his waist, and Ellery watched the muscles in his back flex as he worked. For all the folklore about drug users being pale, scrawny types, Axel had always been quite the eyeful. In fact, laboring away in his current state of undress, he reminded her of something she'd seen before. Where, though? In the athletic world? No. Sculpture? No, though there was a marble statue of Hermes in the Met that had always annoyingly reminded her of Axel. Then she had it: There was a huge Art Deco mural of gold and gray glass from the thirties on the façade of that building in downtown Pittsburgh that showed a puddler, a steelworker who stirs molten iron with his ladle, with his shirt off. At night tiny lights twinkled on it, showing the sparks from his fiery work. It had always fascinated her, and Axel had the body to carry it off.

Ah, Pittsburgh. She had to admit, there were still some things here that made her smile about the place. She still wasn't exactly sure where she was, but given the grainy scent wafting through the room and the fact that Axel was involved, she suspected she was either in a brewery or a meth lab.

"Morning," he said. "Would you like some coffee?"

"God, yes."

He chuckled and climbed down the ladder. What on earth had happened to her last night? The last thing she remembered clearly was asking Axel for a pill.

Jesus, how did he do it? She felt like she'd spent the night in a rock tumbler. Gingerly she moved her hands, feeling the surface on which she was curled. The mattress was made of burlap and appeared to be filled with tiny beans.

She tried to focus on the red letters printed on it: "Vienna Malt." Then she gazed down. She was five feet above the ground. Axel had laid her on a pallet of malt.

He returned with a mug.

"Can I just sniff it? I'm afraid to sit up."

"Poor Pittsburgh." He gave her a woeful smile and held the cup near her nose.

She peeled the burlap off her mouth, which seemed to have been glued into place with dried drool. God, she must look like hell. She got up on an elbow and felt her stomach roil.

"I think I'm going to throw up."

"Doubtful," Axel said. "I'm pretty sure you're running on empty there."

A snippet of him holding her hair popped into her head. So did a prayer for a comet to hit the earth. "I already . . . ?"

He nodded. "Ten times, at least."

Great. She banged her palm on her bedding. "So, what's with the kitty litter?"

"Kitty litter," he said with mock insult. "You are sitting on one of the most lovely things on earth."

"I always knew you were an ass man."

"Your ass, while remarkable in many ways, cannot impart a sweet honey molasses flavor to beer."

"I'd say you have no idea what my ass can impart to beer, but since I apparently can't remember exactly what happened last night, I'm not sure I'd be on solid ground." She held out her hand and, with his help, pulled herself to a sitting position, though a silent timpani banged away behind her forehead in complaint. She took the coffee and noticed a disconcerting freedom of movement.

"Do you, um, happen to know where my bra is?" *My hundred-dollar bra?*

"Wish I could take credit," he said, heading back up the ladder, "but you really wanted that T-shirt."

She looked down. *The Monkey Bar: Where Girls Come to Play.*

Oh, *Christ.*

"And my dress?"

"You *really* wanted that T-shirt."

She put a hand on her forehead. She had a vision of jerking her way over the heads of the crowd, which would certainly explain why her shoulders were singing with pain. But why did she smell like men's cologne?

Then she remembered the hand up her shirt, and a searing flush of embarrassment came over her. "Did we . . ."

He turned to her, very still. "Did we what?"

She squirmed. More images slipped over the floodgates. A man. Joe? John? Jake? His hands under her shirt, then her shirt up to her neck. Oh, good Lord!

". . . get what we needed for the story?"

Axel returned his attention to the vat he'd abandoned. "*I* did. I'm not so sure about you. Though you were conducting quite an interesting interview toward the end."

Axel must have seen it. She had no idea how she had ended up here, but at some point he must have found her. "I'm remembering a guy," she said at last.

"Pretty unforgettable."

"Not exactly Harold."

Axel considered. "No."

"How bad was it?"

"Let's just say your breasts probably have their own Twitter following at this point."

"Oh, Jesus."

"Hey, it beats Ashton Kutcher."

She rubbed her temples, wondering how each of her teeth

could hurt separately. "Axel, what the hell happened to me?"

"Delayed adolescence? You know, it's sort of like always getting immunized for the flu: You build up no tolerance. When the big one hits, you're wiped off the planet."

"Are you saying my young adulthood was sheltered?"

"Have you heard of *The Boy in the Plastic Bubble*?"

"Hey, I know how to party. Look at my shoes. . . . Oh, boy, where's my other shoe?"

"I was a little curious about that myself."

She sipped the coffee. It was strong and hot, not unlike the guy who had made it. "Hey, thanks for taking care of me."

He shrugged. "No problem."

"And now can you tell me what we're doing in a brewery?"

He laughed. "I don't know what *you're* doing in a brewery, but *I'm* cleaning."

"Cleaning? The man who never picked up a single sock? Who ate cereal out of a saucepan when he ran out of bowls?"

"Works for photographers, not so much for beer. This is Brendan's place."

Oh, yes, she remembered Brendan, Axel's party-boy college friend. "So, why are you cleaning? Can't Brendan just get a cleaning person to do it?"

He scooped the mug from her hand and took a long gulp. She felt a tingle where his hand had brushed her skin.

"First," he said, returning the coffee to her and threading his arms back into the shirt, "brewing *is* cleaning. Sure, it's not the glory part, and it's a pain in the ass, but it's about ninety percent of what a brewer does. Second, I'm hoping to buy this place soon."

She lowered the mug. "What?"

"I want to make beer." He buttoned his sleeves.

"And leave New York?"

He laughed. "Yes. And leave New York."

"What about your work?"

"I figure I'll still do some freelance stuff. But this is my dream."

"I-I-" She didn't know what to say. She knew he liked beer and had homebrewed while they were together, but to do it full-time? That seemed so unlike Axel. Of course, what did she really know about him anymore? "But you're going to live in Pittsburgh?"

"I know it's hard to imagine, but it *is* possible to be happy outside New York. I don't really like the publishing business. I'm not going to miss it."

He'd said this without a touch of venom, but Ellery couldn't help but feel the words applied—if not particularly, then in general—to her.

"Where will you live?" she asked.

"For a while, at least, upstairs. There's an office and a storage room up there. All I need is a bed."

This was more than her bruised brain could process. New York would be different without him. While she'd taken care not to cross his path, she'd always known he was there, and in some ways the way he'd worked to stay on top of his game had inspired her to be better too. And now Axel would follow his dream. She felt a sudden emptiness inside.

"Gosh, I certainly wish you the best."

He smiled, a nice crinkly eyed one. "Thank you. That means a lot." He hesitated. "It's funny about dreams. You think you're happy doing one thing, and then something happens. . . ."

"What happened?" she said, instantly alert.

"I just meant in general," he said. "You reach a point when you find you want something else, and the desire can be so powerful."

She made an affirming "Mm-mm" and smiled.

"You've always followed your dreams. That's one of the things I loved about you, you know. The *Sill*, New York, *Vanity Place*. Is there anything left for you to even dream about?"

She considered telling him about the Lark & Ives position, but decided against it. "You know me," she said. "There's always something around the corner."

"Well, whatever it is, I know you'll nail it."

"Thanks."

"Now, I hate to rain on all this fun, but it's getting close to noon and we have a flight and I still have to dump the yeast and then get you back to the hotel to pick up your stuff—that is, unless you're willing to spend the rest of the trip in jeans and a Monkey Bar T-shirt."

"Believe me, if you saw what else was in my suitcase, you'd understand why that isn't such a bad idea."

"But I'm pretty sure that laptop's going to come in handy on assignment. Speaking of deadlines, did I hear you mention you'd started to write?"

God, what had she said to him? She remembered sitting down to type, but she didn't remember anything about romance coming out of her fingers. "It's, ah, coming along."

Something in her tone must have alerted him, for he gave her a long, considering look. "You *are* going to write it, aren't you?"

Ellery stiffened. She didn't like to be backed into a corner, especially when it came to her work, especially by Axel. The assignment sucked, which was exactly what Black wanted, but that didn't mean she had to do it. Not if Carlton Purdy was going to get his bow tie in a double knot over it. She was pretty sure she'd rather explain to the folks at Lark & Ives why she didn't have any article at all in next month's issue of *Vanity Place* than explain why she had written a freakin' ode to romance novels.

"Yes," she said. "Of course."

He nodded. "Good."

She ran a hand through her slightly matted and malt-smelling hair. "I don't suppose there's a shower upstairs."

"What? The renewal of your soul wasn't enough?"

"Axel. Is there?"

"Of a sort."

She cringed. "Spiders?"

"No walls."

"Oh." She relaxed. "That's not a problem."

"Not for a woman who stared down the garbage can of hell, I suppose. What was I thinking? Make it fast, though. I'll be done dumping the yeast in fifteen minutes and then we've got to go."

Axel listened to the thunder of the water upstairs. He found the notion of a naked Ellery in his brewery quite enthralling—so enthralling, in fact, that he'd found himself at a total standstill twice when he should have been working. Crafting beer all day, crafting interesting interludes all night—now, *that* would be the way to live.

He didn't know why he hadn't told Ellery about the

diabetes when she'd asked what had happened. He supposed he was still getting used to the idea himself. Perhaps if he were a little more confident that whatever this thing with her was becoming would last . . .

Of course, he also remembered the way that guarded look had come over her face when he'd asked her about her dreams. In that flash, he'd felt the same small sting of being shut out that he'd sometimes felt when they were together.

The shower stopped and the sound of her toweling off inspired yet another pause, this one involving a vision of a snowy night, a Hudson's Bay blanket and a bed far more forgiving than a bushel of Vienna malt.

"Axel?"

He jumped. "Yes?" She had crept down the stairs without a sound. Her hair hung in damp tendrils and her face was scrubbed a moist pink.

"I feel tons better—though fresh panties would hit the spot."

He held up a finger and dug with his other hand in his pocket. Then he handed her the red thong.

She gazed at it, hypnotized. "I'm not even going to ask."

"My lips are sealed. Listen, I need some help."

"Sure, what?"

"I'm going to up the pressure in the tank by putting the CO_2 line to it." He pointed to a gauge at the top of a nearby fermenter. "We need to get the yeast out. It's all used up. Kaput."

"Like me after last night."

"No comment. The pressure compacts the yeast inside into a manageable mass. When I give the word, you open the valve at the bottom and it slides out into the tub there. Got it?"

"Sure." She knelt down and gave him a thumbs-up. "Ready."

He climbed the ladder and increased the pressure. It generally needed to be about five pounds per square inch to get the soggy yeast to coalesce. He waited a minute then turned it off.

"Okay," he said. "Try it."

She opened the valve. "Nothing."

"Okay, close it tight. I'll turn it up a little more." He turned it up to ten and tapped his foot, counting.

"So what does a manageable mass of kaput yeast look like?" she asked.

"Pudding. A barrel-sized serving of sticky, smelly chocolate pudding."

"Yum."

"Definitely not yum." He turned the pressure off and signaled her to try it again. "Actually, it reminds me of one of the funniest things I ever saw. We like to refer to it as the Bugs Bunny syndrome."

She opened the valve and shook her head. "'Bugs Bunny'?"

"When you build up the PSI," he said, turning the pressure on again, "the yeast slowly creeps down the side and amasses at the bottom; then, when you turn it off and open the valve, it slides out."

"Yeah?"

"But if you forget to tighten the valve at the bottom and the pressure gets high enough, you get something very much like what you might see in—"

An explosive wet boom filled the room, and Ellery stood there, mouth open, arms outstretched, dripping from head to toe with a thick, bready slag that also covered the walls from end to end except for the silhouette of one perfectly shocked Ellery.

"—a Bugs Bunny cartoon. Maybe we can make time for another quick shower."

CHAPTER TWENTY-ONE

Tarmac, Philadelphia Airport

"Seat belts fastened?"

The smile the flight attendant bestowed on Axel was instantly replaced by a look of pinched surprise and she drew away from Ellery. The woman's hand flew to her nose and she hurried to prep the next row for takeoff.

"I told you I still smell," Ellery cried in horror.

"It's just a little malt," Axel said reassuringly. "Very European."

Ellery wore one of Axel's shirts and a spare pair of his jeans belted with a long piece of torn burlap. Since she hadn't also asked to borrow a pair of his briefs, he assumed she was either panty-free or wearing a red-sequined thong, and empirical evidence certainly suggested she was bra-free. The brewery cleanup had taken so long, they'd barely made it to the airport in time to catch the plane to Philly, which meant the opportunity to change into the clean clothes they had snagged from her hotel never materialized. And then their flight had arrived late, which meant they'd had to run to catch the flight to London.

She'd showered again at the brewery, but the shampoo had run out, and she'd refused to even try the industrial soap Brendan used in the vats, even after Axel told her it was the same soap they use in the Żywiec brewery in Poland. In any case, Axel liked the smell of malt on her. Girl plus beer. The only thing better would be a few notes of Porterhouse.

"Are you getting Wi-Fi here?" he asked.

She stopped typing and checked. "Yep."

"Mind if I borrow it for a minute? I need to dash off a quick note."

She frowned. "What's wrong with your phone?"

"Left it in my bag."

She saved her file, minimized it, and handed him the laptop. Then she pulled a magazine out of her tote bag.

It was considerably past eleven a.m., and he hoped Black would be broad-minded about his deadline. Axel fired up Gmail and began to type.

> *Major progress on the piece. Ellery jumped in with both feet, even going so far as to cross the famed Vamp monkey bars herself. On the Team Britta/Team Ynez front, she has fallen firmly in the Ynez camp. In short, full speed ahead. I am amazed at her transformation. I can literally smell the scent of the chase on her.*

He chuckled at that one.

> *The story arc is building, and as far as preparation*

He stole a glance at the article she was reading: "Five Easy Ways He Can Heighten Your Orgasm."

*she has completely submerged herself in the genre. I've
attached some pictures to whet your appetite.*

Then he added his sign-off, slipped the thumb
drive with the memory card from the camera into
the USB, uploaded a few of the shots he'd taken the
night before—including one of Ellery on the platform, victoriously flashing her Monkey Bar T-shirt to
the crowd—and sent the whole thing off to Black. A
few hours late, but it ought to hold the old codger. He
logged out of e-mail.

As an afterthought, he logged into Facebook, found
Jill's profile and sent her a message with that last photo as
well, adding, "Never tease your sister again: See what it
leads to" as the body.

Ellery was still deep into better orgasms—an excellent
state in which to find a woman, he considered philo-
sophically. Then again, based on what he remembered
about Ellery—and his recollection was quite clear on this
point—if her orgasms had gotten any better, she'd have
exploded.

Perhaps, he thought, with a satisfying mental pat on
the back, her more recent boyfriends had been lacking.
Then he remembered the sight of the TAG Heuer guy in
the hallway, and it reminded him of what his high school
hockey coach had told him after Axel had been ejected
from his first playoff game: It doesn't help to be a great
shooter if you can't get on the ice.

He reached for the thumb drive so he could return the
laptop to her, but the sight of the Word icon at the bottom of the screen stopped him. Had she been working on

the story? Guiltily he clicked on the icon and the document opened to its title page.

> "*Going to the Mat: The Literati's Love-Hate Affair with Irving*"

As titles went, it wasn't bad—it acknowledged Ellery's snobbery concerning the romance genre while paving the path for her rebirth as a fan—but he was scratching his head, trying to figure out who the hell Irving was. He knew Harold, Ynez and Britta. Jemmie was the guy from that Scottish romance, though he didn't think Ellery had cracked that one yet. He wondered if Irving was the author of *Vamp*. Despite all the hoopla about it in the press, he wasn't sure he'd recognize the name of *Vamp*'s author even if he saw it.

"I'm sorry," the flight attendant said, and Axel jumped. "You're going to have to put that away."

He saved Ellery's file to his USB, yanked out the device and closed the laptop. Ellery gave him a look of mild boredom and took it from him. "I hope they don't wait too long after we take off to serve dinner," she said, slipping the laptop into her tote. "I'm finding myself a little hungry."

"Throwing up a dozen times will do that for you."

In twenty minutes they were in the air, on their way to Heathrow.

"I think I'm going to sleep." He balled up his coat.

"I might too," she said, grabbing her laptop, "as soon as I finish some stuff."

"So, if you're sleeping and I'm sleeping, does that mean we're sleeping together?"

She didn't turn her head, but he saw the corner of her mouth rise.

He went on, "I mean, I didn't know this was going to turn into one of those *Year of Living Dangerously, We don't even know if we'll be alive tomorrow* assignments, but if it does, I'm game."

"I'm pretty sure we're not going to be running for our lives doing a story on vampires and Highland warriors. It's not that kind of a piece."

"Big talk from a woman who doesn't know where her shoe is."

She reached for her purse and pulled something out.

"What's that?" He was starving, and Ellery had always carried mini Kit Kats with her.

"Carob soy bar," she said, holding it out. "Want one?"

Gah! He shook his head politely.

All of a sudden he remembered what his sister had said that had been niggling at him. It had been when they were talking about Jemmie, the Highlander in *Kiltlander*. "It's *magic*!" she'd squealed. "Honest to God, I don't understand why more men don't read it. Don't they understand they could get any woman they wanted if they just acted like Jemmie?"

The idea intrigued Axel, but was what she'd said even a reasonable assertion? He considered what he knew about romance novels, which admittedly wasn't much, though his knowledge had increased considerably in the last twenty-four hours. First, women seemed to love them. Not all women, of course—he looked at Ellery, who for many reasons, not all of them good, was in a category all by herself—but a decent number. Second, even if a woman didn't love romance novels, they all loved romance. Apart from the clichéd flowers and candy, however, what actually constituted romance was rather foggy to Axel. He felt like champagne had to be involved, and a lot of necking, which brought back the memory of that dark Monkey Bar hallway with an unhappy wallop. Third, just talking about the romance novels with the cashier at the bookstore had earned him a phone number. Fourth . . .

Hm. What else did he know about romance novels?

Oh, that's right: Fourth, *Kiltlander,* the very book his sister was recommending as a primer on seduction, had actually helped him score with Flip Allison in college.

One, two, three and a pretty interesting four. Maybe his sister was right.

He cleared his throat, and Ellery, who was reclining her seat back, looked at him. "Yes?"

"Do you have those other books I gave you?"

"They're in my tote."

"Mind if I take a look?

"Knock yourself out."

He leaned down, dug under a bottle of water and a sweater and found *Kiltlander.*

Ellery eyed him curiously.

"I'm trying to get a feel for shooting possibilities," he said.

"Shooting possibilities, huh? Maybe you'll get your wish, after all. The trip's starting to sound more and more like *The Year of Living Dangerously.*"

CHAPTER TWENTY-TWO

Ellery scratched her nose and gazed out the airplane window. She had missed the interviews she was supposed to get at the Monkey Bar. She knew she could make up part of that loss by interviewing Kate and Jill, since they were such big *Vamp* fans, but she was also planning to call the bartender there and talk to her as well. Axel, of course, had gotten her name.

She examined the other two books Axel had given her, including the one she'd had to wriggle out from under his arm after he'd fallen asleep. She refused to reopen *Vamp*. She was highly suspicious of the effect it had had on her in that fleeting hour of reading, and she had placed it in the category of things that were bad for you but had the illusion of being good, like high-fructose corn syrup, anything by the Pixies and Axel Mackenzie.

She picked a book at random and turned it over to read the description.

An ambitious writer discovers that bad-boy painters are as timeless—and irresistible—as their art.

Not bad, she had to admit, listening to Axel snore. She certainly liked the "ambitious writer" part. And who didn't love a story about an artist? She thought of *The Great Man,* Kate Christensen's wonderful novel about a pain-in-the-ass painter as told through the eyes of his mistress, his wife and his sister. Now, *there* was a narrative!

Ellery sincerely doubted, however, that this novel would hold quite the same place in her regard.

The cover was tolerable—at least, there was no half-naked man clutching the heroine like a pairs skater about to execute a throw. Instead, there was just a woman in a low-cut pink gown. If Ellery didn't know better, she'd swear the gown was Restoration-era, though she'd assumed all romance novels were set in some timeless place in the past when kilt-wearing Highlanders roamed the earth like packs of wild dogs; in some not-too-distant dystopian future when vampires roamed the earth like packs of wild dogs; or exactly in 1811 for the start of the Regency era.

She jumped down further in the description.

> *A few hours posing on Sir Peter Lely's modeling*
> *chaise—*

Hey, wait a second. Peter Lely was a real painter. They didn't put real people in romance novels—why, she didn't know for sure, but she assumed it was because real people somehow kill the mood. She reflected on this for a moment and found herself inexplicably sorry Ynez and Harold hadn't been real people.

She returned to the description.

*A few hours posing on Sir Peter Lely's modeling
chaise leads to a night of seductive passion*

Now, there's an effing surprise.

She was interrupted by the appearance of a young boy, perhaps four or five, in the aisle beside her. He had dark hair and inquisitive green eyes and bit his finger in some vestigial remnant of toddlerhood thumb sucking. He was dressed in Power Ranger pajamas, which made her smile. Jill had loved the Power Rangers as a child and had dressed as the pink Power Ranger for several Halloweens running. Ellery wasn't aware that a new generation had come to worship at the Ranger shrine.

"Hey, there," she said.

He nodded, uncertain.

She assumed his mom or dad was making a bathroom stop and he'd wandered from his seat. "You a Power Rangers fan?"

He pointed to the red Power Ranger on his sleeve.

"You like the red one? Did you ever use a Zord?"

His eyes sparkled and the finger came out. "I have a Tigerzord. I wish it was a Mega Winger. My grandma got it for me. It's the old kind," he added with a touch of disappointment.

"Well, the old ones were more powerful, you know."

"No they're not."

"Oh, sure," she said. "That was back when Zordon invested them with megapowers. The Zords now are good, but not like before."

His eyes widened. "Really?"

"Absolutely. My sister Jill really liked the pink Power

Ranger when she was little. She's as tall as I am now."

"What are you reading?" He inclined his head toward her book.

"Um . . . grown-up stuff."

He turned so that he could see the cover. "What's it about? That girl looks like you."

Ellery turned the book over. The heroine had red hair, a body that was rocking a size zero dress and legs as long as the Ohio River. "Really? Which part?"

He pointed to her face. "You have pretty eyes. My mom has pretty eyes too."

"Is your mom around?"

"She's sleepin'."

"Ah." Ellery took a quick look down the aisle and spotted a woman curled over the armrest, mouth agape. "Does she know you're unbuckled?"

"I had to pee. What's your book about?"

"Well . . . it's about a man who falls in love with a woman."

The boy chewed his lip, took a long look at Axel's sleeping form then returned his gaze to the book. "Does she love him back?"

"I think."

"Is it like *Beauty and the Beast*?"

"Hmm. Probably." What man didn't have a few Beast-like tendencies, after all?

"Will you read it to me?"

The boy's face was painted with eager, innocent desire, and Ellery melted. "Sure."

He leaned in and the finger went back in his mouth. She could smell the sweet, soapy scent of his skin and feel the heat of his body. She remembered how hot Jill had always seemed when she crawled into Ellery's bed. It had been a long time since she'd had the pleasure of a child's attention.

She found the start of a random chapter and began.

"The Beast," she said, conjuring from her imagination, "was very alone and longed for someone to love him. He had been cursed by a wicked sorceress, whom he had offended. His punishment was to spend his life as a beast until he could convince a woman to love him."

Ellery paused. The boy gazed at the page, considering. Then he pointed to the paragraph from which she had been reading.

"That word is 'Peter,'" he said matter of factly, "and that one is 'breast,' not 'beast.'"

She clapped the book closed. "You read?"

He shrugged. "Some stuff. I like *Curious George* best."

All righty. "Say, ah, it would probably be best if you didn't mention this to your mom. Maybe *you* could tell *me* a story—about the Power Rangers, maybe."

"Henry?"

The bleary-eyed woman hurried up to them.

"I'm so sorry," she said, taking her son's arm. "Was he bothering you?"

"Not at all. We were trading Power Rangers stories." Ellery tucked the book under her arm.

"C'mon, Henry," his mom said. "We've got to get back to sleep. Tomorrow's going to be a long day."

"Nice to meet you, Henry," Ellery said, holding out her hand.

The boy shook it solemnly.

As he walked away, Ellery felt an odd pang of longing, as if a better world had come her way but slipped through her fingers. She wondered what it would have been like to hold Henry on her lap. She wondered what it would have been like to hold any sort of baby on her lap.

With a sigh, she returned to the book's back cover.

> *A few hours posing on Sir Peter Lely's modeling chaise leads to a night of seductive passion, then Cam returns home and discovers his betrayal.*

Ellery put the book down and looked at Axel. Betrayal came in so many flavors. There was the soul-throttling betrayal of adultery, the quick lightning strike of a lie and the dull but aching grind of being taken for granted. But Axel's betrayal had been different. Sure, there had been the daily exasperation of living with a man who didn't take care of himself and whose need to party at all hours and go wherever his camera led had left her feeling inconsequential and vaguely prim.

But the constant drinking and shooting and spending time with his friends had meant she couldn't count on him.

If she had told him that, he would have said, "Well, just tell me when it matters." But life doesn't work like that. You have to have a track record. And when she'd found out she was pregnant, she was paralyzed with fear. Fear that she wasn't ready, fear that Axel wouldn't want a child, fear that the career she'd been building would be compromised, fear that she was barely raising Jill properly. The one thing she hadn't been afraid of was that Axel wasn't ready. That had been a given.

She wondered what would have happened if she had told him. She had been planning to, though it had taken her weeks to decide what she wanted. Then almost as soon as she decided she *did* want the baby, she lost it. That was the night she couldn't raise Axel on his cell when the pain started. Her anxiety had grown as the cramping worsened, and by the time she was doubled up in pain, she was petrified and had no one to turn to.

She'd driven herself to the hospital—foolish, she thought now, but in her terror-soaked brain, it had made sense—and walked, bleeding, into the emergency room, carrying her laptop so that she could work while she waited to be seen. That, too, had been foolish, for she was rushed into an ultrasound and then into a room to be prepared for surgery. She'd been quaking with fear, remembering too much of her mother's frequent hospital stays before her death, and wishing Axel had been there to hold her hand.

Everything about a surgery, especially an unexpected one, seems calculated to disempower. She was stripped of her clothes, her dignity and, with the insertion of the IV, her ability to move around. She'd curled up like a child, in pain and alone. When they'd asked if there was anyone she wanted them to call, she said no, and was wheeled, crying, into the operating room.

She'd been furious she'd had to face that alone, furious that she'd had to endure that feeling of powerlessness without an advocate at her side. She'd expected Axel to find her missing at home and try to call. But he hadn't, because he hadn't arrived home. He didn't stroll in until the middle of the next afternoon, long after she'd been released from the hospital.

He said his phone had been stolen, that he'd found the perfect shot of the Sixteenth Street Bridge but had needed to wait for the moon to be right, and then he'd fallen asleep.

Well, she'd had enough of the Sixteenth Street Bridge, and the faces of the commuters at the bus stop at Liberty and Wood, and the way the light hit the leaves at Point State Park—as well as the beer and the drugs—and she'd had it out with him: not about what she was really mad about, but about everything else.

He'd been surprised at first. Their fights had been brief and sporadic—her complaints about his late nights and partying, while frequent, had been mild—and his surprise had turned to shock when she demanded he move out. But he had, especially after she'd made it clear she would not be changing her mind. Within a week he was out of her life forever—or so she had thought.

Turning in his sleep, Axel barked his long legs against the seat in front of him, made a wuffle of complaint and settled his head in her direction.

Ellery's memory of their time together was complicated. They'd been in love, or an adolescent version of it, and she'd been working hard, often in conjunction with Axel, to build her career. In her head, the memory was a heady hodgepodge of late-night typing, take-out Thai, IKEA furniture and really great sex. The fiery breakup seemed such an incongruous end to it all that it sort of played in her head like slow-motion Super 8 footage of a butterfly flapping from flower to flower until it landed on her palm and dropped a poisoned stinger in it.

Automatically she curled her fingers, feeling the imagined sharpness.

It would have been stupid to have the child. What a mess she would have brought a baby into. It was just as well she'd miscarried, but when she let her imagination wander, she could still sometimes re-create that thick, slightly nauseated sense inside her and the feeling that she and Axel had been meant for some higher purpose.

He scratched his belly.

Some higher purpose.

She cleared her head and returned to Peter Lely and his star-crossed heroine. She hoped the sex made up for the unhappiness. She'd had enough betrayal to last a lifetime.

CHAPTER TWENTY-THREE

Wow, did sex make up for the unhappiness!

Right now, Peter, who had turned out to be considerably more entrancing than Ellery's art survey class in college had bothered to mention, had his lovely heroine pinned up against the wall of his studio's balcony and was doing something Ellery was fairly certain wasn't a common painter technique during the Restoration and frankly wasn't sure could even be done. The heroine faced a choice of suggesting removal to the couch for a more thorough bit of underpainting or risking brick burn and quite possibly hip dislocation. Ellery couldn't remember the last time she'd faced such an interesting choice. Her options lately ran more along the lines of news or bed, quit or be fired—

"Chicken or pasta?"

"What? No. Oh. Pasta, I guess." Lots of room to grow in Axel's pants, she thought, and then giggled, thinking how very different a meaning that phrase could have, especially in light of what she was reading.

Axel, who had awakened at the first scent of dinner,

looked up from his book, pointed at the chicken and gave Ellery a look.

"Something funny there, Pittsburgh?"

She wiped the smile from her face and shook her head firmly. The last thing she needed was Axel knowing she was thinking about his pants.

The meals were served, and Ellery picked up her fork and returned to the book.

It seemed the heroine didn't have to make the choice, for when Peter finished tending to her outdoor needs— he was an early forerunner of the plein air tradition, apparently—he did exactly as Ellery had been hoping and carried the lucky girl inside for the final touches.

Suddenly warm, Ellery fluttered the top of Axel's borrowed shirt up and down before reaching above her to adjust the air.

Axel eyed her with curiosity.

The trouble with the characters having sex was that Peter believed his heroine was in love with him . . . well, at least in lust. And she was, but she had also come with the intention of prying some information out of him, and when Peter eventually realized that, he was going to be devastated, especially since the heroine was the first woman Peter had had any interest in since the death of his wife several years earlier.

Ellery flipped the page, hoping that Peter wouldn't figure it out or that the heroine would change her mind.

"Are you going to eat that?"

"Eat what?" she said, jarred by the interruption.

"Em, that." Axel pointed to a hunk of lasagna sitting on her fork. "It's been hanging there for five minutes."

She gave him an irritated *hm* and popped it into her mouth.

"Sorry. I was afraid it might attract flies, eh?" He smiled.

"What are you up to?"

Axel, who had picked up *Kiltlander* again, paused. "Just getting ideas for locations."

"Locations?"

"Yes."

"You spent half an hour looking for locations? It must have been a page-by-page search."

"Just doing my job. Speaking of which"—he leaned in closer, and for an instant Ellery, who was more romance-addled than she'd realized, thought he might kiss her— "mind if I take a look at yours?"

He meant the book. She exhaled. However, she was particularly reluctant to let go of Peter before she knew if his heart was going to be broken. "I . . . I . . ."

"C'mon, Pittsburgh, how long does an examination need to be?"

She sniffed and handed it to him.

"Do you like it?"

She looked around. "What? The book?"

"Yes," he said with heavy sarcasm. "The book."

"You know I don't read stuff like that."

"That's not an answer."

" 'Like' doesn't enter into it. I was reviewing the text, trying to identify the devices specific to the genre." She thought of the wall of the balcony and wondered exactly how uncomfortable bricks would be on one's back. "There are certain conventions authors follow that may help explain the overwhelmingly positive reaction romance novels seem to engender." The image of Peter dropping the spent heroine on the wide, low couch and stripping off his shirt, those whiskey-colored eyes signaling his intent, swum in her head.

"Do you have anything you want to add to the locations?" Axel asked.

"Locations?" She wondered what the servants would have made of the distinctive sounds.

"Ellery?"

"Oh, God, sorry. Yes. Peter Lely's studio, if it exists. I think it was in Covent Garden somewhere. Actually, I think the inside of any Restoration-era town house near Covent Garden would do, assuming it has a balcony. And bricks."

"Wow. That's pretty specific."

"I thought you liked specific. Do you still need it?"

"What? The book?"

"Yes," she said, imitating his sarcasm. "The book."

"I, ah, guess not." He handed it back uncertainly.

"Then I guess we're set." She settled back into her seat and found her page.

They were kissing—those hard, hunger kisses that taste like mistakes. Ellery's mind wandered, feeling those determined lips on hers, their pungent mixture of sadness and lust. She tempted them, teased them, bit them—

She jerked so hard, the tray shook.

She'd bitten Axel. On the lip. Last night. She was sure of it.

With a sidelong glance, she scanned the battlefield. There it was. That curved red contusion on the stubbled skin above his mouth. Those were definitely tooth marks.

Oh, God, what else had she done? And why hadn't Axel said something? And what about Joe/John/Jake?

She scoured her memory for details, but it was all too fuzzy.

She couldn't take it. "Axel."

"Mm."

"Did we kiss last night?"

He turned the page he'd been reading without looking up. "That would be a yes."

"Before or after the other guy?" She prayed before. After seemed to leave room for too many other possibilities on the malt sacks in the brewery.

"After."

"Did we . . . ?"

"No."

No? Her ego bridled. Why not? But while the soft grassy green in his eyes radiated sympathetic warmth, it revealed nothing.

"Was it me kissing you," she asked, "or you kissing me?"

"I'd say it was pretty equal."

All right, then. So Harold and Ynez had had the power to get her to strip half naked, come on to a stranger and lock lips with her ex-boyfriend. You wouldn't hear anyone making that claim for John Updike or F. Scott Fitzgerald.

She didn't care for the unsettling footing this put her on with Axel, but there didn't appear to be a remedy for it. Already the air between them was crackling with some sort of odd potential energy, though Axel, reading his book, was oblivious to it all. She wished she could recall more about the kissing. The only thing she could remember clearly, apart from the nip, was a disconcertingly clear sense that even if they hadn't done it, she would have if he'd given her half the chance.

"Well," she said primly before settling back into her seat, "all I can say is that pill must have been pretty magical."

He grunted and returned to his reading.

CHAPTER TWENTY-FOUR

London Hilton, Park Lane

Axel stared at the rain beyond the window, turning over her words. Magical pill, eh? That's what she thought had inspired that kiss? He was half tempted to tell her the pill had been ibuprofen, but the point was if she thought that was the origin of the kiss, nothing he could say would make a difference.

Despite the fact he suspected he might learn something on the topic of dealing with uninspired kissing partners from Jemmie, the words on the page could not hold his attention.

And in any case, what he had already learned from the man could, well, fill a book.

Jemmie was quite the hero. In the few chapters of *Kiltlander* that Axel had been able to read, Jemmie had, in no particular order, dislocated a shoulder, killed a marauding English soldier, fought off six more with nothing but a barrel stave and a targe, rescued a child about to be hanged, captained a vessel at sea, held his breath underwater for almost two minutes, taught a priest how to use a dagger, beat a dirty card player at his own game, winning a brothel in the process, authored a pamphlet on liberty, escaped from the king's secret prison, sworn a vow to honor his dead brother and lost his virginity to his new wife.

Sadly, Axel lacked the skill to do any of those things except dislocate his shoulder, which he'd done once with a Homeric amount of crying, and lose his virginity, though that had happened so many years ago, it didn't seem to be of much practical consequence.

It was enough to make a man feel quite humble. Which was a shame, given the fact that he was stretched out on the couch in Ellery's room.

He had managed this enviable feat by entering a different check-in line in the lobby, waiting until she disappeared into the elevator, stepping out of line, counting to two hundred, appearing at her door and telling her there was a problem with his room. She'd agreed to let him stay until the front desk called to say his room was ready, and since he wasn't registered nor had any plans to be, that was likely to be a long time—long enough, at least, for him to capture a nice long nap.

He would pocket the per diem and now had the chance to watch Ellery walk around, fresh from the shower, in the hotel's fluffy towel, waves of damp black hair streaming down her back.

"So the appointment at London College is confirmed," Ellery said, looking at her phone.

"Great."

"And I've put together a list of questions. I figure we just need a few head shots of the professor. Maybe one of the college."

"Can do. And the book club meets at seven."

"And I have those questions too. But I have got to get a quick nap if I'm going to make it through the evening."

He watched the sway of her towel over those fantastic legs. "Always the best way to tackle jet lag."

In the chapter Axel had just begun, Jemmie was heading into battle and, things being what they were with Highlanders, felt the need for a quick, er, respite in his new wife's arms. Axel had never headed into battle but felt there were very few things that couldn't be improved with a quick respite.

However, Jemmie wasn't technically in her arms. Her arms were on the wall of an abandoned cottage and Jemmie's appeared to be stuffed deep in her gown, drawing her nipples "into sweet, hard musket balls" as he stood behind her. All fine on that front—Axel could even roll with the musket ball analogy given the incipient battle—but according to the author, her gown wasn't the only thing Jemmie was deep inside of. Even that, Axel *might* have been able to accept, but the author had made the point several times that Jemmie was a good ten inches taller than his wife.

"How tall are you?" Axel asked Ellery.

"Five six," she said, continuing her unpacking. "Why?"

"No reason." Axel was six foot one. That was a seven-inch difference there. And while Axel had certainly made the same sort of approach with Ellery before, they had been fully horizontal at the time, ensuring the battlefield on which they met was, if not level, then at least contiguous.

"Lemme ask you a question."

Ellery made a slightly bored "Mm?"

"Would you be flattered or offended if someone described your nipples as 'musket balls'?"

The unpacking stopped. She gave him a curious look. "I'm going to have to say no one's ever asked me that before."

"I'm not saying I'd describe them that way, of course."

She lifted a brow. "How *would* you describe them?"

Oh, boy. A minefield. "Er, rubies?"

She shook her head, the shiny strands of black moving like beaded fringe. "Clichéd."

"Summer berries."

"Minor improvement."

"It's been a long time. Perhaps if you could refresh my memory. . . ."

"Nice try." She smiled, then paused, hesitant. "So at least *you* didn't see anything at the bar last night."

He had seen her ample assets in that damned hallway, but he knew that isn't what she meant. "Oh, no. Like the other hundred and seventy-two people there, I was definitely a beneficiary of a grant from the Ellery Sharpe 'Incautiousness "R" Us' Foundation."

She groaned.

"Don't worry. It was tastefully done and integral to the character."

"Character?"

"Determined ingenue achieving her martini-inspired dream. Very *Flashdance*."

"You're such a Pittsburgher." She slipped into the bathroom to change.

"I take that as a compliment," he called. He felt his

phone buzz with incoming e-mails and checked it. Christ, he'd forgotten Black. This was not the way to win friends and influence people. Axel was still considering his response when Ellery emerged in a black see-through blouse and purple bustier over his jeans.

"Wow," he said, and got up to hit the now-empty rest-room himself.

She tugged the burlap belt tighter. "I need to go shopping."

"Not on my account."

"Hey."

He stopped. Her face held an interrogatory look. "Yes?"

"I have a question," she said.

He shrugged. "Okay."

"If I was leaning against this wall here"—she leaned against the hallway wall and moved her back up and down it a little—"how hard would it be for you to, say, hold my leg up in the air?"

He frowned. "Not hard at all."

"Because my yoga teacher—I do a lot of partners yoga now—says that's a really hard move for a man."

"Like this?" He caught her knee and lifted until her thigh ran perpendicular to the ground.

"Sort of. I think it's more open."

"Open?"

"You know. Pressed to the side."

He pushed the knee back a few inches. "Like this?"

"Yes."

"I'm afraid I'll hurt you."

"You won't."

He pushed until her skin touched the plaster. He could smell traces of grapefruit on her hair. He wondered if he could get into her partners yoga class.

She closed her eyes and lifted her chin toward the ceiling. Her hair fluttered in the air currents from the heating vent.

"Oh, *yes,*" she said. "That's it."

There was something odd about the way she'd said it. "Hang on."

Her lids popped open. "What?"

"What are you doing?"

"Nothing."

"You're thinking about having sex."

"No I'm not." She flung her leg to the ground.

"You're thinking about having sex with someone else," he said, then added uncertainly, "You *are* thinking about having sex with someone else?" If she was thinking about having sex with him, he could happily accommodate her.

"I don't know what you're talking about," she said stoutly, but there was a twinkle in her eye, and when she tried to hide it, she began to giggle. "Stop looking at me."

He laughed too. "Yoga, is it? Partners class?"

"I can't help it." She convulsed in laughter. "There was a scene in the other book."

"I know!" he agreed. "Mine too!"

"On a balcony, and I mean, can you even get your thingy in when you're standing like this?"

"Wait, wait. Try this one." He turned her toward the wall and lifted her hands above her head, threading his fingers in hers. "You're a foot shorter than I am, okay? And I'm able to lift my kilt and enter you? I mean, am I as long as a broadsword? Maybe if it was articulated, you know, like one of those big buses—"

"Stop!" she howled. "I'm going to wet my pants."

"Wait, there's more. I'm lifting my kilt, I'm hammering away down there like a Scottish John Henry and I'm cross-armed across your chest, teasing your nipples into musket balls?" He brought his hands over her breasts, and suddenly he didn't want to laugh anymore.

She didn't move. He could feel his heart pounding, and the scent of that damp hair was making him stupid.

He squeezed, and the scant weight of the flesh settled into his palms. The boning of the velvet bustier through the sheer blouse entranced him as did the stiffening of the flesh beneath.

"Take it off," he said.

"What?"

"All of it."

He skinned the blouse off her, and her hair swung loose as it fell. Then he undid the bustier bow and loosened the laces. He wanted to see those breasts fall free, just as he had the day before.

She pulled the velvet over her head, and he caught the soft mounds, letting the nipples graze his palms.

She turned to kiss him, a long, needy kiss that set his balls on a slow burn. Then she held up a finger and walked into the bathroom, her long, straight back an intriguing counterpoint to the easy bounce of her breasts. He loosened his belt. This wasn't going to take long. In a moment she emerged, naked except a pair of impossibly high stilettos.

He was hard instantly. Those curved hips and that neat

triangle of fur were stunning. She held out a condom and he took it. She turned, jutting that lush bottom toward him, and put her hands back on the wall.

He brought his arm around her, holding both breasts, and unzipped his fly. She pressed her hips against him. The heels brought her ass right up to his lap.

Reluctantly he released her breasts and let his hands trail down to her buttocks. Cupping them, he imagined a moment or so from now when he'd split the dark seam below. He wondered if she'd inhale the way she used to when he entered her and whether the delicate throaty cries, so close to tears, would drive him to the edge of beautiful heartbreak.

He caught her around the waist and brought his fingers to her crease. Her wild shiver nearly spent him, but he found her bud, warm and stiff, and plied it lightly. She twisted on his fingers, more practiced than he remembered, and the movement enflamed him with jealousy. He hated that other men had touched her, hated that she'd known their pleasure. Once he had thought what they'd had was forever, and a part of him ached for that feeling in this joining.

But he wanted her. He was powerless to stop.

He bit her ear, enjoying the tug of her flesh while his hand made her mewl and squirm.

"Axel," she whispered.

Her skin was so warm, and the hair on her nape rubbed his cheek softly. He released his hand and her head fell forward with a pant.

He dropped his jeans and briefs and stepped out of them.

He tore open the condom. He didn't want to use it, wanted to ask if he could feel her again, just as he remembered, but a careful sideways glance from her seemed to answer his unspoken question, and he unrolled the latex along his length.

She leaned into him as he entered, and the animal in him sprung to life. He buried his hand in her hair, clutching a handful as he moved.

She stretched like a cat, pushing to bring herself closer.

He bent, thrusting deeply, and found that silky triangle again with his fingers. She groaned, surprised at his touch. Her cheek was against the wall now, and he could see her eyes pressed tight, the pleasure apparent in her flushed skin and open mouth.

It took all his strength to delay his release, but he wanted to feel her tremble.

He caught her nipple and teased it lightly. Her hips began to jerk. "No," she whispered. "No."

Then she convulsed and he twisted the nipple tighter, drawing her peak higher. She shuddered once, twice, and with the third he thought she might collapse, so he caught her hips and held her wiggling against him.

Every nerve in him screamed for relief. He turned her limp body around and caught her leg. The heels helped, and he slid back inside. He tore off his shirt to feel those breasts bounce and gave her the first hammering blow. The nipples skimmed his chest, tightening his balls.

But this wasn't how he wanted her. He wrenched himself free, lifted her in his arms and carried her to the bed. In an instant he was on top of her, his tongue deep in her mouth. She wrapped her arms and legs around him, responding feverishly. Slowly he drew away and sat up, settling himself over her waist. She was breathing deeply, watching him with her temptress's eyes.

He palmed her breasts and brought them together, squeezing them over his length. Slowly he moved, dying in the tight, pleasuring warmth, savoring the heft in his hands. He bucked, feeling the release score his spine. When he could breathe again, he fell alongside her, groaning.

"As always," she said, "you consider the experts, then go them a step better."

He laughed, but his laughter was only half felt. Something had been missing. The ebullient young woman who had approached their lovemaking with unflagging joy was gone, replaced by a cooler, more self-contained partner. She had not gasped or cried. Perhaps he was the one who had changed. But to him every motion had felt as raw and powerful as it had when they'd first fallen in love.

He thought of the end of that wonderful time, that call he had answered, the ring that had interrupted his packing that day. It had been unusual for him to answer: the landline had been hers, but he'd lived there long enough for some of his own calls to come through on it, and there had just been something unusual in the tone of the ring, as if the caller were urging him to lift the receiver.

As he looked back, he must have thought it was her, calling to tell him she'd changed her mind, that he did not need to remove himself from the apartment and her life.

But it had been a nurse from a doctor's office, a doctor whose name he didn't know. The nurse had asked for Ellery, and when he'd said she wasn't home, the nurse had asked his name. He'd given it, curious, and she'd paused for a moment before saying, "Oh, yes, I see it here. You're listed as husband and next of kin."

"Yes," he'd said, feeling the hairs on his neck rising and choosing to be deliberately vague in his correction. "We live together." He heard the shuffle of paper. "Is there something wrong?"

"No. Not at all. I was just checking her privacy options. Will you please let Miss Sharpe know the report shows the procedure was complete? She should have no more problems."

"The procedure." He had tried not to make it sound like a question.

"Yes, the D and C. Everything is clear. No remaining products of conception."

Products of conception? "Okay," he said uncertainly.

"You'll be able to conceive again," the woman said, her voice suddenly reassuring. "You should have no problem."

He'd put down the phone, head spinning, and sat, unmoving, for a quarter hour before he noticed his surroundings again. *Had Ellery been pregnant? How long? Had she had an abortion? A miscarriage? Had the child been his? What part, if any, had this played in their breakup?* He'd felt as if he'd taken a hard kick to the gut. Each time he'd reached for his cell phone to call her at her aunt's, where she and Jill had escaped for the weekend, he'd stopped, uncertain he knew the woman he was calling.

She rustled next to him on the hotel bed, pulling the sheet over them both and curling into his shoulder with a happy sigh.

Axel gazed at the gleaming dark espresso of her hair, shot through with glints of chocolate and plum. That time seemed so long ago, though the thought of it would come back to him in an unhappy rush that took his breath away and he'd find himself pulling up those photos on his camera, scouring her face for clues. He would tell himself it didn't matter, that what was done was done, and in a quarter hour he'd be distracted by something and the memories would retreat.

He'd never expected to find himself here again by her side or with his arm in its usual place around her.

"Well," she said with a smile in her voice.

"That about sums it up—though if I'd had to pick one word, it might have been 'brava,' eh?"

She looked at him and grinned. "Thanks. You were pretty wonderful yourself."

He exhaled happily and pulled her closer. He had started this tired, and their liaison had rendered him deliciously numb. His lids were so heavy, he could barely hold them open, and the scent of her hair was like a pleasant sort of ether carrying him off to a distant wonderland where he didn't have to worry about what any of it meant. Even if everything was different when he woke up again, every inch of him—*every* inch—would go to sleep happy now.

She got up on an elbow, allowing a whoosh of cool air to hit him, and he opened his eyes. "Hmm?"

"Bathroom," she said, getting to her feet. "Back in a flash. Then let's sleep."

He sat up, grabbed a tissue and disposed of his condom, trying not to imbue her determination that he wear one with anything more than the usual worry about STDs.

In the old days he would have lit a joint, or at least a cigarette. Now he just had to count the hours from his last shot of insulin or, for a really grand time, check his blood sugar levels. There was nothing like coming down with a serious chronic illness to really shake up one's view of life. But the diagnosis had only served to put the last nail in a lifestyle he'd already grown out of. Once, playing hard had been the reward for working hard. These days, the work was its own reward. And he found the hours after work becoming ones he wished he could fill with something more meaningful. He listened to her in the bathroom, remembering the year he had called her his.

With the book club set for seven and a visit to London College planned before that, he knew they'd only sleep a couple hours, and he decided his blood sugar would be fine until then. He reached for his pants and found his phone. Then he pulled up his e-mail. Jill had replied to his Facebook message. "I can't BELIEVE IT!" she'd written. "Please, please tell me she still has the shirt."

Axel grinned and wrote back, "I don't know. It's been pretty hard keeping any shirt on her lately. Next time you see her, ask her about dumping the yeast." He hit SEND, then called up Black's e-mail from before the flight and typed,

> *Ellery's research continues. She has wrapped herself around the subject and has been banging away since we arrived.*

I'm here all week, folks.

> *I have probed her a little bit—it was admittedly*
> *a very quick review—but I liked what I saw.*
> *She also reviewed my stuff and found it deeply*
> *penetrating.*

He backspaced over the last line, then changed his mind and put it back in.

"You're e-mailing?" Ellery had emerged from the bathroom

"Just something about an assignment," he said vaguely.

"Bed?" she asked, slipping between the covers.

He quirked an inquisitive brow.

"Sleep." But her look suggested while sleep was it for now, the future definitely held promise.

"Sounds heavenly." And as he shut off the light, he wondered what, if anything, it all meant.

CHAPTER TWENTY-FIVE

Blue Lagoon Geothermal Springs, Iceland

Black waved the hot steam away from the top of the water, clutched his ballooning bathing trunks and reread the last line of Mackenzie's e-mail.

"What?" Bettina lay half submerged in the hot, milky blue pool beside him, eyeing him like a crocodile.

"I'm not quite sure. I have the oddest impression of having just read porn."

"For heaven's sake, put that thing down. I didn't come here to watch you fiddle with your BlackBerry. I can do that on videoconference. I still don't understand why you chose this godforsaken place."

"It seemed about equidistant from London and New York, my love."

"The Presidential Suite at the Royal Savoy in Madeira is equidistant. Rio is equidistant. Iceland is an unattended petrol station on an ice floe. For God's sake, the place looks like it was bombed."

"It's one of the largest areas of geothermal activity in the world. It's practically one of the Seven Wonders."

"It's practically a nuclear waste dump. I can see the power plant right there." She made a scornful noise and swam in a slow circle in front of him. Black watched her pale locks stretching hypnotically over a clingy red suit and felt his own trunks tighten.

"It's one of the few places I can be sure we won't run into anyone we know," he added. "And you only had a day before your conference."

She *hmm*ed, relenting a degree.

"Besides, there's a lovely fireplace in the bedroom."

With an enigmatic smile, she ran a finger along the edge of his waistband. "Are you going to put down your e-mail?"

He obeyed instantly. "It was about your article."

The croc eyes lit with interest. "When can I read it?"

"Well, my dear, it takes—"

"You're not going to disappoint me, are you?" She leaned back just far enough to pierce the surface with her hardened nipples. "I want to read it."

He tried to ward off the incipient erection, heart racing, as the headline INTERNATIONAL INCIDENT flashed through his head. "As soon as I have it."

"Do you think you can get it by Friday? A draft, at least."

He felt her hands on his suit, tugging, exploring. He clutched the wall behind him. "I'll try."

" 'Try'?" She held up a finger. "I can hold my breath underwater for two minutes. Why don't you show me what *you* can do for two minutes?" She grabbed the BlackBerry, placed it in his hand and slid slowly down his body and out of sight.

CHAPTER TWENTY-SIX

St. Paul's Church, Covent Garden, London

Axel clutched his jacket against the rising wind and gazed curiously at the phone screen. He had a general idea of what Black meant by "Send maniscip ttttonit. oNo excusssssssssssssssssssssssssssssssssssssssssssssssssssssss," but fifty-two "S's"? Had he been typing with an eggplant?

He turned his gaze to Ellery. The London College connection had canceled on them, and Ellery had immediately suggested that they head for Covent Garden instead.

She had been surprisingly untransformed by their brief assignation. He'd woken after an hour and hopped out of bed to begin a quest for something to appease his rapidly falling blood sugar. When he'd returned, apple in hand, she'd already gotten dressed and was reading. Not a word had been spoken regarding the moments before they'd gone to sleep. If Axel had had anything more than two extremely mediocre beers on the flight over, he'd have sworn he'd blacked out and imagined the whole thing. Not exactly the long-lasting impression Jemmie would have left.

She was holding one of the books Axel had given her,

looking carefully from the page to the church façade and back again. He hoped this meant the article was under way, at least in her head. He was going to need to share something with Black soon.

He sidled up beside her, and she slipped the book under her arm.

"You know," she said, pointing to the sweeping covered portico of the church, "this was where the first casualty of the Great Plague of London was buried. It also happens to be the place where Henry Higgins meets Eliza Doolittle."

"My goodness," Axel said. "*Vanity Place* permits references to *My Fair Lady*? Do you have to wash your mouth out with cognac when you're done?"

"I was thinking of *Pygmalion*."

Axel bowed, acknowledging her victory, but couldn't help adding, "Which, of course, was a very fine romance itself."

Her eyes narrowed. "Do you think?"

"Yes, of course," he said, surprised. "Don't you?"

"I was never sure if they ended up together."

"That's where faith comes in, Pittsburgh. You have to read, well, if not in between the lines, then at least after the words 'The End.' Of course they end up together. They each realize the mistakes they've made and change. Sometimes you have to let your heart write the epilogue."

"I guess that's always sort of been the difference between us. With me, it's my head that writes that stuff." Ellery looked away, flushing. Henry Higgins and Eliza Doolittle ended up together? She had read the play three or four times and though she'd never admit it to Axel, seen the musical, too, and she'd never seen the ending as happy. She wondered, not for the first time, if something inside her was missing.

She'd awakened that afternoon in a happy, dream-like state, letting the bits and pieces of their lovemaking wash over her, easily silencing the critical voice in her head that whispered, *Major mistake!* Then she'd rolled over and discovered he was gone. When he'd finally returned, he was devouring the apple he said he'd picked up from a store across the street. She was sure that wasn't the reason he'd left. She'd had more than enough experience to know the meaning of Axel's disappearances. Then he'd sauntered directly into the shower without a word about what had happened between them.

Now the voice was whispering, *Have you considered getting "Gullible" tattooed on your ass? It would make more sense than what you just used it for.* Of course, a tattoo would only add to her prick-related woes.

Axel slipped the camera off his shoulder and began adjusting the dials. "You say this is part of one of the books?"

"Yep."

"You seemed pretty driven to come here. Is there anything in particular you want me to get?"

She shook her head. What she really wanted was to find the gravestone. The one belonging to Peter's dead wife. The one he came to visit near the start of the book. But she wanted to do it without Axel looking over her shoulder.

"I'll just work on some background shots, then."

"Sure," she said. "Sounds good."

He paused. "You don't need me?"

"No."

She wandered past the church's front entrance, which she had heard the tour guide proclaim was not really the front at all, just an appropriate façade to face the piazza, and found the peaceful tree-lined park in the back, criss-crossed with brick paths and inviting benches, where the graves seemed like they'd be.

A few moments of looking was enough to tell her that no one seemed to be buried there at all. She stopped a man in a cassock walking purposefully toward the church door and asked him where she might find the grave of Peter Lely's wife.

"Lely, is it?" said the man, a textbook example of a ruddy-cheeked Englishman.

"The painter, yes. His wife."

The man's mouth twitched. "Aye, I know him. He had a fine artistic eye for the ladies of the court, did he not?"

Ellery nodded, though she did not add that her knowledge of that had been gleaned from a romance novel.

"Are you with the photographer?" he asked. "I saw you talking together earlier. This is a lovely place for pictures."

"We're working on a story. For a magazine."

"Ah." The priest's face turned solemn. "In regards to your question, yes, Peter Lely is buried here, and his wife may be as well, but there was a great fire in 1795, which destroyed most of the headstones. We have no idea where in our midst he is, except to know he is here."

"Oh," she said, disappointed. "Well, thank you."

In the book, a heartbroken Peter comes to ask forgiveness of his dead wife. And while Ellery wasn't far enough along to know what he had to ask forgiveness for, she had found the scene heartbreaking. She knew from her own experience how painful it was to regret something one couldn't change.

She nodded her thanks to the man and made her way to one of the benches, thinking about all the sorrow that this small garden had seen and how, despite all that, it still managed to exude the most peaceful, welcoming air. It was as if the power to be comforted was stronger even than the inclination to mourn.

It was nearly five, and the November sun was setting, painting the bricks with a golden-pink wash and warming her back. She hoped Peter and his heroine would find more happiness than she and Axel had. As she withdrew the book from her purse, she remembered that when she'd stopped reading, Peter had been about to come face-to-face with his lover for the first time since discovering that she had pursued him to secure information, not because she found herself attracted to him. Though whatever the heroine's intended reason might have been for striking up a relationship with Peter initially, Ellery was absolutely certain the woman had fallen in love with him before their first evening together was over.

Despite the heroine's betrayal, Ellery knew things would work out between the two: That was, after all, the essential nature of romances. Yet, she couldn't imagine how they would overcome such an obstacle and in fact found herself unable to believe it was even possible. And so, with the tension between the lovers at least as strong as that between Ellery's critical eye and her reader's eye, she found herself once again drawn in to the story.

She was jerked out of her reverie a short time later by the priest.

"I do beg your pardon," he said.

Ellery put down the book and wondered vaguely where Axel was. "Is the church closing?"

"No, we have choir practice tonight. You're welcome to stay. I did a little checking on Lely, and I wanted to share it with you."

"Oh?"

"We still don't know where his grave is, but the other priest here reminded me of what we do know about him. He is buried here, and his wife is, too, though there is some question as to whether or not she was his wife."

"Really?" How like a romance novel to not have its facts straight, she thought, with a private ironic smile.

"Well, the record is not clear. What we do know, however, is the woman died giving birth to their son in 1671."

"Oh, my." Ellery felt the emptiness inside her swell like a sponge dipped in water.

"And the son died a few days later. Imagine the poor man's devastation."

"I . . . I can't."

Ellery felt slightly dizzy, the way she did whenever another person's tragedy seemed to catch her in its wake and drag her along on its harrowing ride. The thought of Peter at that headstone, feeling the monumental pull of everything he'd lost, of the wife and the child . . .

"Miss?"

"What?"

The priest was staring at her, concern on his face.

"No, I'm fine." But she wasn't, and for a reason she

couldn't explain, she felt tears starting to well. "Oh, dear." She hurriedly wiped them away. "It's just that the story is so sad. . . ." But she couldn't stop crying. The more she wiped, the faster the wetness seemed to stripe her cheeks. She tried staring directly into the priest's face to reassure him and perhaps herself, but the tears continued.

"Are you all right?"

"Yes. I must just be tired from the flight over." She dug into her purse for a tissue.

"Perhaps you should . . ." He gestured toward the church.

"No. Thank you. I'll be fine."

He left her, and without an audience her last vestige of self-control vanished. She wrapped her arms around her waist and wept.

A moment later she heard the sound of hurried footsteps. She turned as Axel reached her, breathless, and knelt at her feet. The priest stood in the distance.

"What is it?" Axel said softly.

"I don't know," she said, crying.

He slid onto the bench and pulled her next to him. She laid her head on his shoulder and cried.

Why had things gone so wrong for them?

Chapter Twenty-seven

Mullen's Bar & Grill, Pittsburgh, Five Years Earlier

"I want to go home," Ellery said, raising her voice to be heard over the din.

Axel shook his head, not understanding, and lifted the beer to his mouth.

Brendan's band was in the midst of their sound check and the heated riffs of "Tumbling Dice" were mixed in with the *ploink, ploink, ploink* of the bass player, a drum arpeggio, screeching feedback on the speakers, the clank of glasses and the general noise of the crowd. The cigarette smoke was making her queasy and she was afraid she knew why. Her period was overdue.

"Go home," she said, louder. "I want to go home."

Axel's face fell. "C'mon, Pittsburgh. We just got here."

"I know, but it's eleven, and I don't feel well."

He sighed and looked at his watch. Then he waved for the check.

"I can drop you off, eh?" he said. "But I can't stay. I'm doing a shoot with the sanitation workers. Have to be there at four."

She watched him dig through his pocket, then pop something into his mouth.

"I'd really like you to be at home tonight."

"Sanitation workers, Pittsburgh. If there's one rule in the photojournalism world, it's 'Never keep a sanitation worker waiting.'"

The check came and he laid down a twenty. Brendan yelled, "Ax, you're not leaving, are you?"

Axel inclined his head toward Ellery and made the motion of driving. "I'll be back," he called, and led her out.

She hated feeling like an obligation. She made her way through a fog of smoke and had to forcibly swallow a gag. The next issue of *City Sill* was due in the morning, and she'd had a pregnancy test kit hidden in her purse since before dinner, hoping to get home to use it.

The idea of being pregnant terrified her, though there was a vein of something like amazement there as well. All her life she'd felt like she'd come from something broken. Her father had left, and her mother had worked hard to give Jill and Ellery the semblance of normal family life. But then she'd gotten sick and died, and Ellery had inherited the job of trying to hold the family, or what was left of it, together. She knew she'd taken good care of Jill, and Axel was fitting in well, but it still felt like she was treading water. Nothing had ever happened that had made Ellery feel as if she might be building something permanent. Until now.

She emerged into the cool air of the street with Axel behind her.

"I'm sorry you're not feeling well," he said.

"It's probably a bug or something. I still have to finish my piece for the *Sill* and write the editorial."

What was the point of saying anything until she knew? Even then she thought it would be better to wait until the doctor had confirmed it and the most dangerous period for a miscarriage had passed.

Axel pulled her into the lonely glow of a streetlight and searched her face, his eyes dark and earnest. "Why did you want me home tonight?"

"I want you home every night, Axel."

He held her gaze a beat, then laughed and put his arm around her. "I love that about you."

CHAPTER TWENTY-EIGHT

The Rosemary Hotel, London, Present Day

Axel held open the door. The smells of hops, fire smoke and garlic hung over the well-worn wood of the bar.

Ellery gave him an uncertain look. "A pub?" He'd told her this was a hotel, but Ellery knew a pub when she saw one.

"I told you I had friends in London." He pulled off his scarf and led her to a stool.

"I knew you had friends in pubs in London. What you told me was you had friends with connections to book clubs."

"Tell her, Simon."

The publican, a bald, scarred-cheek brute who looked like an escapee from a Guy Ritchie movie, moved the bar rag from one arm to the other. "'E's not lyin', luv. The Rosemary Readers meet here every Thursday night at seven." He pointed to a table in an alcove in front of one of the establishment's diamond-paned windows. "Right there in the snug."

Ellery's plan was to have these women serve as the

panel of readers she'd interview for her article. She'd talk to them as a group, asking stuff like "What makes romance different than other genres?" and "Why do readers read romance?" and hoping the insights of the group would provide a good hook for the story. She'd begin to draft the article tomorrow on the train to Edinburgh even though she still felt no certainty she was willing to have this published with her name on it.

"Axel, will you be wanting a pint? We have a good oyster stout."

Ellery grimaced. "Oh, God, do those words even go together?"

"Oatmeal, I think," he said to Simon. "Maybe a nice Scottish Borders?"

Ellery considered the incident in the garden outside St. Paul's. After some nose blowing and cheek wiping she'd recovered her composure, but she'd dared not tell Axel why she'd been crying. She wasn't even sure she understood it herself. She'd just passed it off as a combination of jetlag and bad airplane lasagna.

"As you like," Simon said. "And for the lady?"

"Coffee," she said firmly, hoping Simon hadn't been expecting Axel to answer for her.

Simon nodded and disappeared into the back.

Axel and Ellery took seats at the bar.

"This is where those in the know stay," he explained. "Very popular with the *GQ* crowd. It's cheap, convenient and friendly."

"Ah." Ellery grabbed a bag of potato chips off a display and tore it open. "I hope they have something good to eat here," she said, popping a chip in her mouth. "I'm starving."

Truth was, she hoped getting something in her stomach would settle her down a bit. Ever since this assignment had begun, she'd felt like she'd been on a bender. Okay, technically, she *had* been on a bender. Well, maybe "bender" wasn't the right word. "Adventure," perhaps. But an adventure that led to a public striptease that led to a shortsighted session of carnal origami with Axel and an unexpected bout of tears? That was a lot for someone who considered herself pretty level-headed. She looked at Axel, thinking about their unorthodox scene in the hotel room, and held out her forearms, remembering the coolness of the wall beneath them.

"Trouble?" Axel asked with what she would have sworn was a twinkle in his eye.

"No," she said, placing her arms squarely on the bar.

Simon placed two sloshing glass mugs in front of them. Axel lifted the lighter-colored of the two and sniffed it inquisitively. Then he tilted it toward her.

"To a great story."

She lifted hers reluctantly. "It's not hot," she said, looking at the contents.

He frowned. "It's not supposed to be."

She sipped and nearly gagged. "It's not coffee!"

He looked horrified. "Did you want actual coffee?"

"I ordered coffee."

"Well, we were talking about stout. I'm pretty sure Simon thought you meant coffee stout."

"Coffee in *beer*?"

"You betcha."

"Jeez, is there anything you people won't put into it?"

He scratched his cheek, considering. "Peppermint.

Tried it once in a holiday stout. It's not as merry as you might think."

Ellery, whose need for caffeine was stronger than her desire for a more traditional delivery method, took another swallow. She could feel Axel looking at her.

"You sure you're okay?" he said.

She nodded, unwilling to meet his eyes. She looked instead at his lean wrist and the dusting of russet hairs along his taut, tan arm and the way his first two fingers lifted and lowered slowly over the counter. He was on the precipice of asking more, and she threw out an invisible wall of unapproachability to keep him from doing it.

His fingers stilled and, with a sigh from their owner, tightened around the handle of his mug and disappeared from her sight.

"I have to hit the men's room."

"Of course you do."

"Meaning?"

"Nothing." There was no point in arguing about it.

When he disappeared, she asked Simon for a menu. He cocked his head toward the chalkboard on the wall next to the framed picture of the Tottenham Hotspur Football Club. "Game Pie, Ploughman's Lunch, Fish and Chips," the board read, as well as something referred to mysteriously as "Whelks."

"How are the whelks today?" she asked.

"Garlicky."

"Darn. I'll have the fish and chips." At least that was readily identifiable. "Side salad?"

He shook his head.

Of course not. Perhaps if she asked for a lettuce stout.

Her phone rang. It was a work number. She took another draft of her beer abomination and answered.

"Ellery Sharpe."

"I heard you were naked in Pittsburgh." It was Kate.

"*Half* naked. Please tell me you're not in a pitch meeting."

"Manicure. Which half?"

"My left half. Jesus, can the manicurist understand English?"

"I think so. It's Jill. We met in the park for lunch."

"Hiya, sis!" Jill called in the background. "Nice boob action!"

"Yeah," Kate said. "Great for the résumé."

"Nobody knew who I was," Ellery said. "And the only pictures were Axel's and he took those after I had the T-shirt on."

"Yeah, after he picked his jaw off the floor. Pardon?" Kate added, obviously talking to Jill. Then to Ellery: "Oh, no. Jill assures me there are plenty of pictures of you online looking, well, positively empowered."

"Pictures!" She sat up so hard, she nearly fell off the stool.

"Pictures?" said Axel, who had just returned.

Kate said, "Oh, yeah. Apparently you need only go to Twitter and search for 'Ynez army' and you'll find links to tons of 'em. Oh, hang on. . . ." Kate was listening to Jill again. "I'm told 'boob empowerment' works too."

"Oh, *great*."

"Is that Kate?" Axel said, hearing her tinny voice coming out of Ellery's earpiece. "Is there an issue with the pictures? Tell her I have a bunch if she wants to look them over early."

"Soooooo," Kate said. "The million dollar question is: How empowered did you get with Axel?"

"The photos are looking *great*." Ellery hugged the phone tighter to her ear. "Axel can send you what he has if you want to look them over now."

Kate laughed. "Ask him if he's been on Twitter lately."

"No, no, it's no problem. He says he'd be happy to share them."

"I'll bet he would. Maybe you two should get yourselves into a dark room and see what develops, you lover, you."

"Did she say 'cover'?" Axel edged closer, any vestige of manners gone. "God, I'd love a cover. Who would we shoot? Bettina Moore? Or maybe that woman who wrote *Vamp*?"

Ellery said, "I know who I'd choose to shoot," and Kate giggled.

"Yes, I promise he'll send what he has. Gotta run. Bye." Ellery hit the END button.

"A cover would be great," Axel said.

Oh, Jesus. The only thing worse than writing the damn article would be seeing it make the cover of *Vanity Place*. She'd be laughed out of New York.

"Kate sounded eager for details," he said.

" 'Eager' doesn't begin to describe it. Better send her what you have tonight."

Simon put the fish in front of Ellery. Axel motioned for a similar order for himself and grabbed one of her chips. "God, I love this stuff."

"They're yours. I'm only going to have a couple."

He found the malt vinegar bottle and made himself a

puddle at one end of the plate and followed that with an artery-tightening snowstorm of salt.

"How are you feeling about whelks?"

The chip stopped before it reached his mouth and his eyebrows rose in happy arches. "They have whelks?"

"God, what is it with you British Empire people?"

"Technically, Canada is not part of the British Empire—not anymore, at least."

"You still have the queen's picture on your money."

"Think of it as plaid pants. If you don't wear plaid pants at a country club, no one will know you belong."

"Is that how it is?" She knew for a fact Axel wouldn't be caught dead in plaid pants *or* at a country club.

"Yes. And Americans are like the slightly vulgar out-of-town guests you bring who shout to the caddy from the patio of the tea shop."

"Slightly vulgar *independent* guests, you mean. We fought for it, you know. Didn't wait for it to be handed to us along with the lyrics to 'O Canada' and a box of Tim Hortons doughnuts."

"Mmmm," he said happily through the chip he was eating. "Doughnuts."

The sky had turned a dark gray on their walk from Covent Garden, and Ellery was not surprised to hear the clap of lightning followed by the immediate rumble of rain.

"Great." She gazed at the empty snug. The pub itself was nearly empty. "First the London College woman cancels and now I just know the book ladies are not going to show."

"They'll show," Simon said, returning with Axel's dinner. At this point Axel had moved Ellery's plate in front of him and was digging into her fish. The pub man paused for a moment, then slid the new plate in front of Ellery. "The Rosemary Readers never miss."

"Hm."

Simon ducked under the bar to attend to the fire in the room's small hearth when a crashing jolt of thunder heralded an even harder downpour.

"This day's going to be a total waste," Ellery grumbled, and immediately regretted it when she saw the look that came over Axel's face. "I meant as far as the article is concerned."

"Ah." He sucked a stray bit of fried batter off his finger. "You need to think more positively."

"That was positive. Otherwise, I'd have said our careers are finished and we're doomed to walk the cheerless halls of the unemployment office, begging for jobs taking school pictures and writing obituaries."

"There's the Ellery I know. You're not going to eat my fish, are you?"

She paused, fork in the air, and gave him a look. Then with a flourish she bit into the firm, white plank and let the steamy, oily, salty morsel melt on her tongue.

"Pretty good, eh?" he said.

"Fantastic."

"So at least the night's not going to be a total wash?"

His eyes glittered when he said it, and she hid her flush in a quick slug of coffee-beer. "Except for the fact that the women aren't going to make it. Nobody comes out on a night like this if they don't have to."

"They'll come."

A man opened the door, shook off his rain slicker and

said, "Anybody own the Ford Estate Wagon parked on the corner? The storm drains have overflowed. Looks like it might be carried off with the rain."

"Wanna bet?" she said to Axel.

"That depends." He gazed at her from a bent elbow, liquid eyes alight with mischief. "How interesting do you want to make it?"

When she found her breath, she said, "Ten bucks."

He shook his head. "Not even close to interesting."

She could feel the warmth rising on her cheeks. "Twenty?"

"Simon," he called, not breaking her gaze. "How much are the rooms upstairs?"

"Sixty quid."

"How does sixty quid sound?"

She shifted. "Pricey."

"What does it matter? You're going to win, right? If they don't show, you win. But if they do . . ."

She wasn't quite sure what she was agreeing to, but she had a sudden keen interest in the weather. She finished the fish, leaving the chips for Axel, and munched on the single leaf of lettuce that had come on her plate. "So, ah, how close to seven o'clock are we?"

Axel checked his cell phone. "Forty minutes. I'm going to get set up."

"And I'm going to sit by the fire and put together an outline for the piece."

"Speaking of that," he said, his posture changing subtly, "where do you stand?"

"Stand?"

"On the piece."

She rolled her eyes. "I think you know where I stand."

"I meant in regards to writing it."

"It's in process."

She hiked her backpack onto her shoulder and was about to step away, when he added, "Can I see it, do you think?"

"What? The draft?"

"Yeah. You know I always enjoy reading your stuff."

She shrugged. *Not much of a risk,* she considered, *since I haven't written a single word.* "Sure."

The truth was, she still wasn't sure what she was going to write. Harold, Ynez and Peter, not to mention that conniving bitch Britta, had certainly engaged her—far more than they should have, she thought uncomfortably. But it had been a false engagement. A borrowed interest related to sex and love and honor, topics generally not tackled in real books, or if they were, they were done in a drier, most distant way, when the stuff at risk wasn't so bloody heart-stopping and you weren't sitting on the edge of your seat wondering what, if anything, Peter was going to do once he found out his heroine intended to write a tell-all biography of him and—

She unzipped the backpack and reached inside for the book. Dammit, it was *Kiltlander.* She must have left the one with Peter Lely in it in the hotel room.

She was about to return *Kiltlander* to her backpack when a phrase on the back caught her eye: "Can their fragile love survive the blow?"

Hm.

She didn't think they meant a hurricane or the act one so often associated with romances, though the bare-chested Highlander did look particularly rubber-legged. Settling into the chair, she read the book's description. It seemed Jemmie, he of the wobbly knees, had had his eighteenth-century world upended with the unexpected arrival of a smart, determined and apparently shocked woman named Cara who'd accidentally traveled to his time from the twentieth century. Time travel? Well, there's a plot you don't find too often in nominee lists of the National Book Awards. She put it right up there with superheroes, talking dead people and giant crabs that attack New York. Nonetheless, nothing in the description explained what sort of blow their fragile love had taken.

She bit her lip, looking from the notebook in which she should be outlining to the book. Reading was part of the work she needed to accomplish in order to write the piece, she reminded herself.

She opened the book and turned to the first page.

Chapter Twenty-nine

Axel had finished setting up his camera in the corner of the empty snug. He would do some standard shots with the tripod, but he thought he might try some free lensing too. With the darkness of the bar behind the women, he'd be able to catch a real sense of liveliness and movement—that is, if any of them were willing to brave the downpour.

He was glad he had eaten. Not only had the fish been fantastic, but he'd been feeling a tad lightheaded. He'd probably dosed himself too high, which had made his blood sugar drop like a lead weight and could have sent him into a potentially life-threatening insulin shock if he hadn't eaten.

He looked over at the hearth. The chair wings obscured his view of her, but he knew what he would find: the focus in her eyes, the slim, self-assured line of her back as she wrote, the curl of her leg beneath her.

He was glad to think she *was* writing. And since it sounded like she was willing to let him look at her draft, he wouldn't have to tax Black's patience much longer. Axel might be leaving New York, but he wasn't leaving photography, and those who defied Buhl Martin Black could find themselves on the outs in the magazine world.

He considered the incident at St. Paul's, remembering with a niggling guilt the pleasure he'd felt holding her even though he had no idea why she'd been crying. Women were a confusing lot, and Ellery more than most. Trying to understand one was like trying to catch a piece of shell in a bowl of raw eggs: The more you tried, the more it slithered away. At least, that's what Jemmie had said, and Axel certainly agreed.

As for the rest of Ellery's mixed signals . . .

He didn't know what this afternoon in the hotel room had meant to her, but that had always been the trouble with the two of them. There was magic in those haughty blue eyes, but too often they hid more than they revealed.

He grabbed a camera and focused on the chair. He liked the contrast between her poised arm and the foot moving unconsciously to find the warmth of the fire. He got off six or seven shots; then, catching Simon's eye, he held up his empty mug and made his way to the hearth.

"Eeee!" she shrieked, startled.

"Sorry, I was just—" He saw the book in her hand. "I thought you were outlining."

The door opened. A portly woman of about fifty with orange-red hair, a cheery smile and flushed cheeks entered. She had a book in her hand.

Axel met Ellery's eyes.

"That's not all of them," Ellery said.

"All of them, is it?" He accepted a new mug from

Simon and nodded his thanks. "I didn't realize that was part of our bet. How many readers are we expecting tonight, Simon?"

"Six. Here's two more now."

Axel chuckled at the look on Ellery's face, unfolded himself and clapped her on the shoulder.

"Let's get to work."

CHAPTER THIRTY

The two new arrivals turned out to be sisters, Marabel and Isabel. And fortunately both they and Ginger, the older woman, had already read and loved *Kiltlander*.

"But wait," Ellery said under her breath, stealing a glance at Axel to ensure he was out of earshot. "Cara's married back in the twentieth century, right? To a decent guy?"

"Yes, she is, lass," Ginger said, grinning.

"But she's being forced to marry Jemmie in his time."

"Indeed." Marabel giggled.

"So she'll be married to both of them?"

"I could imagine worse," Ginger said. "Especially if you had a husband who only put the boots to you the odd nights Fulham wins."

The women laughed and Ellery blinked. She'd never been pulled into a story like this. She couldn't believe Cara was going to sleep with another man while she was married to someone else. In Philip Roth, sure. But a romance? Part of her was shocked, part of her was turned on and *all* of her wanted to see the scene when Jemmie took off that kilt. She knew she should be asking questions like "When did you start reading romances" and "What do you think romances do for women," but first she had to satisfy her desperate need for information on Jemmie and Cara.

"What exactly is Cara going to do about it?" Ellery demanded.

"What can she do?" Ginger said. "If she doesn't marry him, both of them will be put to death. It's her only choice."

"But is she going to *sleep* with both of them?" Cara had fallen back in time after climbing the hill of an ancient burial mound in Scotland called Cairnpapple, and Ellery could imagine—she could hardly *stop* imagining—that although Cara was being held prisoner in the past, she could conceivably figure out how to get back to her own time, and then where would that kilt scene be?

"You're going to have to read it," Isabel said. "More happens after the wedding night."

"Then there *is* a wedding night?"

The women met each other's eyes, sharing a secret so heady they looked like they'd each swallowed a Roman candle.

"What?" Ellery said. "What?"

"It's a good scene," Ginger said enigmatically. "One of the best."

"Ever," Marabel added.

Ellery felt a strange electricity racing from her heart to the tips of her fingers, like she wanted to grab the book and run to the ladies' room. She could hear the people in the bar talking around her, but she wasn't processing the words. Her ears were buzzing, and she wondered if this was what Axel felt when he'd taken some amazing drug.

"But I *have* to know. I mean, is it like"—Axel appeared at the edge of Ellery's vision, fiddling with his lens—"other forms of genre writing? Does romance do something different for you than, say, mysteries do for mystery readers?"

Isabel, clearly the older and more reserved of the sisters, frowned, confused at the sudden change in topic, but said, "Well, mysteries seem to be about serving justice and—"

"You know what?" Ellery said. "I forgot I have to make a call. Why don't you go ahead and start the book club. I'll be back as soon as I can."

She slipped *Kiltlander* and her phone under her arm unobtrusively and slid out of the chair, though she caught the look of interest on Axel's face.

She flew down the hallway to the restroom and was thrilled to discover a well-lit three-stall setup, which meant she could curl up on one of the toilets without inconveniencing anyone. Years of training had made Ellery an extraordinarily fast reader, and soon the book was ringing out a steady *shhhp* every thirty seconds or so. The wedding scene was fifteen pages. She could get through it in under ten minutes.

Cara, it seemed, realized that she and Jemmie had no other choice but to marry. She believed Jemmie was equally as pragmatic. But while Jemmie was more than willing to do as their captors required, he told her frankly that he wanted her, that the marriage was not a hardship for him but something that he truly desired.

Cara couldn't deny she had feelings for Jemmie. He had saved her from a marauding clan and had been willing to give his life for hers when they were captured.

Even if they were able to escape, Cara had no confidence that she'd ever be able to make her way back to Cairnpapple or even that Cairnpapple's magic could be prevailed upon to work for her return. She fretted as the priest was called.

Beyond the stall door, sounds of footsteps came and went but nothing could induce Ellery to stop.

As the ceremony began, Jemmie pledged his love to Cara and swore that he would protect her with his life.

Ellery made an involuntary sigh. That is what was at the heart of true love, wasn't it—between a man and woman, a parent and child? It was as simple as that: the knowledge that you would give your own life to protect another. And here was this young Highlander, able to understand that sentiment and voice it.

Dammit, what was Cara going to do? Jemmie pulled out a knife and cut a line across his palm.

Ellery gasped, and someone in the adjoining stall said, "Are you all right?"

"What? Yes, yes. I'm fine."

A blood oath was what he proposed. Cara looked at her hand uncertainly.

Oh, do it, Cara. Do it.

Cara agreed, and after a second quick cut, they held their palms together, blood intermixing, while Jemmie said a prayer in Gaelic.

Ellery could hardly breathe. She wanted things to work out between Jemmie and Cara, wanted their love to triumph, but how could there be any hope for their relationship when they came from two entirely different worlds and Cara's world was calling to her?

Cara made it through the ceremony and found herself alone with Jemmie in the small room their captors had provided. They talked until they had exhausted all the conversation they had. Jemmie told her that from that day forward, his primary obligations in life were to keep her safe and make her happy.

Ellery wondered what it would be like to feel such protection. Heck, the closest she'd ever been to such a feeling was . . . She straightened. The closest she'd ever been was when she lay in Axel's arms at the Warhol that first night. Oh, why couldn't life do a clean sweep of a memory like that once you moved on, sort of the way a new profile picture replaces the old one in each old Facebook post?

Jemmie's kilt was warm and thick, and Cara's fingers shook as she found the belt buckle that held it around his body. Jemmie asked Cara if she was ready. She was, and they kissed.

"The plaid will warm us, lass," he said, and threw the heavy wool over both their shoulders, tucking it around them until she could feel the warmth of his body. Then he asked her if she would be patient with him and revealed his shocking secret.

Ellery banged the door of the restroom so hard exiting that Axel, who had just turned down the hallway, was afraid for a moment she'd taken it off its hinges. He saw the impending path of the freight train and jumped out of the way, but she swerved to a stop and jabbed her finger into his chest.

"Is there a plaid for Clan Mackenzie?" she demanded, eyes as bright as candles.

Flustered, he took a second to respond. "You mean a tartan? Yes."

"Why didn't you ever tell me?"

She didn't wait for an answer, just continued her mad rush down the hall, calling as she went, "Whatever you do, don't interrupt us! I'm at a key point in the interview!"

He picked up his phone, which he'd dropped when she'd slammed the door. *Well, I'm glad to see she's taking the article seriously.*

"Jemmie's a *virgin*?" Ellery cried when she reached the snug. The women, now numbering five, stopped their conversation and laughed.

"Ha!" Ginger said. "And you said you were on the phone."

"*Kiltlander,* right?" one of the newer arrivals said, smiling. "God, I love that one."

"Isn't Jemmie amazing?"

"Told you it was something." Marabel grinned.

"He's a *virgin*," Ellery repeated, barely able to contain her fascination. It was inexplicable. It was titillating. It was *mesmerizing*. Her brain was like a bottle of champagne that had been shaken too hard. If she didn't get someone to uncork her, she was going to pop.

"How could he be a virgin?" she said. "He knew how to kiss Cara well enough to make her toes wiggle?"

"My boyfriend in the fifth form could make my toes wiggle," Isabel said, grinning, "and I know he was a virgin because in sixth form we took the plunge together."

Ellery laughed. Suddenly she felt almost as close to these women as she did her friends at work. *I guess the shared experience of a romance novel can be the same kind of bonding experience.*

But Jemmie a virgin? She could accept this on an intellectual level but not on the revved-up emotional one she found herself on. "Jemmie's a warrior. He's fought in battles, led his clan. Surely there were women clamoring to sleep with him when he returned."

"You made assumptions, my dear," Ginger said. "A dangerous prospect for a reader—or any woman, for that matter."

The other new arrival said, "Jemmie has a highly developed sense of what's right and wrong—"

"Oh, I *know*," Ellery said.

"—and I think he just wanted to wait until he could join with the woman who would be his wife."

"It's just so . . . wonderful." Ellery sighed. "And he loves her so much. I feel like I don't want to do anything but read it. I'm Ellery, by the way."

"Ginger was telling us about you," said the one who'd been detailing Jemmie's sense of honor. "I'm Pansy. And this is Madge," she added, gesturing to a white-haired woman a few years older than Ginger. "I know just how you feel. The first time I read *Kiltlander*, I stopped doing housework, I stopped cooking, I stopped doing anything except reading. I'd run to the attic to hide so my kids couldn't find me. At one point my son was wandering the upstairs calling for me. I just held my breath, hoping he'd think I'd left for the post office. I felt bad," she said.

"Well, only a little. But it didn't matter because I wasn't going to stop."

"That's nothing," Madge said. "I called off work when I got near the end. Lost thirty-two quid that day. Didn't dare tell my boyfriend."

Ellery nodded. "I don't want to tell mine, either. I mean, not my boyfriend. The photographer."

Every head turned.

Across the room, Axel was sipping a club soda, gazing absently at the group. Under the gaze of five sets of eyes, he froze.

"Don't look, don't look, don't look," Ellery whispered. The women's heads snapped back.

"He's your photographer?" Madge said. "He sort of looks like Jemmie."

"What?" Ellery peeked through her fingers. "No."

"Sure. He's tall. And scruffy. Remember, Jemmie's dirk had been taken from him and he couldn't shave for Cara on their wedding night. And isn't that a wee bit of red in his hair?"

"I . . . well . . ." Ellery narrowed her gaze. There *was* a bit of red there.

"He said he was your boyfriend."

"That's not true, Izzy," Marabel said. "He said he had hopes. You see, he was taking pictures of us while you were gone, and Ginger said her youngest daughter was holding out for a handsome one and would he be interested? He said he was honored but that he was pressing his suit with someone else."

"He said that?" Since when did Axel talk like someone out of a romance novel?

"Oh, yes," Marabel said. "And Pansy was the one who asked if the someone else was you: You'd make such a handsome couple, after all."

"He didn't answer," Pansy said, "but his cheeks turned a pretty shade of pink."

So much for journalistic detachment.

"But why can't he know about *Kiltlander*?" Isabel said. "He's working on the story, too, isn't he?"

"Well, yes, but . . . It's sort of hard to explain." *Not really,* she thought. *You're a big fat snob and a hypocrite to boot.* Then she fell upon a workable response. "He thinks I should be writing. Our deadline's Monday. And all I want to do is immerse myself in Jemmie and Cara. Who knew happy endings could be so wonderful?"

The table fell eerily silent.

"Why are you all looking like that?" A nervous shiver went down her spine. "You are not telling me that Jemmie and Cara don't end up together!"

Their gazes shifted in five different directions.

"No, no, *no!*" Ellery said. "I won't have it. How could I have chosen the one romance that doesn't end with a happily ever after?"

Ginger patted Ellery's shoulder. "We're not saying it doesn't end with a happily ever after"—Ellery's heart soared—"but we're not saying it does, either. There's more to a happily ever after than 'happy,' and you're just going to have to get there on your own."

Ellery thought of Tess of the d'Urbervilles dead on the gallows; Jay Gatsby shot by a jealous husband; and Juliet stabbing herself with a dagger after finding Romeo dead.

"But don't worry," Isabel said. "There's some good stuff

along the way, including several historic battles, cameos by both Voltaire and the king of France—"

"Sex in a moonlit river," Marabel interrupted, "sex bent over a tree; sex in a boardinghouse where Jemmie is both drunk and more than a little jealous; and," she added, eyes glittering, "a *very* fine spanking."

"He *spanks* her?" The cork didn't just pop, it blew the bottle into a thousand pieces. Ellery squealed, "Are you effing *kidding* me?"

Isabel, clearly irritated at her sister's interruption, said, "Believe me. It's not as fun as you'd think."

Marabel whooped. "Sounds like the voice of experience talking."

A crimson flush as well as a barely suppressed smile spread across Isabel's cheeks. Ellery's jaw dropped. Isabel, a nice but mouse-colored forty-something who could have been the poster child for "unremarkable," got spanked? Ellery had to admit she was a little envious. The most outrageous thing that had happened in her bed in the last year was when a stink bug had fallen into it from the ceiling.

These women were not at all like she expected romance readers to be. She liked them, which made her feel pretty guilty about the contempt she'd felt.

The women were still laughing when the pub's door creaked open. Ellery looked over nervously. Six would mean a full contingent of book club members, and Axel would win his bet, but it was a balding man with fogged-up glasses, wearing an easy smile and a slightly shabby rain coat.

"Hello, Roger," Simon said, and the women attempted to rein in their giggles.

Roger wiped off his glasses and made his way to the

snug. Isabel sat up straighter and gave him a little wave.

"Glad you're here, Roger," Ginger said. "We're a bit stalled on the current topic. Could probably use a switch." She gave the other women a broad wink on the last word.

"Indeed." Pansy's mouth twitched from the strain of trying not to laugh. "You could almost say we've hit bottom."

Roger gazed at the knot of chortling women, confused. He had to be Isabel's husband. Ellery looked at the clock. Could that much time have passed? Was it already time for the book club to end?

"What is it?" Roger grinned good-naturedly at the guffaws, though he clearly had no idea why the women were laughing. "What?"

Simon appeared with a mug of beer, placed it in his hands and gave him an interested look.

"Izzy told us you like to smack her fanny," Marabel said quite distinctly.

Roger coughed a little as a wave of red lapped at his jowls. The whole bar was listening now. His smile didn't falter, but Ellery did notice a vein of pride creep into it.

"Ah. I see. Well, why not? It's a damned fine fanny, after all, and a little tanning now and then warms us both." He lifted the mug to cheers from the room, including those of Isabel, who scooted down the bench to give him room.

When the table quieted, Ellery said, "I know you're almost done here, but I have just a few more questions."

"We're not done," Pansy said, frowning. "We've barely begun."

"Aye, sorry I'm late." Roger slipped a book out of his coat pocket—the same book the rest of the women had in front of them.

Ellery gulped. Roger *was* number six. She looked to see if Axel had noticed. He had. He put down his glass, spread the fingers of his right hand, added his left thumb and gave her a sparkling look.

Holy crapola.

She turned back to the group.

"You're a man." Her voice was shaking a bit from the realization that her evening, like her afternoon, was going to be taking a very surprising turn.

"I am, aye," Roger said amiably. "Thank you for noticing."

The women giggled.

"But why are you reading romance?"

He chewed his lip for a moment. "Simple, really. I like the stories. I read my first—when was it, Izzy? About ten years ago. Izzy and I had been married, oh, a good number of years then and, truth be told, had begun to drift apart. Oh, Izzy doesn't mind me telling this story," he added, evidently in response to Ellery's look of concern. "We've told it many times. She loved romances, always had them stashed around the house. I knew she was thinking of leaving me. We hadn't talked about it, but it was clear she was unhappy, and I didn't know what to do, but I knew I didn't want to lose her. I picked up a book she'd finished and decided on a whim to hide it, wondering for an instant if someday that might be all I had left of her. I'd always been a big reader. I love mysteries—Sayers, Tey, Christie, Rankin—and historical fiction: I teach history at the local school and, oh, the battles and intrigue! When Hornblower captures the Witch of Endor in Nantes . . ." His face took on a faraway glow.

Ellery, who knew enough of Horatio Hornblower to

conclude that the *Witch of Endor* was a ship, not a person, smiled. She, too, understood the joy of getting lost in a story.

"I had no plan, really, when I began to read Izzy's book," Roger continued. "I just thought that if I did read it, I'd at least have something to talk to her about. As it turned out, it concerned the Battle of Trafalgar, and the hero was a man longing for a woman out of his reach. I thought the action was well done, but what appealed to me more was the battle the hero was fighting for his soul. He loved the woman so much that if he could not conquer her heart, he knew he would die. Which, of course," he added as tears welled in his eyes, "was how I felt about Izzy."

Izzy reached out, laid her hand over his and squeezed.

"She found me reading it that night. I think she was as surprised as you." He smiled at the memory. "But it was the first real conversation we'd had in a long while."

Izzy's eyes, which had been filling as he spoke, reached their capacity, and a tear striped each cheek. It was so sweet, Ellery wanted to throw her arms around both of them.

"Something changed that night for us," Roger said, "and I'm very grateful for it. What surprised me even more is I loved the book. There were still battles and heroes and life-or-death choices, but it added the fight for the inner empire too." He touched his heart. "I liked that."

Marabel twitched a brow. "It's enough to make a man say, 'Bottoms up,'" The giggling began anew.

Despite Ellery's burgeoning respect for romances and their readers, this still wasn't an article she wanted to write—not when Carlton Purdy was holding up the final decision so that the board of Lark & Ives could read her next *Vanity Place* piece. She could just see the look on the board members' faces. There was a reason people read romance novels in the bathtub—other than the obvious one, of course—and that was so nobody else saw them doing it.

A hand clasped her shoulder. Axel crouched beside her chair, creating a cozy circle of intimacy with his body. Instantly the chitchat next to her seemed like it was miles away.

"Hey," he said.

She could see the long muscles running down that forearm and smell the faint scent of beer on his breath. The electricity between them was so strong, the hairs on her arms stood on end. Did he feel it too? Was she the only one susceptible? Or was that the reason he steadied himself with a hand on the chair?

"You doing okay over here?" he asked.

"Yep."

"Not to work a pun to death, but you must be whipped."

The gleam in his eye reminded her that the minute she stopped working, a sixty-quid room awaited. "No, I'm okay."

"Can I bring you something to drink?"

"An actual coffee would be fabulous."

"Will do. I've gotten all the pictures I need, so whenever you're ready . . ."

Why did those forearms have to look so damn sexy? "Sure. Give me fifteen minutes more with them and then we can work on the story."

He made a small snort, unbent and kissed her on the head. "Nice try, Pittsburgh."

CHAPTER THIRTY-ONE

Axel parked himself at the bar, letting the scent of her hair float through his head. Sixty quid. A quick tumble up stairs. Something very fast and very wrong. Then a moonlit walk to the hotel and a long sleep curled up beside her. Life couldn't be better.

The rain had stopped, and the place was starting to fill. He loved the sound of a bar at full tilt: the clink of glasses, the screech of chairs, the hum of the crowd. Hell, he even liked the heady scent of cigarette smoke, which he only caught when the door opened, for smoking was banned indoors even in England now. There was energy in a place like this, some of it so primed for action, the smallest slight could set off an epic brawl; but, hey, that's what life was for, right?

"Mackenzie," a surprised voice said. "I'll be damned."

Axel turned. The man was Barry Steinberg, fellow beer aficionado, kick-ass writer and partier extraordinaire. Axel had worked with him on a number of pieces at *GQ*. Steinberg wrote for *Slate* now. They had gone drinking many times together, but as Axel had begun to shrug off the life of late nights and hard living, he'd found Barry's company increasingly hard to take.

Axel nodded at his colleague. "Glad to catch you before the local constabulary discovers you're in town."

"Sit, sit. What are you drinking?" Barry opened his wallet, peeled off a ten-pound note and waved it at Simon.

"Club soda, my friend."

"What?"

"I'm trying to cut back."

"Relying on better drugs now?" His gave his friend a collegial elbow to the ribs.

Axel let his eyes drift to Ellery. "You could say that. What are you in town for?"

"That conference I was telling you about. Starts tomorrow. And then an interview with Ian McEwan. You?"

"A shoot for *Vanity Place*. Probably my last. The oatmeal stout is excellent, by the way."

Steinberg gave his friend a narrow look but ordered the stout. "What do you mean, 'Probably my last'? Your last with *Vanity Place*?"

"Maybe my last anywhere. I'm buying a microbrewery."

"No way! No *way*!" He held out a fist and Axel bumped it with his own. "Axel Mackenzie and all the beer he can drink!"

"I'm pretty excited." *Though, of course,* Axel thought, *all the beer I can drink adds up to exactly two eight-ounce glasses a day.*

Steinberg said. "Actually, I may be moving on to bigger and better things myself."

"Oh?"

Simon put down another mug and Steinberg picked it up to look at the foam. "I may be running my own magazine."

"Whoa! Congratulations. Where?"

"It's a new rag. I'll get to build it up from the ground floor. And they're pouring millions into it. It's from our friends at Lark & Ives."

"Well, that's worth drinking to." Axel lifted his glass.

"You can't toast with club soda. Barkeep, bring this man a beer. A big one."

Simon looked at Axel. Axel gave him a minute shrug.

"So, when do we get to celebrate?" Axel asked, picking up his club soda.

"End of the month. The board makes their decision then. It's down to two candidates, me and this other woman. Actually, you may know her. Ellery Sharpe?"

Axel nearly choked. Ellery was down to the final round for a publisher's job and she hadn't said anything. Not a word. "Yeah, I know her."

Steinberg made a silent whistle. "Have you seen the bod on that one? Man, I could hit that anytime. Maybe, if she loses the job, I can put her on my staff, if you know what I mean." He gave Axel a shove.

Simon put down the beer and Axel lifted it. Their mugs clanked and Steinberg took a long swallow. Axel drank without tasting and pushed the mug away. She hadn't lied. He couldn't fault her for that. She just hadn't been willing to share herself with him. His mother once said it wasn't the fights that destroyed a relationship; it was the silences.

"Purdy says she's working on something amazing,"

Steinberg said. "Which is why I'm over here chasing the McEwan story. I've gotta outgun her."

"I doubt it will come down to a single story," Axel said darkly.

"No, seriously, man. It's gonna be a freakin' shoot-out in front of the board there. I wish I knew what she was working on."

Well, that certainly helped explain Ellery's reluctance to do the romance piece, he thought, though he wished she would have considered taking him into her confidence. "Sorry. Can't help you."

Axel felt slightly queasy, enough to wonder if he had dosed himself too high on insulin, but decided it was only the impact of hearing this from Steinberg. From the corner he could hear a certain note in Ellery's voice rise occasionally above the noise of the crowd. He wondered if Steinberg would recognize it. If he did, he'd go over there, and Axel knew it wouldn't take his friend longer than a minute to figure out what sort of story Ellery was working on. Then he'd carry the news back to Lark & Ives, gloating like a fox that had swallowed a hen.

Axel gazed into the head of the beer for a long time. Then he took a deep breath, drew his stool forward so that his body blocked the view of the snug and said, "Let's get the hell out of here. I'm ready to party."

CHAPTER THIRTY-TWO

London Hilton, Park Lane

Ellery wept. Stupidly. Though why she'd been surprised, she didn't know. When she had wrapped up her questions at the table, Axel was gone. Simon told her he'd run into an old friend and left with him soon after.

So she lay flat on her stomach on the hotel bed—such a short time ago *their* bed—and let the disappointment run out of her like water from a faucet. She rarely cried. As a young girl, it had been out of a wish to not add to the burden of her hardworking mother. After her mother died, it had been to keep Jill from feeling any more than she already did that the world was a terrifying and uncertain place.

But now that Ellery had started, she couldn't stop. She cried for her lost mother; for the fear of losing a job she wanted so badly; for making such bad choices with men; and for that little boy on the plane, who, in a different world, could have been hers.

And when she'd finally exhausted her tears, and her eyes felt as dry and worn as heaps of gravel, she went to sleep.

A light knock on the door awakened her. She looked at her phone. Four o'clock. An early night for Axel, she thought bitterly. She stood up, slipped on her coat and opened the door.

He looked like shit.

"Sorry," he said, and stumbled by her to the bathroom. When the echoes of his retching died away, she tapped on the door. "Axel?"

He opened it, wiping his mouth, his eyes as pink as newborn rats.

"I guess I owe you an explanation."

She opened the hotel door. "Get your things and get out."

CHAPTER THIRTY-THREE

Train to Edinburgh

Ellery lifted her eyes from *Kiltlander* to gaze abstractedly at the East Anglia scenery streaming by her window. Two rows down, on the opposite side of the train's aisle, she could see the top of Axel's sleeping head. In four hours they'd be in Edinburgh, which also happened to be where Jemmie and Cara were heading in the story, though they, at least, seemed to be taking some pleasure in each other's company.

She'd never expected Axel to make the train, and it had been with considerable surprise she'd seen him jogging down the King's Cross platform, duffel in one hand and camera equipment bag in the other.

Their tickets had been for adjoining seats, but Ellery had found an empty seat next to a nice older man who was getting off in Stevenage. She'd watched Axel find his way to their seats and stop when he discovered they were empty, his thumb drumming against his thigh. She'd lowered her head, returning to the book, not caring whether he saw her or not. The next time she'd looked, he was collapsed in the seat, asleep.

Jemmie and Cara were on horseback, having escaped their captors, and were enjoying their postnuptial bliss. Ellery had found their electrifying wedding-night scene salve for her battered emotions. Cara had been as shocked as Ellery about Jemmie's untouched state, especially given the fact that before Jemmie had fallen in love with her, Cara had come upon him lip-locked with some young Scottish chick who had then screwed her bottom firmly into his lap.

Jemmie, wearing his linen shirt and nothing more, had explained to Cara that holding on to his virginity had been a tribute to his father, who had often spoken to his young son about the honor a man bestows on his chosen bride by waiting. The story had melted Cara's heart as well as Ellery's. Unsurprisingly, Jemmie had found his first taste of fornication quite addictive, and Cara had accommodated his every curiosity, to Ellery's *immense* satisfaction.

Sometime after her seatmate had gotten off at Stevenage, Ellery was distressed to discover the young couple running into storm clouds, both literally and figuratively. They were returning to the clan castle where they'd first stayed on their long journey, and Jemmie told Cara he needed to see the young woman—she of the firmly screwed bottom—to explain why he had married Cara.

No woman wants to hear that a marriage to her requires explanation to anybody, and Cara had gone darkly silent. Ellery wanted to believe Jemmie was doing the right thing, but the truth was, neither she nor Cara knew enough about him to be fully confident their hopes would be rewarded.

Don't do it, Jemmie. Don't disappoint her.

A body dropped into the seat next to her. It was Axel.

She stood immediately to squeeze by him. He caught her by the wrist.

"Sit."

She gave him a look and he let go of her arm. But she sunk slowly into her seat.

"I'm sorry I left you at the pub," he said. "I had a reason."

"You needed to party."

"If I'd needed to party," he said, eyes flashing, "I could have done that with you. I told you I don't do that stuff anymore."

"Except last night."

"Last night was an exception. For you."

"For *me*?"

Axel had a way of squaring his shoulders when he was angry that made him look like he was made of steel. She thought of that puddler in that Pittsburgh mosaic, shoulders bared, red-hot sparks of fire glinting around him.

"I ran into Barry Steinberg last night," he said. "He's in town for some publishing conference. He told me he was in the running for a new job."

Her gaze dropped to her shoes. "Is he?"

A stillness came over Axel that sent a chill through her. He stood up.

"The reason I disappeared with Barry," he said, "was to keep him from finding out what you were working on and taking the news back to Lark & Ives. But it would have been a lot easier on both of us if you had been willing to share your situation with me. I'll be staying at the Albany Hotel in Edinburgh. Call me when you decide what you want to shoot."

He stalked away.

Ellery sat unmoving as the tidal wave of guilt crashed hard into the breakwater of her conscience. Had she owed him the truth about Lark & Ives? Technically the answer was no. But she of all people didn't want to live on the razor-sharp edge of technicalities. The truth was, if he'd been one of her other friends, she would have confided in him, especially after he'd told her about chasing his own dream with the microbrewery.

She got up to go after him, letting the book fall to her seat.

He wasn't in their assigned seats. Scanning each row, she made her way down the line, threading her way quickly through the university students playing with their phones, businessmen reading the *Financial Times* and well-organized travelers queuing at the end of each car as they approached the stop for Peterborough.

She found him in the alcove at the end of the second car, slouched against the window, watching fields littered with the remnants of last summer's harvest slip by.

She wasn't sure if he'd seen her until he said, "I've always distrusted fall. The way it carries this false patina of abundance and color, as if the party will never end."

She thought, *The party would never end if you were in charge,* but held her tongue.

"But autumn fruits are hard," he said, "and the pumpkins rot, and you end up living on the memory. And that's the part I don't like."

She felt like an icy November wind was blowing right through her.

He turned to her. "Do you even have the faintest intention of writing the article?"

•

"Of course. It puts me in a very awkward position, but—"

He caught her hand and turned it over. Then he dropped a USB drive in it. "I saved what you were working on on the plane. Twenty-four hours ago. Maybe less. I shouldn't have done it, but I wanted to see what you were writing. I looked at it this morning. It's an article on John Irving."

Her hand was shaking. "It isn't a real article. It's what I wished I were writing."

"Of course it is." He took a deep breath and shook his shoulders, as if he were purposefully letting go of something. Then he looked at her, eyes softer. "If you'd like, I'll tell Black the article's off. I can't work. The light's not right. The subject doesn't interest me. You know, prima donna at work."

"No," she said firmly. "If it's going to get called off, it'll get called off because of me."

He considered this, then gave her a short nod.

"So we're okay?" she said.

His gaze went back to the passing fields for a moment, and he sighed. "I love you, Ellery. Probably always will."

Her throat started to tighten. "But?"

"But you shut me out. I don't mean just Lark & Ives or even the Irving article. You certainly have a right to your privacy. But even when we were together, you threw up this wall between me and the stuff that really mattered. When I found out about the job you're going for, I felt the same thing. I just can't do it again. Not anymore."

"What are you saying?"

"I'm saying I think we should just stick to the article."

He waited for a reply, but she couldn't think of anything that would satisfactorily explain why keeping a clear line between her public and private desires made her feel safe, nor did she expect an answer to satisfy him even if she could.

In the end, she said nothing, and he shook his head and left.

CHAPTER THIRTY-FOUR

Less than an hour outside Edinburgh, the train was barreling down a particularly rough stretch of track, and each hitch of the car thumped Ellery's hip torturously against Axel's thigh. As punishments go, it was an unjust one, he considered, stealing a look at her as she typed. After all, he'd only accelerated what would have happened eventually.

They hadn't spoken since the talk in the vestibule. Oh, they'd exchanged pleasantries—"Could you pass my jacket?" "Is there any water left?"—each trying to show that the words in the vestibule had been forgotten; but they hadn't *really* talked, and it struck Axel quite forcibly that they might never really talk again. After they'd broken up five years ago and would see each other in the hallway of one publishing company or another, they'd always been able to say what they were feeling, even if what they'd been feeling hadn't been exactly pleasant. He would hate to lose what they'd been able to re-create these last few days. But he also knew he couldn't go on feeling that there were parts of her she'd never share with him.

Part of Axel wanted to steal away to the lounge car to lose himself in one slowly sipped beer, but another part couldn't bring himself to stand. Would he ever feel her next to him like this again?

He had drunk himself into oblivion the night before. He could have chosen to divert Steinberg with a more moderate amount of alcohol or none at all, but he'd been hurt. Why couldn't she open up to him?

He rubbed his neck, where the tingling pinched nerve, dormant since Tuesday, had returned. He could feel the microbrewery slipping through his fingers. Who knew what Ellery would or would not write? He growled. Why did everything with her have to be so difficult?

Glancing at his watch, he considered what remained of their assignment. Today was Friday. Once they arrived in Edinburgh, the plan had been to make a quick visit to the sociologist, who lived in a small town on the outskirts of the city, then jump back in the rental car and head to the Highlands for a day of shooting. But Ellery had asked to delay the start of the trip north until Saturday morning, saying she wanted to see Cara's time portal. This was the first time Ellery had shown the slightest interest in any of the books he'd given her, and while he'd been surprised, he'd been smart enough not to show it.

According to the author, the portal was an ancient burial mound in the Lowlands of Scotland called Cairnpapple. However, as with most ancient spiritual places, it had been as much a place for primitive desires to be sated as it had been for connecting with mystical forces—at least, according to Jemmie, and who was going to argue with him?

Axel's father, a churchgoing Scotsman who had emigrated to Canada as a boy, would have pooh-poohed the magic associated with such places. But his mother—a geologist at the University of Toronto—loved that sort of stuff. He remembered her fascination with the petroglyphs in Peterborough and, as they hiked around Baffin Island one summer holiday, how she'd touched each *inuksuk*—those rocks stacked by the Inuit to look like pointing figures. She'd told Axel and his sisters that the piles pointed the way to food or water or shelter for travelers. But it was the way her eyes twinkled each time she added her own pebble to the extended arms that had left Axel with the distinct impression she'd felt their use went beyond the mere practical.

Axel gazed into the distance, considering the idea of ancient connections and crossroads in time. While not strictly a believer, Axel had always felt the world could use a little more magic and, therefore, thought it best to keep an open mind.

Of course, he understood why Jemmie would find the place sacred, given that the woman who'd first upended his life, then fallen in love with him, had emerged from the place. Axel wondered with a rueful smile if that's why he'd always had such warm feelings for Pittsburgh.

He was already starting to work through the creative issues with shooting Cairnpapple in his head. Would there be enough light? Could he go wide-angle or even three-sixty? Cara's appearance had occurred during a full moon. Would it be better to shoot it at night?

The conductor was making his way down the rows, letting the passengers know they were reaching the last stop before Edinburgh.

Axel opened *Kiltlander*, trying to remember where he'd left off. Then he remembered why he'd stopped reading. Not only had Jemmie seemed capable of powers beyond those of an everyday mortal, it had dawned on Axel that there was no way this story was going to end happily. No matter how much in love Jemmie and Cara were, they belonged to two different worlds. Axel believed in magic to a point, but the same magic that had drawn them together was sure to pull Cara back to her rightful place, just as Jemmie would be pulled to his. Axel was in no mood to have his heart broken. His cell phone buzzed, reminding him he needed to get a draft of something to Black soon. *Hell.*

The conductor stopped next to Axel, smiling at what he assumed to be a happy young couple and jingling the change in his pocket.

"I heard," Axel said. "We'll be ready."

" 'Bout forty minutes by my watch," the conductor said as the train lurched. He looked at Axel and nodded. "Bit of a rough patch. It'll smooth out before we get there."

"I hope."

Chapter Thirty-five

M8 Motorway, Scotland

The magnificent hill of Edinburgh proper had given way to the gentle rises of the outlying suburbs as the rental car made its journey west. Ellery had never been to Edinburgh before and regretted that her career seemed to bring her within an arm's length of so many good things without actually delivering them.

Axel checked the rear view before gliding into the next lane. She felt as if she'd been pushed off the edge of a steep cliff and was tumbling in slow motion to the ground. He was here in the car with her—and as always, unerringly polite—but she knew their relationship had changed. She hadn't wanted him back in her life, and now she didn't want him to leave. No wonder he'd had it with her.

But surely, after all the time they'd spent in each other's hearts and each other's hair, he couldn't have picked now to say good-bye. She refused to believe it was over.

"Have you ever been to Edinburgh?" she asked hesitantly.

He chuckled, turning the wheel a degree to follow the road's curve. "Yes. Once. For a crazy week the summer after my junior year of college. We were backpacking across Europe and decided on a whim to attend the Fringe Festival. Let me tell you, Edinburgh is a town that knows how to party. I should show you the pictures sometime."

She wondered who the "we" had been, though she'd bite her tongue before she'd ask. She also wondered at Axel's pronunciation of the city's name. "Say it again."

"What?"

"Edinburgh." She knew enough to know it wasn't pronounced like "Pittsburgh," with a hard "g" at the end. She'd always said "Edinboro," putting a "burro" at the end, but Axel's pronunciation was something even more.

"Edinburgh," he said, making the "boro" into a "burr" with a rolled "r" and the tiniest bit of an "uh" at the end, like a vocal subscript to the rest of the word.

"Oh," she said, inexplicably delighted. She didn't know he could roll his "r's"—or that he knew what was evidently the preferred Scottish pronunciation.

"My dad was a Scot, remember. 'Dammit, Ax,'" Axel said in a blowsy Scots voice, "'ye don't call it "Pittsburg." John Forbes named the place, and the man was from Dunfermline, for the love of Jesus. It's pronounced "Pittsburrah."'"

Ellery laughed. "I wish I'd known your father."

"He was quite a character."

She looked at her phone and shifted.

"Thinking of calling Black?" Axel asked.

"Maybe. It's too early there yet." How did he read her mind? If she had a different take on the article or wasn't going to write it at all, this would be the time to tell her boss.

"Today's the last chance to catch him before Monday."

"I know. I have his cell phone number."

The motorway was busy, and they fell into silence as Axel wove his way through the unfamiliar car brands and the odd, foreshortened British lorries.

"Lark and Ives, huh?" he said when the road cleared. "Impressive."

He'd said this in an upbeat tone, graciously trying to show that his harsh words on the train were now water under the bridge. Nonetheless, she felt her ears start to buzz.

"Yep. It's pretty cool just to be asked to interview."

"For what it's worth, I think you'd make a great publisher. Steinberg's a prick. They'll never choose him."

"Right, because no pricks ever get to be publisher."

They both laughed, and for the first time since the night before, Ellery felt a little better.

"I think it's great you're going after what you want," he said. "I hope you know that."

"Like you," she said.

"Like me. Right."

Yep, each of them pursuing a dream that would leave them with four hundred miles separating them. Couldn't be better.

After a quarter hour of driving past hedge-trimmed homes, parks and big-box stores, Axel made a turn off the main highway and the countryside spread out before them. This was starting to look like the land of Jemmie Forster.

Axel fumbled with the printed directions, and Ellery took them from his hand. "Hotel first?" she asked. "Or sociologist? What do you prefer?"

"You know I'd never miss a nooner with a sociologist if I have the choice."

Ellery rang the professor, a Dr. Albrecht, who not only

was indeed ready to see them but was just about to put on tea and asked if they would like to join her.

With a nod from Axel, Ellery agreed, adding to him after she hung up, "Does tea include food?" Her stomach was growling so much, she sounded like one of Jemmie's hunting dogs.

"God, I hope so. I could use a big English fry-up."

"It's almost noon. I doubt she's going to be offering you breakfast."

"You underestimate my ability to inspire."

Ellery might underestimate his ability in a number of areas, but she knew with utter certainty that was not one of them.

They drove past the heart of the town to where the houses were replaced by cottages and fields scattered with sheep. November, railing against the coming winter, had pulled a sunny, warm day out of her quiver, and the gentle hills gave a decent illusion of green.

"There!"

"What?" He slowed the car.

"There's a sign for Cairnpapple. Look! And there it is."

"Shall we?" He was already turning into the small car park at the base of the hill. At the far end sat an industrial-looking Quonset hut with a sign that read, VISITORS' CENTER CLOSED FOR THE SEASON.

"Just screams Neolithic, doesn't it?" Axel parked and they emerged. The field that led to the hill appeared to be part of some farm, for the grass was dotted with dairy cows, and several of them lowed, irritated at the intrusion.

Feeling a frisson of excitement, Ellery approached the stairs leading to the rise. This was where Jemmie had first met Cara, and for a reason she couldn't explain, she was as nervous as if she were about to meet Nabokov or Hemingway. She'd never fallen so deeply into a book before. It was like the story kept one hand on her heart and the other on her gut and alternated which one it would squeeze. In the part she'd been reading on the train, Jemmie and Cara were confronting the possible end of their relationship as Jemmie led her back to Cairnpapple so that she might return to the life she'd left behind.

Axel was already snapping pictures. As always, he turned and snapped one of her, and she flushed.

She walked to the bottom of the stone steps dug into the side of this squat, almost flat-topped hill and looked up. There were perhaps a couple hundred paces between her and the highest point, which was supposedly the tallest thing for miles. At the top, a grass-covered burial mound marked the summit. It was not visible from where she stood, but she knew it was there because she'd seen it as they drove up. Moreover, she carried two different descriptions of it in her head: one from Cara as she arrived, panicked to find herself in a world she didn't recognize; and one from Jemmie as he led her back, heartsick at having to say good-bye.

When Ellery's train had pulled into Edinburgh's station and she'd closed the book, Jemmie and Cara had been within sight of the place. Ellery didn't know what choice Cara would make or even if she'd have a choice. There was no guarantee that the magic of the place would allow her to go in the opposite direction.

Poor Jemmie. He'd be devastated to lose her.

Ellery remembered Ginger's words: "There's more to a

happily-ever-after than 'happy,' and you've just got to get there on your own."

Well, the women had certainly been right about the other parts of the book. That had, in fact, been a very fine spanking. She felt warmth spread across her face.

"Red cheeks," Axel said. "A sign of the devil within. At least, that's what my dad used to say."

Cara's red cheeks had been caused by a different sort of devil, and she hadn't spoken to Jemmie for two days after it had happened.

"I, um . . ."

"Going up?"

He wanted her in some of the shots. He always liked people in his pictures to give what he was shooting human scale.

"Yeah. Sure." She hurried up the path to the clicks of his shutter.

She reached the long, flat summit and saw the mound, rising like a wide nipple from the hill below. The mound had to be ten feet tall and fifty feet across. A gravel-topped ridge surrounded the base. In a wider circle sat a line of stone, and beyond that a grass-lined ditch perhaps six feet deep was visible. Whatever rituals had been performed here had been massive, indeed.

But Ellery could feel none of the power of the place, which distressed her. In the distance was the town, crossed with vehicle-lined streets, and the motorway beyond that. She could see the smokestacks of a factory, several water towers and, when she turned in the other direction, a cell tower that bisected the sky.

Whatever magic Cara had felt when Jemmie scooped her off the ground at their first meeting was missing for

Ellery. She felt such a rush of self-pity for this absence, she turned and started back, running directly into Axel.

"Whoa," he said, catching her so she didn't fall. "What's up?"

"I'm going to wait in the car. Take your time." She hurried down to the parking lot and plopped onto the passenger seat, betrayed by an excitement that now felt silly and unworthy. The ancient current was something only true lovers felt.

Well, if that isn't a sign, I don't know what is.

She picked up the phone. She'd put this off long enough. She needed to come clean with Carlton Purdy.

He answered on the first ring. "My goodness, you're up with the songbirds."

"I'm in the U.K."

"On the Irving interview?"

"That's what I wanted to talk to you about." She cringed, knowing what would come next.

"Talk away, sister."

"Do you think the board would be very disappointed if my next article was on something else? You know, the requirements of commercial magazines sometimes mean that writers—"

"Oh, gosh, of course not. Don't sound so glum. I mean, it's not like you're going to tell me it's on Stephen King, are you?" He laughed.

"Stephen King?"

"Sorry. It's a bit of an inside joke here. The publisher before me pitched the board the idea of doing an issue each year on genre writing. He wanted to have Stephen King be a guest editor. It was the only board meeting where the publisher was asked to step outside. We still call getting fired 'getting Kinged' around here. What's the article going to be about?"

"Um . . ." Her mind was a blank. She could hardly say romance novels now. "Let's say the impact evolving forms of writing have on readers."

He made a snoring noise. "Sorry, I fell asleep. Time to jump ship, darling. Well, it's too bad about Irving, but the board will have your DeLillo piece to chew on. Is that all you were worried about?"

"Ah . . . yes."

"Tally-ho, then."

"Tally-ho." Ellery ended the call more depressed than she'd started it. She couldn't write the article as Black wanted it. Her chances of landing that spot at Lark & Ives would be reduced to zero.

Axel opened the driver's door and swung into his seat. "You're sure you're okay?" He leaned into the back to drop his camera into his bag.

"Yes. Listen, I'm going to tell Black I can't write this."

"Seriously?" He started the car.

"Axel, a literary critic and her discovery of romance novels? I'll be a punch line."

He sighed. "El, I understand why you don't want to do this, but I really think if you just wrote the damned thing you'd do a fantastic job. Black thinks you have the power to change readers' minds. So do I. Lark & Ives will see that."

"I appreciate you saying that. I do, really. But I just have to handle it my way, okay?"

"Of course." He dropped the clutch and hit the gas, leaving only the disapproving rumble of gravel to fill the silence.

CHAPTER THIRTY-SIX

Thistle Bed & Breakfast, Bathgate, Scotland

"Romance novels are artifacts," Dr. Albrecht said, her iron-gray bob framing incisive blue eyes and dimpled cheeks. "They capture and document the evolving mind-set of late-twentieth-century and early-twenty-first-century vimen." The diminutive German scholar, perched on a stool in her equally diminutive kitchen, was chopping vegetables for pea soup with the ferocity of a battling Highlander.

"Exactly," Ellery said, carefully dodging the carrot shrapnel. "They're not literature."

"I didn't say that."

Axel and Ellery had arrived fifteen minutes earlier, but Axel said he'd spotted a barn on the property that had looked particularly interesting—"Afternoon light," he'd called as he exited the car—though she'd had the sense a wish to be alone was more his motivation.

She'd seen the look on his face when she told him the news. Dammit, why did she value his opinion so highly? But her decision wasn't going to stop her from doing the interview with Dr. Albrecht. The way she looked at it, the sociologist had some interesting things to say, and Ellery was a reporter. She could always give another writer her notes. Besides, she was starving.

"So you think they are literature?" Ellery said, grabbing a stray carrot.

"I suppose if vun *vuz* going to eliminate them from the hallowed world of literature, it would be for their overused plot drivers; the central conceit of characters overcoming impossible odds to fall in love; and happy endings—"

"Exactly."

"—in vhich case you'd have to eliminate Chaucer, Jane Austen, Dorothy Sayers, and half of Charles Dickens as vell."

"But wait," Ellery said, thrown for a loop, "what about the sex?"

"You're right. Toss out Shakespeare, Toni Morrison and Philip Roth too."

"But—"

"The characteristics you identify vith good literature— unadorned, complex prose, dark themes, moral ambiguity—are constructs of the twentieth century. And," she added with a sly smile in Ellery's direction, "very male-driven."

Ellery frowned. *No, that's not right.* "Shakespeare was dark."

Dr. Albrecht waved her hand. "Shakespeare could do anything. That's like basing expectations for your nephew's soccer league on David Beckham."

Sociology, literature, soup and soccer. A real Renaissance woman here.

Dr. Albrecht used the side of the knife to bulldoze the mountain of vegetables into a waiting bowl. She reached for a bag of onions.

"That's going to be a lot of soup," Ellery said, darting her hand in to grab another nibble. She was strongly hoping the eating part of the day would begin soon.

"I'm expecting a lot of people."

"Ah. But you have to admit, some romances aren't very well written."

"Some literary novels aren't very vell written. A lot of them, in fact. Or have you had a different experience?"

Ellery flushed. Scads of books came across her desk for review every week that could be described as nothing short of dreadful. "I-I-"

"I encourage my students to agree on vhat defines a good novel before they begin to pass judgment. About the only thing they can all agree on is that the story should capture 'true' human experience. Now, admittedly it's been a long time since I vuz a young girl, Miss Sharpe, but as far as I know, falling in love still falls under that umbrella."

Ellery thought of Jemmie and Cara in sight of that hill. She thought of all the times she had turned to find herself in the sights of Axel's lens, his eyes twinkling as he caught her unaware. She wanted to believe Dr. Albrecht, but the woman who had battled her way almost to the top of the literary journalism world just couldn't.

"But is it worthy of a novel?" Ellery asked.

"If people read it and love it and find true human experience reflected back from the pages, who's to say vhat is and isn't vurthy?"

"It's just . . ." Try as she might, Ellery couldn't formulate an argument to counter that. "I guess I never thought about it that way."

"Most don't."

Dr. Albrecht was nearly halfway through the onions before Ellery recalled her manners. "Hey, what am I thinking? Let me help. I can help chop."

"Not a problem," the older woman said. "You have notes to take."

Ellery looked at her notebook, where she'd written exactly four words: "Shakespeare," "soccer" and "Axel's eyes."

"Right." She crossed out that last entry.

A large pot of broth was simmering on the stove, and the waves of garlic and onion scent were filling the kitchen. Ellery shoved her hunger aside, and as she considered what to ask next, she let her gaze drift to the kitchen window and down the winding road that had led them here.

"Are you aware that a scene from a very popular romance novel takes place no more than a quarter mile from your house?"

Dr. Albrecht's face broke into a wide grin. "*Kiltlander*. Oh, yes."

"You *read* them too? I mean, not just for research?"

She laughed. "Vell, I've certainly read *Kiltlander*. Could hardly put it down."

Ellery leaned over, knocking her notebook on the floor and speaking low and fast. "So, does she leave or doesn't she? They were just within sight of the mound twenty pages ago, when Jemmie's nemesis arrived and then it was an escape on horseback till they were cornered in an empty church, and someone now has taken Cara hostage and Jemmie is offering his life in exchange for hers."

"Oh, I remember that scene. It gets vurse before it gets better," Dr. Albrecht said apologetically.

"But they're not going to hurt Jemmie, are they? I mean, the man's been after him since the start of the book—earlier, even." Ellery caught a quick breath and felt the words tumbling even faster from her mouth. "This cannot be how it ends. Is Cara going to pick to stay and try to rescue Jemmie, or is she going to go? The women in the Rosemary Readers said there's more to happily-ever-after than 'happy' and then their eyebrows got all weird and they wouldn't say anything more. If Jemmie dies for her, I'll kill him."

"I don't know," the sociologist said with a waggish lift of her brow. "They did sacrifice a lot of people on the top of that hill."

Ellery moaned, and her hostess laughed. "I don't think you need to vurry about Jemmie dying. But Cara and Jemmie have other pretty big hurdles to get across—vun in particular."

"What?"

Dr. Albrecht's face grew serious. "There's a child."

Ellery's head split like an atom in a thousand directions. Where do they have a child? In the future? In the past? Is it Jemmie's? Was Cara pregnant when she arrived? Or is it Jemmie's by another woman? Had he lied about his virginity? Ellery fought every instinct to grab the book and run for the bathroom right now.

"What happens? C'mon, you have to tell me."

"I can't tell you, or rather, I shall not. The pleasure in any romance comes from the not knowing."

Ellery considered the unhappiness she'd been feeling since Axel threw their relationship into question. Nope, she thought. Not a single iota of pleasure. Dr. Albrecht might be an expert on love stories, but she was no expert on love.

"Oh, pleeeeeease," Ellery begged. "Just a hint."

"A hint, aye?"

"*Yes.*"

Dr. Albrecht held the knife in the air, considering. "How about this: Vithout forgiveness, there is no love. And in the end, it is vurth every hardship."

"*What?* No! That's not a hint."

"It's better than a hint. It's the whole story in a nutshell."

"*Gah!*"

Wiping her hands on her apron, Dr. Albrecht smiled. "Here. Let me get you that tea I promised." She found the teakettle and plugged it in, and Ellery went to the window to see if the rise of Cairnpapple was visible beyond the sun-dappled fields.

"Vhere are you staying?"

"I can't remember. It's in Bathgate, though. We haven't checked in yet." She found if she edged to the side and ducked a little, she could just make out the top. She wondered what it would be like to live close to something that had played such a critical part in a beloved book like *Kiltlander*.

"You know," the older woman said, "it's a common misconception that romance readers are unhappy in love. The readers I see most inflamed by *Kiltlander* are the vuns who are just falling in love."

She met Ellery's eyes and Ellery flushed. "That wouldn't be me," Ellery said, at which point Axel appeared in the window, gave Ellery a big smile and continued toward the front door. She flushed harder.

"Mm-mm," the sociologist said, making that uniquely Scottish sound that seemed to mean anything from *Interesting* to *I don't believe you* to *I think I may have left my iron on*. The woman at the newsstand in the train station had made the same sound when Ellery had told her they appeared to be sold out of the *New York Times*.

Ellery crossed her arms. "You know, you give off a distinctly Scottish vibe for someone who's clearly German."

"I don't think vun can avoid it." She gave Ellery a sly smile. "Perhaps it's Cairnpapple."

"How long have you lived here?"

"Vee moved here ten years ago."

"Is your husband a professor too?"

"Vuz," the older woman said. "He passed away the year before last. That's him, in the picture." Ellery looked at the frame, nestled between the flour and sugar canisters. It was the two of them, somewhere in a field. The man was tall, with red-blonde hair, and he had his arm wrapped protectively around his petite wife. Ellery smiled.

There was a soft knock at the door. "There's your young man now."

"He's my photographer."

Dr. Albrecht was already running to the entryway. "Come in, come in. Velcome. Vee vere just sitting down to tea."

"Fantastic barn," Axel said, greeting his hostess and ducking under the lintel. "And there's a distillery next to it! That's what I call hospitality." He stopped, gave Ellery a quick look and lifted his nose to the air. "My stomach's growling. Is that bacon I smell?"

"No, but, goodness me, let me make you some," Dr. Albrecht said. "You two probably haven't eaten, have you? You just took the train up this morning. I'm so sorry. This party tonight has me all a-hoo."

"Oh, no," Axel said. "Please don't go to any trouble. It's just when I opened the door, it brought back memories of my grandma making me one of those marvelous English breakfasts."

"Bacon? Fried eggs? Mushrooms?" Dr. Albrecht inquired. "I can make vun for you right now if you'd like."

"That would be great." Axel gave Ellery a canny smile. "Miss Sharpe, you too?"

"Please call me Ellery. And, yes, me too. Dr. Albrecht, let me introduce the photographer working with me. Axel Mackenzie, this is Dr. Gertrude Albrecht."

He held out his hand and Dr. Albrecht shook it. He outscaled her by a good fifteen inches, so it looked a little bit like she was shaking the hand of the Popeye float in the Macy's Thanksgiving Day Parade.

"Mackenzie," the professor repeated. "You're Scottish?"

He dropped into his father's voice. "From the great kingdom of Fife, aye. My father, eh?" he added, switching back to his own laid-back Canadian accent. "I'm from Toronto."

"Oh my God," Dr. Albrecht cried. "Are you a forty long?"

Axel blinked. "I beg your pardon?"

"A forty long? Do you vear a forty long suit?"

He gave Ellery a slightly alarmed look. "Yes, actually, I do."

"Forget the hotel. You two can stay here. I need a man in a kilt tonight."

Now it was Ellery's turn to blink.

"I rent the barn out for céilidhs—parties," Dr. Albrecht explained. "There's a business conference over in Livingston. Tonight is their big event. They bus over to the distillery for a vhiskey tasting, then adjourn here for supper and music. It's the damned Americans—pardon me, Ms. Sharpe—they love a man in a kilt, and part of the deal is I'm supposed to supply them by the handful."

Vivid image, Ellery thought, choking a little on her carrot. Then the image of Axel in a kilt danced into her head, and she swallowed hard. The vivid images were raining down like fireworks in July.

"But I'm three shy of my usual six," Dr. Albrecht continued, "and I have Angus's kilt here from the cleaners—Angus is my postman—but he's got the flu. Four would be so much better than three. Please say yes. The rooms are on me."

Axel looked at Ellery and shrugged. Ellery hoped the insane desire to see Axel in Jemmie-wear wasn't written all over her face. She felt like a kid who'd just been handed the key to FAO Schwarz. "Sure," she said nonchalantly. "Why not?"

"Do I have to do anything?" Axel asked.

"Have you ever poured a beer?"

"Oh, once or twice. But I'm a very quick study."

"Excellent. Vhy don't you carry the bags upstairs vhile I start breakfast?" She went to the tiny check-in desk at the bottom of the stairs and looked at the rack of keys. "Vill you be vanting one room or two?"

CHAPTER THIRTY-SEVEN

Ellery would have preferred if Axel's answer hadn't been so swift or unequivocal. He had softened it with a regretful shrug in her direction, leaving her to imagine . . . what? That he was sorry it had come to that?

She looked from the book in her lap to the phone lying on the chintz comforter. She had adjourned to her room after their fry-up and the conclusion of the interview. There, she'd tried to call Black, but she'd had to leave a message. At this point she just wished she could get it all over with, Axel included, and get back to New York. The waiting left Dr. Albrecht's wonderful breakfast sitting heavy in her stomach.

She could hear Axel on the other side of the wall, and—despite the fact that Jemmie had Cara pinned underneath him in the first clean, warm and unsupervised bed of their marriage—the sound left her feeling decidedly blue. For the last few years she had thought of Axel like she did a writing deadline: You knew it was out there, but you didn't want to think too much about it. But apparently he was more like a deadline than she'd imagined, for the only thing worse than having an Axel was having no Axel at all.

He was unpacking his duffel. She could hear the drawers squeaking. He'd always packed his clothes neatly in drawers, even at a hotel. She supposed it had been part of his upbringing, with four sisters and a well-organized mother supervising his every move. She remembered the way he would change around his sisters, transforming into this boyish, put-upon charmer, angling for a fair share of attention in his mile-a-minute family. It was a side of him she had loved, and the thought of it sent a twinge of sadness through her.

She thought of what Dr. Albrecht had said about the evolving mind-sets of women. . . .

She stopped. What Dr. Albrecht had said! That was it! Her way into the article!

"Hold that position, you two," she whispered to *Kilt-lander*. "I'll be back." Then she picked up her laptop, turned it on and fired up Word.

Her fingers were just above the keyboard when she caught sight of her e-mail icon blinking and decided she should probably at least scan her messages first. Who knew? Maybe they had run out of space for the article. Maybe Black had retired. Maybe aliens were planning to take over the *Vanity Place* building.

There were dozens of messages in her in-box, but none with an intriguing subject line like "Alien Readiness Plan" or "Buhl Martin Black: The End of an Era." There was a Facebook message from Jill saying that, based on the picture Axel had sent of Ellery in the Monkey Bar, the trip seemed to be turning out to be even more interesting than Jill had hoped and that she was curious as to whether the wardrobe selections had had any influence on the proceedings.

"Ha-ha." Ellery considered digging in her hard drive to find the video of Jill lip-synching to Britney Spears's "Oops! . . . I Did It Again" during her sixth-grade talent show and post it in response, but relented. However, the image of that god-awful red leotard and fishnets did remind Ellery that she was going to need an outfit for the party tonight.

The halter dress Kate and Jill had packed—emerald green, silky and cut to her navel in the front and even lower in the back—would probably be okay if she could borrow a safety pin and a wrap from Dr. Albrecht. It might be a warm November day, but she wasn't going to sashay around a Scottish hoedown with a dress whose back fell into what Jill liked to call "the ass headlands."

There were a few e-mails from Kate, most of them work-related, which Ellery scanned, but one had a subject line that made her sit up: "Jill?" it read. Kate had just sent it an hour earlier.

Ellery opened the e-mail.

> *Hey, girl. Would love to hear how things are going on that special project—oh, and the article too. Ha! Hopefully, the Whopper turned out as hard as you usually like them.*
>
> *I enjoyed spending time with Jill. She left for school this morning. I hesitated to write because I didn't want you to worry, but I noticed that she seemed quieter than usual. The only time she was*

her regular self was when we were gossiping about
you and Axel, and, of course, that didn't take up
more than five or six hours. I asked if school was
going okay, and she said she thought she'd be on the
dean's list this semester, so there doesn't seem to be
any trouble there. Her roommates are fine and so is
her work-study job, but there was a definite change
in her demeanor when I asked about boys. I don't
know if you know anything, but I thought it might
be worthwhile to mention to you. I tried subtle and
overt. All I got was "Everything's good."

Kate

Unsettled, Ellery reached for her phone and dialed Jill. She didn't answer. Ellery looked at the clock. It was ten a.m. in New York. She left a message asking her to call if she got a chance and added, "Nothing important" before hanging up.

Jill had had a couple of on-again, off-again boyfriends her sophomore year of college and another guy she'd dated through most of the winter last year. She hadn't mentioned anyone this year, but that wasn't unusual. Jill played things pretty close to the vest until she was ready to go public. Ellery supposed this was a natural reaction to having had a father who had high-tailed it out of the family as soon as he could, and she tried to respect her younger sister's guardedness.

Ellery returned to the keyboard, more distracted than she would have wished, to try to explain why women like romance.

CHAPTER THIRTY-EIGHT

Like Jemmie, Axel was coming to the firm conclusion that women were impossible to understand, and that what they liked, clear and immutable one day, turned into formless mist the next.

On the train, Axel had followed Jemmie and Cara through their near return to Cairnpapple, their capture, their escape and several sex scenes eye-opening enough to reaffirm his belief that a woman's imagination could be a very frightening thing. And now, after having downloaded the e-book to his phone, he found himself totally bewildered by Cara's incandescent fury at Jemmie for his determination to chase down the villain and exact his revenge for their mistreatment of her.

Foolish man! she had cried. *If I wanted you to die for me, I'd have killed you myself.*

This to the man who had saved her life? Inexplicable.

Axel laid down the phone and paced to the window. He could hear Ellery tapping at her keyboard in the next room. Writing? After all her protestations, was he to believe she was now sitting in a bed-and-breakfast in Bathgate, Scotland, writing an article on romance novels? Doubtful. She was probably finishing the piece on John Irving.

Did women ever make sense?

His phone buzzed. He reached for it and groaned.

"Hey, Brendan. What's up?"

"Look, the guy who made the counteroffer? He's raised the bid another six grand. I don't want to be a jerk, Axel. I'm going to sell the brewery to you, but I really need to know if you're going to buy it, because if you're not, I don't want to miss this."

Axel took a deep breath. It was hard letting go. "Take the offer. I won't have the money."

"Seriously?"

"Yep. I took a bet on something that's not going to pay off. I was going to call you today anyway."

"Aw, man. That sucks. You would have been great."

Yeah, I would have. "Thanks. The stars weren't aligned, I guess." The phone beeped in his ear. "Hang on, will you?" Axel checked the display. It was Jill, whose name hadn't appeared there in years, a fact that fanned a spark of curiosity in him as well as one of concern.

"Listen, I'll call you back," he said to Brendan. "I gotta take this."

"No need. I'll tell the guy we're a go."

Axel switched lines. "Jill, hey." He couldn't remember the last time Jill had called him. She had reached out a few times after he and Ellery had broken up, and he'd always been glad to hear from her; but he knew it wouldn't have been proper to maintain a friendship with her without Ellery's involvement, and in any case Ellery had made it clear she didn't want him in their lives, even on the periphery.

"You busy?"

There was something in her voice that made him straighten. "Nope. What's up?"

"I'm in trouble."

By "in trouble" she meant just that. Facing a slate of upcoming finals and ruing a boyfriend who wasn't returning her calls, she was between two positive at-home pregnancy tests yesterday and an appointment to talk about next steps at the college clinic on Monday. Axel would have liked to get his hands on the so-called boyfriend, but he knew that wasn't the relevant point at the moment. She was angry, upset, buckling under the pressure of her senior year and terrified of telling her sister.

She only cried once during the call, and he knew that only because she was silent for a full minute before answering when he asked her what she wanted to do.

The amazing self-control of the Sharpe sisters. Sometimes he wished he could grab them by the shoulders and shake some honest-to-God emotion out of them. But that, he thought with a sigh, wasn't the point, either.

Knowing he was completely out of his depth and fearful of giving advice that would lead her astray, he begged her to call Ellery. Ellery, he said, would never be disappointed with anything she did. But Jill would not relent. Further, she made him swear he wouldn't mention a word to her.

He hung up and stared at the bare limbs of the tree outside for a good twenty minutes before moving. He'd never been a woman, obviously, and despite having grown up around four of them and spent a good part of his adult life in relationships of one sort or another with many more, he couldn't help Jill navigate this with any degree of ability. No matter what she had made him promise, he knew he was going to tell Ellery. She was Jill's guardian. Moreover, she loved Jill deeply and had stepped in without a second thought to care for her when their mother had died.

But he also knew breaking his word to Jill would mark the end of the easy friendship they had just renewed. He wasn't her father, but in the perennial "me versus them" battle every child goes through, his betrayal would brand him with that stain of parental them-ness, permanently changing their relationship.

But there was another complication, one that was perhaps even more responsible for keeping him motionless since the end of the call. He did not want to have any sort of conversation with Ellery about pregnancy.

Even five years later, the unanswered questions still pained him. No matter how he approached the subject of Jill's situation, if he told Ellery, he would be entering a battleground defenseless.

Ellery, Ellery, Ellery.

He rubbed his aching neck and considered what Jemmie might do. He wished his sister had told him which Jemmie the women adored. Was it the wise Jemmie, the courageous Jemmie, the reckless Jemmie? He thought of his sister's words.

Don't they understand they could get any woman into bed they wanted if they just acted like Jemmie in Kiltlander?

Of course, Axel was no longer trying to get Ellery in bed. It wasn't that he didn't want to bed her; he did—and in a way that made his belly contract when he looked at her. But he had finally realized what he needed from her was something more important: her trust. And if she couldn't give it to him, he couldn't be with her.

He doubted the conversation he was about to have with her would earn that trust, and he dreaded the ground they would have to cover, littered as it was with landmines big enough to destroy both of them. No one would come out unscathed. The one lesson he'd gotten from Jemmie was this: If you love a woman, you have to do what's right for her. The only trouble is you'd better be damn well sure you know what's right.

Axel slipped his phone in his pocket, stepped into the hall and knocked reluctantly on Ellery's door.

Chapter Thirty-nine

**"Plugged In: The Future of Publishing" Conference,
Dorchester Hotel, London**

Barry Steinberg let his eyes wander from the intern at Condé Nast, whose breasts didn't quite make up for her long and exceedingly dull story about her sister's wedding in High Line Park, to the face of Bettina Moore, head of Pierrot Publishing, at the far end of the bar.

His head was still muzzy from the night with Axel, but not so muzzy that it blunted the zing that went through Steinberg's heart whenever he saw a mover and shaker. A year ago Bettina would never have made the cut for a summit like this. But having a book that had spent thirty-seven weeks at the number one spot on the best-seller list tended to shake up one's social calendar.

The intern's voice fell to a faint hum, like the buzz of a mosquito, and despite the message his balls were furiously telegraphing to his mouth to make sure he said something to score himself a place somewhere later in her evening, he found himself being drawn to the light of Bettina Moore.

"And the reception afterward was awesome. Everyone got Rollerblades and—"

"You know what?" Steinberg said, tossing a ten-pound note on the bar. "What time are you leaving? I would love to pick this up then."

"I dunno." The intern flipped her hair, smiling. "Maybe midnight?"

"Perfect. Your last drink's on me. I can tell you about the time Norman Mailer and I were thrown out of Farrell's Bar in Brooklyn."

"Really? Wait, who's Norman Mailer?"

He threaded his way down to Moore, who was sipping something pink and girly, and signaled the bartender to make two more.

"Bettina, you look lovely tonight."

He'd heard she was in the midst of an ugly divorce, but she was well over forty, so too old for serious consideration.

"Hello, Barry. You look like shite."

He laughed. "Hell of a night last night. Ran into an old buddy. Axel Mackenzie, actually. You might know him."

It was her turn to laugh. "I sure do. He's here? He's working on an article on romance novels."

"Are you sure? He told me he was doing something for *Vanity Place*?"

"That's the article."

Steinberg laughed.

She gave him a chilly look. "You find that odd?"

"The magazine that likened J. K. Rowling to the Reverend Jim Jones? Yeah, actually. I do."

The bartender put down the drinks. Barry slipped him a twenty and picked up his.

"Yeah, well, it's going to be the cover story," Moore said. "Maybe they're changing."

"Sure. And maybe my Prius will take first place at Le Mans." Strange of Axel to hide the fact he was working on a cover story. He was not one for modesty. He took a sip of the drink. Jesus, it was *gin*. "So it's a photo essay?"

"Hell, no. An in-depth into the enduring power of romance novels. *Vamp*'s going to be front and center."

Stranger still.

"And what have *you* been up to? Nothing good, I'm sure." She smiled.

"Actually, I'm up for that new publisher's spot at Lark & Ives."

"Well, well, well. Congrats."

"I don't have it yet. It's down to me and the critic at *Vanity Place*, actually. Ellery Sharpe."

"Ellery Sharpe?" Moore's lip curled over the rim of her glass. "Axel's working on the piece with her."

Steinberg put his drink on the bar. "Ellery Sharpe? Writing a story on romance novels?"

Moore tossed back her drink and picked up the second. "Yep."

He looked at his watch. One o'clock in New York. Carlton Purdy should be at his desk. "Well, congratulations on the cover story. I'm going to have to tell you: That's the greatest fucking thing I've ever heard."

Chapter Forty

Thistle Bed & Breakfast, Bathgate, Scotland

Ellery cracked the door. It was Axel. There was a look of unease on his face, and despite a brief smile, she could tell he'd rather be somewhere else. She wished she wasn't still wearing his shirt. "Come in."

He stepped in carefully, hands stuffed in his pockets, like he was walking between rickety shelves stacked with glass.

She wasn't sure whether to leave the door open or closed. "What's up?"

He took a spot by the desk and gestured to her laptop. "I heard you working."

"Yep. I've got a rough draft."

His brow peaked and a bit of the stiffness disappeared. "Of what? Not the romance article?"

"Yep."

"Really?"

She shrugged and let the door swing closed. "I debated for a long time. Finally decided to meet Black halfway."

Axel tilted his head. "'Halfway'?" He bent to look at her screen.

"'The Postmodern Reader: Feminism and the Transformational World of Romance,'" he read. "What the hell is this?"

"That's my take on it. Dr. Albrecht gave me a lot of stuff on the sociological aspects of romance novels in the second half of the twentieth century. It's tight. It gives romance novels their due. And it satisfies Black's requirements."

He hit PAGE DOWN and scanned the screen. "'By subverting a woman's desire for fulfillment into easily consumable chunks,'" he read, "'romance novels serve as a psychological break from the trials of everyday life'?" He looked up, horrified. "This doesn't satisfy Black's requirements. Where's the joy? Where's the excitement? Where's the buzz coming from those Rosemary Readers? Christ, for this, I should have been taking pictures of you at a podium."

"Oh, of course," she said hotly, "I forgot. It's all about you and your pictures."

"I think you've been in the magazine biz long enough to know it's nice when the copy matches the photos."

"Well, in this case, the requirement will have to slide. That's the story I'm writing."

"Jesus, Ellery, I've never seen you cut a story off at the knees like this. For God's sake, screw Carlton Purdy. You know you could make this subject sing. If he doesn't like what a respected journalist writes about how women really feel, then he needs to find a new line of work."

"I can't, Axel," she said, each word a tight burst of scorching steam. "I want this job."

"I felt better when I thought you weren't going to write it at all. At least then you were standing on some principles."

"Fuck you."

For a long moment the room echoed with the words; then Axel shook his head, his face an infuriating mix of disbelief and disgust. "Jesus, what the hell happened to you?"

"You, Axel. *You* happened to me."

He strode to the door and flung it open. "Well, you know what? *You* happened to *me* too."

CHAPTER FORTY-ONE

Greenwich Village, Manhattan

Carlton Purdy took off his reading glasses, folded them neatly and placed them in the mid-century Blenko glass eyeglass holder on his bedside table. Tony was almost done with his shower, and he did not like him to be reminded his partner needed glasses. In fact, Carlton equipped himself with everything he could to minimize the fourteen-year age gap between them, including a modest number of hair plugs, a subscription to *Men's Health* and an amazing stomach-reducing undergarment from Slapz called a Bear Hug.

Of course, he wasn't wearing one now. It was after their every-other-Friday lunchtime liaison, and their every-other-Friday lunchtime liaison meant Tony's homemade seviche, *Glee* on TiVo and lighting the Diptyque Green Fig candles.

Tony strode out, his smooth coffee-colored skin still capable of diverting Carlton from even the most intense conference call.

He loosened the towel and snapped it playfully at

Carlton's legs. "Hey, what's with the pajamas? It's show time, amigo."

Carlton grinned. He liked being teased, but he also knew he looked fabulous in his Orvis black Lab pajamas.

"Time to make those dogs hunt," Tony said, and they both laughed.

He dropped the towel on the floor and made a Superman-like leap onto the bed. Carlton sighed, half in response to Tony's amazing abs and half in response to the wet towel on the repurposed oak flooring.

"God, I love those candles," Tony said, taking a deep sniff. "Smells like Fig Newtons." He cocked a brow, and Carlton laughed again.

Tony was fluffing the pillows when Carlton's Black-Berry buzzed. "Here we go." He propped himself on his elbow, waiting for Carlton to answer it.

Carlton picked up the phone on the second ring, but couldn't read the display.

"Are you going to answer?" Tony said. The phone rang again.

"Oh, it's no one I want to talk to."

Tony pursed his lips, eyes glinting, and reached across Carlton to snag the glasses. "I don't know why you don't wear them. You look adorable."

Beaming, Carlton answered in a singsong voice. "Hel-lo."

"Carlton, it's me. Barry Steinberg."

"Barry Steinberg, as I live and breathe. Why would Barry Steinberg be calling me on this overcast Friday? You're not withdrawing your name from consideration, are you?"

Tony whispered, "Lark & Ives?" and Carlton nodded.

"No, no," Steinberg said. "Not at all. I'm calling because I found out something that may be of interest."

"I'm listening."

"I just found out Ellery Sharpe's writing an article on romance novels for *Vanity Place*."

"Don't be ridiculous. I shouldn't be telling you this, but she's writing an article on the impact evolving forms of writing have on readers."

"Yeah, romance readers. Ellery Sharpe's in the U.K. With Axel Mackenzie. They're doing a spread on romance novels, with a focus on *Vamp*."

"*Vamp*?" Carlton sat up so quickly, he knocked Tony off his elbow. Purdy had heard a lot of unbelievable things, but *Vanity Place* running a spread on *Vamp*? It was preposterous. It was *beyond* preposterous.

At the mention of *Vamp*, Tony bared his teeth and began to nibble on Carlton's neck, which Carlton only half tried to stop.

Carlton was conflicted. Ellery Sharpe, upright and reliable, had promised him and his board an article on evolving forms of fiction. Barry Steinberg, perhaps more reliable than upright, had said her article was on, of all things, romance novels.

"You look cute when your lip curls," Tony whispered.

Romance novels were about as likely to find a place at Lark & Ives as a recipe for tuna casserole. Was she trying to sabotage him? If it were true, she was certainly sabotaging herself.

He decided to take a neutral approach.

"Thank you, Barry. I don't think you need to trouble yourself about it. I'll look into it. And I'm looking forward to receiving your piece at the end of the month."

He rang off and Tony said, "You'd better not be receiving his piece. There'll be a duel at ten paces."

"There seems to be something amiss with one of my candidates, Ellery Sharpe. If what I just heard is true—and I can't believe it is—she's writing an article on *romance novels*."

"Oh, God," Tony said in mock horror, "is it catching?"

"Laugh if you will. There are certain things literary critics don't do."

"You know, snobbishness is not exactly your most attractive quality."

"I'm not being a snob," Carlton said, picking up the phone again. "I'm being . . ."

"Narrow-minded?"

"Realistic. The people who read romance novels are—"

"Gorgeous, well cut and currently considering grabbing those pajamas at the ankles and yanking?"

Carlton blinked. "Not you!"

"Oh, yes. In fact, there's a certain red-haired Scottish Highlander who's haunted my dreams for years."

"*Tony.*"

Tony dissolved into laughter. "You're so easy to shock. I love that about you. Please tell me that phone's in your hand because you're planning to heave it into the wastebasket?"

"Let me make just one more call. Please, please, please."

Tony growled good-naturedly. "Make it fast."

"We can settle this in two minutes."

"Then we're going to settle something else," Tony said, flopping back on his pillow. "And I can assure you, it's going to take considerably longer than two minutes."

CHAPTER FORTY-TWO

Thistle Bed & Breakfast, Bathgate, Scotland

Jesus, what an asshole.

Ellery slammed the door and tore off Axel's shirt. *I'll go topless before I'll give him the satisfaction of seeing me in something of his again.*

The phone rang and her heart skipped a beat. But it was neither Black nor Jill. It was Carlton Purdy, and she decided to send him to voice mail.

Axel knocked on the door, and she flung it open, one arm stretched across her breasts and the other ready to stuff the shirt down his throat. "What is it, you asshole—"

The brows on Dr. Albrecht's face flew up. "I beg your pardon. I vundered if you had an outfit for tonight. The party is not formal. Still, there is a certain level of sparkle and shine. I have a neighbor who may be about your size."

Ellery turned and struggled back into the abhorrent shirt. "Sorry. We were having a bit of a disagreement— Axel and I."

"Article writing must be quite challenging."

Ellery noticed a gleam in the woman's eye and felt her

cheeks redden. "He and I are . . . were . . . Oh, it doesn't matter. Let's just say he can be a jerk sometimes."

"They can be difficult, it's true."

"How men think they've earned the right to be such god-awful imbeciles sometimes, I don't know."

"Oh, I meant the Scots. My second husband vuz a Grant."

A Scottish husband? Ellery looked at her, surprised, and her face dimpled. "Yeah, well. Axel's only half Scottish."

"Perhaps he's only half an imbecile as well."

Ellery thought about the article. Admittedly, it hadn't been her most stellar effort. It lacked the passion that usually marked her work. But why couldn't he understand that that was the only way she could have written it? "Maybe," she said, unconvinced.

"There's a scene in *Kiltlander*. It's toward the end, so I von't ruin it for you. But in it a thoughtless action on Jemmie's part has unintentionally led to the destruction of something very dear to Cara—very dear to both of them, in fact. She is furious and has every right to be. In the midst of their argument, they come to the realization that the hurdle of being from two different vurlds is one their love, vhich has already stretched to the point of breaking, cannot overcome."

Ellery dropped onto the bed. "Are you telling me they don't end up together?"

Dr. Albrecht gazed at her over her glasses. "May I observe as a sociologist that, given the prescribed plot structure in romance, the considerable anxiety produced in a reader vis-à-vis the outcome of the story is fascinating to me and quite possibly unique in the vurld of literature."

"Oh my God, are you going to tell me or not?"

"I am not. I am, however, going to tell you vhat Jemmie said to Cara. He said, 'I canna promise not to make mistakes. I can only promise to learn from them.' Vhen you think about it, that's all vee can ask from anyone."

She had done the lines in a Scottish accent filtered through a Teutonic tongue, and Ellery had to bite her cheek to keep from smiling. "I get your point, and I don't disagree, but what does one do when the other person doesn't even seem to recognize he's made a mistake?"

"Stones stop a farmer, not a builder."

"Jemmie said that?"

"No, my husband. And he vuz one of Scotland's finest architects." Dr. Albrecht smiled, remembering.

"How long were you married?"

"Ten years. We met right after he retired in 'ninety-eight. I vuz visiting Scotland to do some research. Married six veeks later."

"Quite the vintage year. Wasn't that the year *Kiltlander* came out as well?"

"No, *Kiltlander* vuz a year earlier."

A sparkle came into Dr. Albrecht's eyes, and Ellery's mind raced. "Wait a second," she said, filled with the thrill of detection. "Your husband has red hair."

Dr. Albrecht didn't respond, but the sparkle shone brighter.

Ellery narrowed her eyes. "Where exactly were you doing your research?"

"At the Highland Games in Stirling."

Ellery's jaw dropped. "You came to Scotland to find yourself a Jemmie!"

"I vouldn't say that exactly."

"Was he wearing a kilt the day you met?"

Dr. Albrecht's face burst into a shining grin. "Och, he was handsome in that Grant red!"

"You evil genius!"

"I vuz studying the Scots warrior archetype," she said primly. "Vun of the first things you learn in sociology is that the only conclusions you can draw must be based on observable, measurable data. I vuz simply adhering to the scientific method."

"Uh-huh. Tell me, did Mr. Grant have any idea he was participating in a study?"

"Such studies must be done blind, of course, but I did learn the familiar Scots warrior fantasy in romance is based on very solid evidence."

They laughed.

Ellery leaned back on her hands. "I'm almost afraid to ask if your research also included such topics as the Western cowboy, the big-city fireman and the English nobleman."

"A lady never tells. Let me just say I found there vuz no need to conduct any further research into hero archetypes after Archie."

"It sounds like your marriage was every romance reader's fantasy."

"Vell, perhaps. Now let us see what vee can do about finding *you* some fantasy. Do you have a dress for tonight?"

Ellery pushed the bathroom door closed with her toe,

revealing the low-cut halter dress hanging on the back. The five-inch spike heels in black patent leather were sitting on the floor.

Dr. Albrecht laid a hand over her heart. *"Gott im Himmel."*

Scared the Scottish right out of her, Ellery noted. "Yeah, it's a little, um . . ."

"Hurenhaft?"

"If that means what I think it means, then, yes. Frankly, it wasn't my choice, but then again, I'm not the one who packed my suitcase."

"Axel?"

Ellery made a short, ironic guffaw. "No. Not a bad guess, come to think of it. But he would have picked a shorter skirt."

"I think," Dr. Albrecht said, "I may have something to help."

She scurried out of the room, and after a moment or two of distant door creaking and hanger squeaking she reappeared with a white angora sweater with three-quarter sleeves whose placket was embroidered with pearls resembling tiny flowers on vines. It had gorgeous loop-de-loop frog clasps. It looked like it had just stepped out of a fifties prom.

"Oh my God, it's beautiful," Ellery said, feeling the silky smooth yarn.

"It vuz my mother's. Try it on. She was about your size."

"With the dress?"

"Yes."

Ellery slipped into the bathroom and emerged a moment later. When she stepped back to view herself in the room's mirror, she saw she'd been transformed from a *hurenhaft* strumpet to a Grace Kelly debutante.

"It's lovely!"

"Vee need a bit more, yes?" Dr. Albrecht disappeared a second time, returning with a box, a pair of scissors and an ancient tulle slip. "My vedding petticoat," she said, holding up the last item.

"It's beautiful," Ellery said after she'd pulled it on, "and I'm honored you'd lend it, but it reaches almost to the floor."

The older woman grinned, held up the scissors, then dropped to a knee and reached for the excess.

"No!" Ellery cried. "Not your wedding skirt."

"Bah. First vedding."

In a moment the emerald skirt was aloft, floating on several inches of bouncy tulle.

"Omigod, look at what it does when I turn," Ellery said. She felt like a princess. "I have a pair of pearl studs. I'm going to pull my hair into a knot. It will be perfect."

"Vun more thing."

Dr. Albrecht pulled back the top of the box, revealing a breathtaking pair of silk flats in navy and green plaid with a rosette atop each toe.

Ellery gasped. They were perfect. They brought everything in the outfit together, and they had the added benefits of being both comfortable and beautiful. Then her spirits fell. "Oh, but I'll never fit into them." Dr. Albrecht had to be six inches shorter than Ellery. Surely her feet had to be smaller too.

"Vee are lucky," the sociologist said, slipping her feet

out from under her pant legs. "My father always called them my little battleships."

She placed the shoes on the floor, and Ellery slipped her feet in. The fit was damned near perfect.

"I can't thank you enough," Ellery said, giving the woman a hug. "I would have hated to be . . ."

"*Hurenhaft.*"

"*Hurenhaft,* exactly."

"Vell, I think a little of *die Hurenhaftigkeit* is always recommended."

Ellery laughed. "I'll do my best."

"And vhat, then, are vee going to do about the article?"

That was code for Axel. Ellery's shoulders sagged. She looked beautiful, but what was the point? Axel and she would never see eye to eye.

"I don't know. I guess I'll keep working on it."

"That's my girl."

Ellery checked the clock. "Ooh, we're getting close. Can I give you a hand with party prep?"

"Do you mean instead of vurking on the article?"

"Yes," Ellery said, chagrinned. "I suppose that's what I do mean."

"I do not need you for another half an hour or so."

You tenacious Teutonic matchmaker, you. No wonder the Germans were able to roll through Paris.

"I may just nap."

"Vhatever suits, dear. I'm sure the article is fine as it is."

Grrrr.

"Actually, there *is* something you could do for me," Dr. Albrecht said, stopping at the door. "There's a large powder room at the bottom of the stairs. It's the public one, as it vur. Everything should be in order there, but if you could make sure the soaps are out, the hand towels are neatly folded, that sort of thing . . ."

"Sure. Anything at all." Anything that meant not working on the "article." As for the actual article, she hoped Black liked it, because she had already sent him the draft.

CHAPTER FORTY-THREE

Upper East Side, Manhattan

Black stood on the balcony of his co-op apartment, shivering. He had snuck away from work, thinking Margey would be at her tennis lesson, only to discover Margey had a migraine and was lying on their bed with an ice pack, a sleeping mask and a serving-bowl-sized glass of pinot grigio at her side, which of course meant he had to feign a gallbladder attack to explain his appearance in the middle of the day. So now, instead of relaxing in his custom-made lambskin Eames lounger with his trousers around his knees, enjoying a nice long, relaxed phone call with Bettina, he was looking over the tops of the denuded Central Park trees, praying his neighbor's damned Yorkshire terrier wouldn't catch him standing outside and go off like an upper-register fire alarm.

He pulled his BlackBerry out of his pocket, willing Bettina to call. No missed calls. No new texts. Goddammit, he was going to freeze his considerable ass off if she didn't call soon. With all the friggin' apps out there, they couldn't invent one that made the phone into a hand warmer?

He had brought his glasses in case she sent a picture. She was known to do that—horribly filthy ones that made his heart leap into his throat and his creaky prostrate ring with the vigor of St. Patrick's bells, and the last thing he wanted if that happened was to wake Margey while digging for reading glasses in the table next to the bed.

He checked his e-mail in case Bettina had contacted him to cancel. She used the name Lloyd Pribbenow and subject lines that depended on the message she wished to convey. There was "Issues with the Franzen piece" (Are you free to talk?), "Did you see this in Publishers Weekly?" (Just checked into the hotel), and "PR Follow Up" (I'm naked on Skype).

Unfortunately, there was nothing from Lloyd or Bettina in his in-box, but there was an e-mail from Ellery Sharpe with the draft of the romance article, which he was glad to see. He'd been pissed with Mackenzie for not answering his e-mails, but from Ellery's cover note, it looked like he'd gotten a damn-near-finished piece. Perhaps Mackenzie had more power of persuasion than Black had been willing to give him credit for.

He was just opening the document when his phone buzzed with a blocked call.

"Hello?" he said, carefully neutral.

"God, Buhl, you're so cautious. Just once I'd like you to answer with 'I've got my dick in my hand thinking about you.'"

"Which, of course, would be the time the head of Human Resources would be calling." Though Black considered he might have to put his dick in his hand soon if it got any colder. "How are you, my love?"

"Bored. The conference was a complete snore. Plus, there were the usual barbs about *Vamp*."

And while Bettina whined about being both lauded and decried in the industry for her success—a situation she had related to Black several dozen times at least—he surreptitiously withdrew the phone from his ear to open the attachment in Ellery's e-mail.

"The Postmodern Reader: Feminism and the Transformational World of Romance"? "What the *fuck*?"

" 'What the fuck'?" came a confused squawk through the speaker. "What the fuck—*what*?"

Black frantically slung the phone back to his ear. "Nothing. I mean, I can't believe they would treat you like that." *That title better pay off with a story so glowingly passionate about romance novels that Teamsters will cry.* He moved the phone in front of him again.

For the next sixty seconds he heard absolutely nothing Bettina said, only the radiator-clanging of his blood as fury hissed through his veins.

Then she said the word "Sharpe."

"What?" he demanded, nearly fumbling the phone. "What did you say?"

"I said Barry Steinberg told me Ellery Sharpe is in line to run the new rag at Lark & Ives."

"She's *what*?" he roared. This was the last straw. "Lark & fucking *Ives*?"

He heard a clunk one balcony over as Misty, the "Terror from Yorkshire," threw herself into the glass of the patio door, leaping six feet in the air and unleashing a barrage of barking shrill enough to curdle brain jelly.

Margey would be up in an instant. "I've gotta go."

"What?" Bettina said, "I can't hear you."

"I said," he repeated louder, "I've gotta go."

"What? What's that noise?"

"It's the goddamned dog!"

Misty was flying back and forth between the kitchen window and the French door to the patio, emitting a drumroll of earsplitting barks whenever she appeared.

"Goddammit," Black said. "Shut the fuck up!"

"I beg your pardon!" Bettina said.

Margey appeared in the living room, sleep mask on her forehead, glaring at him through the patio doors.

"I have to go!" Black cried.

"Don't you hang up on me!" Bettina said.

Misty leapt against the screen, until it finally opened and she landed on the patio, where she swung in a full circle on the Carrara marble before finding her footing and charging directly at him, stopping only when the width of her head kept her from flying through the rails into his neck. He hung up in the middle of a stream of vulgarity from Bettina, just as Margey opened the door and glowered at him.

"Jesus Christ, Buhl, you are the rudest person I know."

She slammed the door.

Black considered his lover, his wife and the employee who had woefully shortchanged him on an assignment and was now trying to steal away to Lark & Ives.

"Bitches," he said.

Misty bared her teeth and growled.

CHAPTER FORTY-FOUR

Thistle Bed & Breakfast, Bathgate, Scotland

Axel examined the kilt in the dry-cleaning bag and the accompanying parcel of accessories without really seeing any of it. Ellery's "compromise" position on the article was ridiculous. She was a far better journalist than that. He hated the way the magazine world worked. And he was still the sole possessor of Jill's secret, a possessor who would soon have to break his confidante's trust by telling it to the one person he never wanted to talk to again.

He grabbed the collar of his shirt, pulled it over his head and tossed it. *Women.*

Bending, he pulled the Dopp kit out of his duffel bag and unzipped it. Then he looked at the contents and scratched his head. With the time change, late lunch and uncertain dinner, he had to figure out if he needed to take any insulin. He pricked his finger and tested it. Two twenty-seven. Yikes. He tore open a syringe and lifted the small glass vial from its special holder. He cleaned the top of the bottle with an alcohol wipe and pinched a piece of stomach between his thumb and forefinger, wiping the flesh too. Tapping the vial, he lifted it into the air and drew out the appropriate amount of insulin. Then he inserted the needle into his flesh and, when the syringe was empty, withdrew it and put everything away.

He turned his attention once more to the kilt. He had worn one more times than he'd care to remember, every April sixth, the anniversary of the Declaration of Arbroath, when his dad would drag them out to the backyard for a picture, his sisters and mother free to wear whatever spring dresses they had at hand, while he and his father would trot out the Mackenzie tartan, complete with brogues, knee-high socks, dirk and sporran. His father would set the self-timer on the camera and hurry to insert himself behind the family. Once the picture had been captured, he would read out the entire Declaration, followed in due course by a broad sampling of Robert Louis Stevenson, Sir Walter Scott and, if he'd dipped into the Canadian Club early enough, Robert Burns.

Axel smiled. He missed his father.

Still, the old man would not have approved of a Black Watch tartan, which was the standard of the abhorred Clan Campbell, but Axel did not hold to the old battle lines. He kicked off his hiking boots, removed his belt and slipped out of his jeans and boxers. Then he wrapped the heavy wool around him, rethreading the belt at his waist. Digging through the bag once more, he pulled out the sporran and fastened it around his hips. The fit was good, though he'd never been a fan of the horsehair. He looked inside, hoping he didn't discover condoms or a phone number or something. Finding nothing, he debated what he should carry and decided on his cell phone and a ten-pound note so that he could buy a couple of beers. Then he dropped the wallet in the duffel and followed that with his discarded clothes.

He sat on the toilet to pull on the thick socks, folding them over the flashes that had been pinned to them. There were no brogues. He hoped his boots would do and laced them up. There was also no shirt. He stuck his head outside the door and was lucky to catch Dr. Albrecht scurrying by.

"Oh, you look grand," she said.

He made a courtly bow, which made her giggle, and asked, "Is there a shirt for this, or do I wear my own?" Not, of course, that his duffel bag held anything more than T-shirts, a couple button-down collar shirts and a sweater.

She held up a finger. "Let me check. I think there is."

She darted away, and Axel looked in the mirror at the two-day growth of beard. He probably should shave for the party. Then his vanity chimed in to remind him Ellery had always preferred him looking, as she'd said, "a little Colin Farrell."

"No one asked your opinion," he replied pointedly to his vanity.

He reached for his shaver, standing firm on the notion he should not attend to Ellery's desires, but then changed his mind.

Oh, the hell with it.

Perhaps he'd take his own "compromise" position, trimming the whiskers into a nice Wilford Brimley or something.

He heard a light tap and the door opened. It was Ellery, and she jumped a foot.

* * *

She felt her heart go off in her chest like a cartoon alarm clock, and if there'd been a wooden beam above her, she would have bonked her head on it. "What are you doing here?"

"I could ask you the same question."

She hoped he wouldn't, since she could barely form a sentence. He looked amazing. He was bare to the waist, his chest covered with its usual light pelt of auburn curls, and the musculature of his stomach rippled and bent as he moved. But it wasn't the nakedness that stunned her: It was the heavy, dark tartan of black, blue and green fanned over his legs, revealing lovely, round knees and *outstanding* calves.

How had she not noticed those calves before? Here she'd been mooning for years over his forearms, and his calves made his forearms look like some anemic appetizer on an erogenous man-part smorgasbord.

"I . . . I . . ." She couldn't take her eyes off him. The effect was overwhelming. "I'm sorry. I was supposed to clean up in here." With effort, she backed out, mortified. Then she stopped and opened the door wider. "Wait a second. Why aren't you changing in your room?"

"Dr. Albrecht kicked me out. Said she needed to clean. Sent me and my dry-cleaning bag down here."

"Ah." The mad German matchmaker at work. "Well, if you don't mind making sure there's toilet paper and clean towels when you leave, I'll just head to—"

"Wait. I want to talk."

He dug a heather-blue sweater out of his duffel and

jerked it over his head. Why is it men always dress like it'll be the last time that item of clothing will ever be usable?

She gave him a look. "I believe I heard everything I needed to upstairs. Sucky article, no principles. Got it."

"'Sucky'? I don't remember seeing that in *The New York Times Style Guide.*"

"Funny. Was there something more you needed to add?"

"Yes, actually."

"Oh, great. Are my teeth stained? Does my outfit bother you?"

He made a point of running his eyes over the skirt and sweater.

"Actually, your outfit is pretty nice."

She harrumphed. Flattery was going to get him nowhere. However, if he flashed that calf one more time . . .

It was getting harder to fit anger and attraction into her jet lagged brain.

"If you have an apology, I'll listen," she said. "Otherwise, you can just—"

"I don't have an apology," he said then added, abashed, "I have a regret. The article is shit, Ellery. You know it and I know it. But I should have been nicer about it."

"Gee, and you still wonder why we broke up."

He bent to zip his duffel bag. Then he gave her a troubled look, and the temperature in the room changed in a way Ellery could not directly identify.

"I need to talk to you," he said. "It's important. Let's take a walk."

She uncrossed her arm and gestured to him to proceed.

Chapter Forty-Five

He was unnaturally silent as they picked their way through trees framed by the pink evening sky, and her pique had been replaced by worry. The leaves crunched underfoot, and even in the unnatural warmth Ellery could smell the iron tang of oncoming winter. Behind them, the sounds of guitar, tin whistle and bodhrán rose on the wind as the band tuned and practiced in the barn. Ahead of them the rise of Cairnpapple shone in the fading light.

Axel paused to help her over a gnarled root. "It's about Jill," he said without preamble.

A spike of fear shot up Ellery's back.

"She's okay—well, she will be." He sighed. "She's pregnant, Ellery. She's scared."

So many questions flew through Ellery's head, she didn't know where to start. She finally decided on, "Who's the father?"

"I don't know. She hasn't told me and I didn't ask."

Told *him*. Ellery felt a kick that made her stomach contract with its ferocity.

"She told *you*?"

"Ellery"—he put his hand on her arm—"the important thing is helping Jill."

She pulled away. "I know what the important thing is."

"I know you do. That's why I told you. I am incapable of providing that kind of help."

"I sure know that."

He flinched, and she knew the remark had hit home.

"I'm trying to do the right thing," he said.

Yes. Yes, he was. He had told her. She was grateful for that. She turned, unwilling to let him see her pain and swiped a palm under her eye.

"When?" she asked.

"I dunno. A month or so ago, I guess. She's not very far along. She just found out."

"When did she call?"

"An hour ago."

"I need to talk to her." She started back toward the house.

"Ellery, wait. She asked me not to tell you."

Ellery froze. It was bad enough to not be told first. But to be kept purposefully in the dark?

"Why would she tell you?"

"I don't know. I haven't talked to her in years. But I know why she doesn't want to tell you."

"Why?"

"She said because you never make mistakes and you wouldn't understand."

The coup de grâce. Ellery had worked so hard trying to

make life perfect for her sister, she'd forgotten to show her that there were ways to work through hard times. Ellery's shoulders heaved, and the next thing she knew, Axel had his arms around her.

"That's not true, you know," she said, crying. "I make mistakes."

"I'd say 'Don't I know it,' but I'm afraid you wouldn't laugh."

She did laugh, and then cried more. She thought of her own fear when she'd found herself in the same unexpected spot. "I have to call her, Axel."

"I know, and that's why I told you. She's going to be royally pissed, but I can live with that."

"What's she going to do?"

"That I don't know. She has an appointment at the college clinic on Monday."

Her breath caught. "An appointment for what?"

"I don't know. Advice."

She pulled away. "I need to call. I have to tell her—" She stopped. "I have to talk to her."

Axel hugged his arms around him as though a cool breeze had blown through. "Ellery, what happened to us? At the end. What happened?"

"Oh, Axel, do we have to do this now?"

"Please. Just tell me. I've waited all these years. Please, tell me."

She shook her head. "It was so long ago."

"I know you were pregnant."

The words hung in the air like mists from an ancient river. "How . . . ?"

His eyes creased for an instant, as if reliving a long-ago

blow. "Your doctor's office called. The day I was packing. To say . . ." He searched for the right words. "To say it was done. I assume that was part of why you ended things. I know it wasn't the only reason."

"Oh, Axel." A heated shame came over her. Five years was a long time to wonder about such a thing, and so many things had changed. "I should have told you." She thought of lying there alone on the hospital gurney. "It made me so sad. I was so afraid."

He reached out but his hand seemed to stop midway. "Was it mine?" he asked softly, and the true horror of his situation hit her.

"Oh, God, Axel! I'm so sorry. Yes, it was yours. I'm capable of a lot of horrible things, but I would never have done that to you."

He was reeling from the news. She could see it on his pale cheeks and in the whiteness of his knuckles.

"And the baby," he said. "You . . . ?"

"I lost it, Axel," she said. "A night you were gone. They had to—"

"I understand."

He sat down on the tree they'd climbed over and put his head in his hands. She'd failed Jill and she'd failed him. That was a lot of failing in one lifetime.

She took a step toward him but was afraid to get closer. "I planned to tell you about it . . . about the pregnancy."

"Did you?" He didn't look up. She could see the rise and fall of his chest.

"I was so happy. I was, Axel. Despite our differences. At first I wasn't sure—I mean, about actually *being* pregnant. I thought I was, and I found to my surprise the thought made me pretty happy. I wanted you to be there when I took the test, but we were out someplace and I wasn't feeling very well, and I should have told you, but all I wanted to do was go home—"

"It was the night at Mullen's, when Brendan was playing." He gazed at her expectantly, awaiting her confirmation that his guess was right.

"Yes, it was."

"And I didn't want to leave."

"Nope."

"And I drove you home and came back."

She nodded. "And then I tested myself and I knew." She looked at him, feeling the sadness of it all. "And then I was mad at you and didn't want to tell you. Oh, God, it seems like such a long time ago and such a stupid thing to be mad about. And once I'd stopped being mad, I wanted to wait. Until I was further along and it was safe."

"Safe." He gave half a chuckle as if nothing between them had ever been safe.

"And then . . . later . . . I began to lose the baby . . ."

"And I was gone again. How did you know—I mean, that something was wrong?" His eyes were as clear as green lochs.

"Terrible cramps. Just terrible. Like a knife in my gut."

"Oh, God. Did Jill know?"

It was Ellery's turn for a regretful half laugh. "No, of course not. If she did, maybe I'm the one she would have called today."

He crossed his arms, staring into the empty fields

beside them. The slow, plaintive notes of "Auld Lang Syne" drifted through the trees.

Ellery glanced back. "Oh, dear, it sounds like they're starting the party."

"I hope," he said, giving her a weak smile, "they don't start the party with *that*."

She laughed.

"I don't understand," he said, regret tinged with awe. "How did you do it? You were all by yourself."

Ellery felt the tears begin to well again. "It was awful. I was so scared."

In an instant Axel was on his feet, holding her tight as she wept. She could feel the rough finish of the sweater's wool and the warmth of his shoulder beneath. He patted her until she stilled.

"I'm sorry I wasn't a very good boyfriend."

She looked up at him, the light of the sunset catching the red in his hair, and went to pat his cheek but found herself kissing him instead. He held her with the tips of his fingers, as if she were porcelain that might break.

A phone buzzed and she broke away, forgetting for a second she had left hers in her room.

Axel pulled his out of his sporran. "It's Black. Christ almighty." He rolled his eyes and sent the call into oblivion.

"I should call Jill."

"Yes. Go, go. I'll walk you back."

"No, there's no point. She won't take my call. I tried before I found you. I got no answer. Then I got a text: SORRY I MISSED YOUR CALL. I'M BEAT. WHY DON'T WE CATCH UP WHEN YOU'RE BACK FROM YOUR TRIP. She's blowing me off."

Axel held up his phone. "She'll answer me." He pressed the screen a couple times, then lifted the phone to his ear. After a second or two he nodded. She'd answered.

"Jill, hi. Listen, I was thinking more about what you told me."

Ellery heard a short, indistinct reply.

"You know the best person to help you with this is your sister." Axel rubbed the spot between his brows. Jill's reply was more agitated.

"Jill, you called me because you needed help, and I have to do what I think is right." He took a deep breath. "I told Ellery."

The agitation turned to fury. Ellery could recognize the sound even if the words themselves were indiscernible.

"Yes, I know a friend wouldn't have done this. But I'm not your friend. I'm a grown-up and I have to help. I'm sorry. Here's your sister. She knows everything."

He handed Ellery the phone, and Ellery patted him on the back. He had done well. He took her hand and kissed it. Then, with a brief wave, he started back toward the house.

Ellery took a deep breath. "Jill," she said into the cool silence, "I'm so sorry. I've been through this myself. I never told you, but back when Axel and I were together, I was pregnant once too. Tell me what happened."

Without missing a step, Axel turned, gave her an approving smile, and continued on his way.

CHAPTER FORTY-SIX

Axel filled the goblet with a nice Spanish Rioja, then grabbed a pint glass, tilted the tap and let the straw-colored Belhaven run down the side, ensuring an adequate but not overly pretentious amount of foam. It had been a long time since he'd been on this side of a bar—he'd practically put himself through college working at the Maple Leaf Tap in Toronto—and it brought back a lot of fond memories.

"What do I owe you?" asked the woman who had ordered the drinks, pulling a handful of bills out of the pocket of her sleek leather blazer. Her cheeks were flushed and he suspected the whiskey-tasting earlier this afternoon had been more than just a taste for her.

"Open bar," he said. "They just announced your company's picking up everything."

"I can think of one thing I'd like them to pick up," she said, and leered at the hem of his kilt.

"Ah, ah, ah." He waved a forbidding finger at her, and she gave him a big smile.

Someone had set up a tip jar, and the woman pushed a bill toward it. "There's ten pounds in it for you if you tell me what's worn underneath."

A white-haired gentleman sitting at the far end of the bar snorted, and Axel sighed, dropping the dirty pint glasses in the suds. "Nothing's worn, I assure you. It's all in perfect working order."

The joke was as old as Cairnpapple—he'd heard his father say it dozens of times—but she burst into giggles and slipped the bill into the jar. "Linda!" she called, grabbing the Rioja and Belhaven. "You have to hear what the guy at the bar said."

Axel shook his head. "Jesus, that's the fourth woman who's made a comment about the kilt. One of them tried to grab it. I feel like I should be getting combat pay here."

The man chuckled. "There's something about a kilt, lad. It unleashes a woman's inner . . ." He groped for the right word.

"Beast?"

"Man, I'm afraid. It's the only time they get to turn the tables on us. The sly looks. The innuendo. It's rather scary to be on the receiving end, don't you think?"

Dr. Albrecht walked up to the bar, gave the older gentleman a close scan from head to toe, then with a point at the bottle of Rioja said pleasantly, "Vhy, Reggie, I don't believe I've ever seen a pair of knees quite so pink before."

Axel peered over the bar. Reggie was wearing a kilt as well, a light-blue one. He gave Axel an I-told-you-so look and pulled the hem a little lower.

Axel poured the last of the bottle and pushed the glass toward Dr. Albrecht.

"Vhere's Ellery?" she asked.

"I doubt she'll be coming."

The sociologist searched his face so hard, he felt compelled to add, "It's not me, I swear. She's on a call. It's pretty important." *Sheesh.* It was like having his mother here. Next she'd be checking to see if his nails were clean. He gave them a discreet look. Not bad.

"I'm glad you mentioned her, though," he added. "She's going to need a flight back to the States as soon as possible, which I guess means a flight to London from here."

"Tonight?"

He thought of the worry in Jill's voice. "Yes, if it's possible."

"Let me run back to the house to check the schedules. There may be time to make the last flight. Vhat about you? Vill you be going vith her?"

He'd be about as handy as mud flaps on a speedboat in that tête-à-tête. "No. I'll finish out here and catch the train as planned."

"And then vhat?" The sociologist narrowed her eyes.

Axel knew she wasn't asking about his London hotel plans.

"I don't know. Hard to say." He had no idea what if anything the kiss had meant, though he had passed on both the food and the Belhaven in order to keep the fresh melon taste of Ellery in his mouth.

Dr. Albrecht made one of those noises his father used to make when Axel said his homework was mostly done, and she scurried off. As he washed the glasses, the band began a rousing version of "Scotland the Brave." He wouldn't have guessed a tin whistle could take the part of the bagpipes in that song, but the little instrument was doing a yeoman's duty. A number of the guests were dancing, and still more were drinking, talking or eating. The barn was a perfect spot for a party. He could see why Dr. Albrecht did a good business in céilidhs.

"So, are you one of the hired hands here too?" he asked Reggie. "Though perhaps I should say 'hired legs.'"

Reggie chuckled. "Oh, no. I own the distillery next door. I've known Gerty for years. Archie and I curled together."

"A curler, eh? I've done a bit a curling myself. More of a hockey man, though. You don't look like a curler. You look more like a rugger. The shoulders, I think. You're not a Scot, though."

"No, just a Northumberland bloke who loves whiskey. By the way, I couldn't help but notice you're not a Scot, either."

Axel felt his ears pinken. "Sorry," he said, dropping the borrowed accent. "Part of the conditions of employment. I feel like I'm a spy or something. Probably not required for you, though."

"No, the kilt's more than enough."

Axel laughed.

"It's quite good, though," Reggie said, "your accent, I mean."

"My father was from Fife but moved to Canada as a child. That's where I'm from."

"Ah, the great kingdom of Fife. Have you been?"

"Never."

"You should go. I recommend Kirkcaldy. A lovely

town. And if you go, I suggest Fyfe Fyre, a great bitter from Fyfe Brewing."

Axel straightened. "You a beer drinker?"

"A man needs something to wash his whiskey down, aye?"

Axel grinned. "I'll drink to that." He picked up his club soda and clinked Reggie's glass, but he didn't drink.

"Not thirsty?"

"Something like that. Say, I almost bought a microbrewery this week."

Reggie raised a brow. "Oh?"

"Couldn't come up with enough money."

"You know anything about brewing?"

"Yes. A lot. Enough to know it's what I want to do."

Three more women approached the bar, and Axel poured a chardonnay, a Coke and another Belhaven, enduring only a single giggled comment about his theoretical lack of underclothes in the process. He was amused to discover, however, that bending for the clean glasses consistently doubled his tip. Perhaps he would end up with a brewery after all.

Reggie signaled for a refill.

"I'm Axel, by the way." He held out his hand. "Axel Mackenzie."

Reggie shook it. "What are you doing in Bathgate?"

"I'm a photographer." He grabbed Reggie's glass and ducked his head toward the tripod and equipment bag tucked into the corner. "I'm here for a story."

"On what?"

"Romance novels."

Reggie nodded. "*Kiltlander*."

"Among others." He filled the glass and set it down again.

"Have I seen your stuff?"

"Probably. I do a lot of magazine work. God, did you see the moon out there? I'm dying to take a crack at that."

"What was the stramash about the lassie?"

Axel made an unhappy grunt, hoping it would be answer enough.

"I see." Reggie sipped his beer. "I've had a run of bad luck myself. My soon-to-be ex-wife wants half of everything."

"Well, fortunately, I've got nothing to be halved. And in any case, we broke up a long time ago."

"Mm-hm."

Axel couldn't quite put a description on what had happened between him and Ellery. He was relieved to know she hadn't cheated on him, though in his heart he'd never really believed it. But another part of him was unexpectedly sad to discover something that would have brought them such joy had been lost.

Right woman, wrong time.

"Reggie," he said, slouching against the wall behind the bar, "it sounds like what you need to do is find yourself the right woman."

"Have, my lad. Two problems. First, I'm na' divorced. The ex-wife's dragging her feet, and it wouldn't be right to ask the new lady until that was settled."

"And?"

Reggie's shoulders settled a degree lower. "And I can't get the new lass to pay me the slightest mind."

Dr. Albrecht ran up to the bar, nodding briefly at Reggie. "There is a flight," she said to Axel. "I'll let her know. How are vee doing on the beer?"

"Tons left. This is definitely a harder-drinking crowd."

"Would you like me to send over a cask of whiskey?" Reggie asked, the eagerness to help written clearly on his face.

"Thank you, Reggie," she said absently, scanning the dance floor. "You can send me the bill."

"No, no, it's on me," he said, but she had already flitted away.

"I see what you mean." Axel pulled out a bottle of aged whiskey he'd found under the bar. "This yours?"

"It is."

Axel put down two shot glasses. If he was going to give up the taste of Ellery Sharpe, it might as well be for a shot of eighteen-year-old Scotch.

He gave each glass a generous pour and picked up his. "To someday figuring women out."

Reggie picked his up and threw it back. *"Sláinte."*

Axel drank his. *And then she was gone.*

"Do you like it?"

The exquisite peaty smokiness rolled past his lungs and into his belly. It was great, but not as good as what it had replaced. "It's marvelous."

Reggie smiled.

"Are you planning to get some dinner?" Axel asked. The caterer had opened a resplendent buffet with a lamb roast, parsnips, potatoes, meat pies, beans, stewed cabbage and Dr. Albrecht's soup. He could smell the garlic of the lamb all the way over at the bar.

"I believe I might."

"What do you suppose those things are?"

Reggie looked toward the platter where Axel was pointing. It was piled high with some sort of dough pockets.

"Pasties, I imagine. More of a Cornish treat than Scottish, but I doubt this crowd will notice."

"They look like pierogies," Axel said, thinking of that delectable Pittsburgh treat. "Only with a pastry crust."

" 'Pierogies'?"

"Rolled dough folded in a half-circle over mashed potatoes and sautéed onions. Fried in butter and served with sour cream. A-mazing."

"Mmmmm. Wonder what they'd be like with neeps and tatties? Are they a Canadian dish?"

"Oh, God, no. Pittsburghian. Not fattening enough for Canadians. Our national dish is poutine—chips topped with brown gravy and cheese curds."

Reggie's eyes blinked dreamily. "This I must try."

"Poutine, a couple of Labatt Blues, the Maple Leafs on the big screen . . ." Axel stared happily into the distance. "But," he added quickly, "pierogies are nearly their equal. I don't know why, but I have a real soft spot for them."

"I don't suppose the lassie's from Pittsburgh?"

Axel's cheeks warmed.

"Mm-hm."

"That's where the brewery I almost bought is too."

"A sort of regional hat trick?"

Axel laughed. "You, my friend, know your sports."

"If only I knew women as well."

"I hear ya."

Reggie climbed to his feet and gave Axel a nod before heading toward the food. Axel grabbed his camera and began to reel off some shots of the band as they wound down, slowing the shutter speed in order to get blurs of movement. There wouldn't be an article—there was little chance Black would publish what Ellery had written—but Axel could probably pull the photos together into something for a travel magazine.

Dr. Albrecht reappeared. "Axel, vill you close the bar? The bigvigs vant to do some speeches during dinner, and they don't vant people getting up for refills until it's over."

"Sure. No problem." He'd worked enough places over the years to know you could always count on the suits to shut down the fun. "Say, is there going to be dancing afterward?"

"Oh, I'm sure there vill be. The place is booked until one."

"Reggie would like the first dance."

She frowned. "Vhat do you mean?"

"The first dance, Frau Doktor. With you."

"Vith *me*?" Her face filled with surprise. Good Lord, how subtle had Reggie been?

"Who else?"

"I, vell . . ." She stammered out a few more sounds, dimples puckered, and fell silent.

"I'll let him know?"

"Yes," she nodded, eyes sparkling. *"Danke."*

Axel closed up the bar, grabbed his camera and found Reggie in the food line. "You're lined up for the first dance after dinner," he said, thumping him on the back. "Make the most of it."

"What? How—"

"I told her where you stand. Knocked her right back into German."

"But the divorce . . ."

"A dance isn't a marriage proposal, pal. Keep it clean."

Axel hitched the camera onto his shoulder and made his way to the guitar player. "Great set," he said; then, slipping the guy a five-pound note, he added, "First song after dinner? Make it a slow one."

CHAPTER FORTY-SEVEN

Ellery pressed the END button and hugged the phone to her chest. It killed her to be half a world away when Jill needed her. But Jill had assured her over and over that the appointment was purely informational and that she was sure her friend, Melissa, would be able to go with her. After Jill's initial hesitation, which had been like a slow stab to the heart to Ellery, she had opened up, relieved to share her burden with her sister. They'd ended the call with Jill agreeing to call back if she couldn't confirm Melissa.

Ellery was trying to keep her mind off the boyfriend, who wasn't returning calls. Jill didn't want to talk about him and said he was "a nonvariable" in the equation. A week ago Ellery might have agreed, but the look on Axel's face when he'd asked if Ellery's baby had been his had convinced her otherwise. How awful for Axel to have spent the last five years wondering whether she'd had an affair or, worse, to think she'd known it was his and didn't want it. She'd carried her anger for so long, nurtured it like it was some bittersweet replacement for the child she'd lost, and all it took was a half hour of mutual worrying about Jill to make all of it seem as inconsequential as leaves blowing in the wind.

She could still feel the spots on her back where his fingers had come to rest as they'd kissed, and all she wanted to do was find him and tell him about the phone call.

He wouldn't have been a horrible parent, she thought, or even a bad one. His heart was in the right place, even if Ellery didn't quite believe his protestations about giving up partying. He had, after all, been out the entire night drinking with that slimeball Barry Steinberg.

How the hell had Steinberg ended up in London at the same time as she and Axel? He was a slimeball, no doubt. But he was also a fantastic writer, and a worthy opponent in this race to the Lark & Ives finish line.

Dammit! She wanted that job. She'd be perfect, possessing just the right mix of administrative and critical skills. She knew just how she'd set up the new magazine too. Not too priggish. Not too *GQ*. With great utility players in key roles. No more specialists. She wanted team players who could pinch-hit for each other. Everyone would learn. Everyone would be challenged. She'd be sitting in that chair, and she could hire anyone she wanted. Heck, she could hire Axel. Why not have the best, right? After all, he was—

Then she remembered.

Axel would be in Pittsburgh, running a brewery. Far away from New York. Far away from her. And while he had said he wouldn't give up photography completely, he'd made it pretty clear he didn't like the magazine industry or New York.

Suddenly, the Lark & Ives confection she'd been rolling around her tongue lost some of its sweetness.

She also reminded herself that she was theorizing well ahead of the evidence. Yes, they'd made love, and, yes, he'd just given her the most wonderful kiss, but he was also disappointed with the article she'd written, which she had to admit he had every right to be. He was aware of what she was capable of as well as she did, and he held her to high standards. Well, at least the standard of truth, and he knew she had learned more about the power of romance novels in the last few days than she was letting on.

She was starting to feel a little disingenuous about not writing the story Black wanted. Hell, she'd been tearing through *Kiltlander* at record pace. Of course romance novels had the power to bring intelligent readers pleasure. It would be foolish at this point to argue anything else. But, oh, how she wanted that job at Lark & Ives . . .

Axel had a more compelling reason to be disappointed with her. He'd spent five years living with pain and uncertainty that she had made him suffer. She hadn't done it consciously, but she'd been the cause of it nonetheless.

The trees were brilliantly lit by the platinum glow of the full moon, and she made her way back to the party.

In the barn the guests were relaxing at their tables or still waiting in line at the buffet, and the incredible mix of smells was making Ellery hungry again. But she wanted to find Axel and didn't see him or Dr. Albrecht anywhere.

A man in his late fifties or early sixties with a shock of white hair and an enchanting pale blue kilt caught her eye. He was standing beside the empty dance floor, shifting his weight nervously from foot to foot and moving his lips in some rosary-like repetition. When she focused her attention on it, she realized he was counting rhythmically: "*One,* two, three, four. *One,* two, three, four . . ."

"Upcoming waltz?" she asked, and he started.

"Indeed," he said. "Though my partner seems to have fled."

"Sounds like a fatal error on her part."

He smiled. "Oh, I'll catch her eventually. The band's going to play half the night. Are you looking for someone?" he added, catching the wide look she was casting around the room.

"Yeah, a guy a little older than me. Brown hair. He's wearing a kilt too."

The man's brows lifted and his smile grew larger. "Pittsburgh, right?"

"How did you—"

"It's a night for good guesses. He's on break. Should be back soon, though. Should I tell him you're looking for him?"

"Yes, thanks. If you see him, tell him I'm going back to the house."

"I'll let him know."

On the way her phone buzzed. She looked down. It was a text from Kate. ARE YOU WITH ELLERY?

Ellery had forgotten the phone she had was Axel's. She dialed Kate's number at work. "What's up?"

"Why are you on Axel's phone? Is he lying there next to you?"

"I'm outside a barn in Scotland."

"Wow, I hope you have some blankets."

"Funny. I talked to Jill." Ellery took a quick look around the yard. Wherever Axel had taken his break, it didn't seem to be around here.

"I was just going to ask. Is everything okay?"

As close as she was to Kate, Ellery wasn't going to share the story. That was going to be up to Jill. "Yeah. Just down about some boy. She'll be fine."

"Oh, good. Thought I was falling down on the aunt front."

"Nope. Your instincts were right. I appreciate the heads-up."

"No problem, my friend. Unfortunately, that's not why I called."

Kate's voice had dropped to a no-nonsense whisper, and Ellery felt a lump grow in the pit of her stomach.

"Black's looking for you," Kate said. "Called your phone. Called my phone. Called Axel's phone."

Ellery looked at the recent calls. Two from Black. Axel must have had his phone on SILENT or he'd sent them to voice mail before he'd handed the phone to her.

"What does Black want?" Ellery asked, knowing the answer perfectly well.

"Near as I can tell, to see you strung up from the Lark & Ives tower."

Ellery winced. He'd found out. Somehow he'd found out. And her compromise romance article was going to be the icing on that already heartburn-inducing cake.

She was surprised Black hadn't figured out a way to have her struck by lightening. She stepped away from a utility pole. "Oh, shit."

"It gets worse."

"Worse than me losing my job?" She wondered if Black had read the article.

"Depends on how you feel about your photographer," Kate said.

"What does *that* mean?"

"Well, Black's pretty angry with Axel too."

"Why, it's not his fault I'm interviewing at Lark & Ives."

"No," Kate said carefully, "but it is his fault you turned in, and I quote, 'a turd wrapped in prose so dull, it could do double-duty as a thermostat manual.'"

Well, that answered that question. "I still don't see how it's Axel's fault."

There was a long pause before Kate answered. "Apparently, Black had enlisted him to help ensure you wrote the kind of article he wanted."

Ellery didn't know whether to laugh or cry. Axel was being paid to coach her on the article? Good God, he'd have known better than anyone that he didn't have a chance of influencing how she wrote her story. She would have noticed anything obvious. And anything subtle—

She froze. The books. The book club at his friend's pub. The kiss.

No. It couldn't be true. There was no way that kiss or his kindness regarding Jill or his heated desire during their lovemaking at the hotel yesterday could have been made-up. She knew that in her soul. Nonetheless, Kate's revelation threw the rest of what she thought she knew about Axel into an uncertain light.

"Ellery, are you okay?"

"Yeah, yeah. I'll be okay."

"I'm sorry. Kinda stinky, huh?"

"Yeah, kinda. If it's true, and I'm not sure it is. But in any case, I've got bigger fish to fry."

"Black's still trying to reach you. You're going to have to talk to him."

"What? To be fired? There's a call I don't mind sending to voice mail."

"You think he's going to fire you?"

"At this point I'm not sure I care. You know, of course, the Lark & Ives thing is getting close, and this may make it a little easier. But I can get writing gigs if I have to." Though she hoped it didn't come to that.

"Oops. I gotta run," Kate said, which was probably code for "Black on the move." "I'll call you back."

Ellery said good-bye and bounded onto the porch of the bed-and-breakfast, through the door and up the stairs. She needed to see Axel's face in order to know how she felt. His door was closed. She knocked, but there was no answer. She tried the door, but it was locked. She ran to her room and found her phone. Eight missed calls: two from Kate, five from Black and one from Carlton Purdy. She was just about to call Carlton when Dr. Albrecht stuck her head in the door.

"Oh, there you are. Vhy are you not vith Axel?"

Nice to get right down to business. "Is he here?"

"He vuz at the barn. Do you mind if I drop this here." It was Axel's duffel.

"That's fine."

She put the bag on the floor. "He said you'll need a flight to London tonight, so you could fly home tomorrow."

Ellery smiled, happy to have found a measure of reassurance in Axel's concern for her.

"There's one at eleven you can still make," Dr. Albrecht added, looking at her watch.

"I probably won't need it," Ellery said after a moment's consideration, "but I'll let you know. The issue seems to have resolved itself a little bit."

"Good, good," the sociologist said. "I have a call in to a friend with a car service to make sure he can get you to the airport. I'll let him know it's on hold."

"Thank you. I should know soon. I have a few calls to make."

Ellery's phone rang, and she shrugged apologetically at Dr. Albrecht, who scooted out. The call was from Black, who was making his sixth try. She considered blowing him off, but what was the point? She'd rolled the dice and lost. Time to pay the house.

"Sharpe here," she said, sinking onto the bed.

The next few moments were a blur of accusations, vodka-soaked fury and an incredible selection of Anglo-Saxon interjections, including several Ellery believed may have dated as far back as *The Canterbury Tales*. Her actual firing was sandwiched somewhere between a tirade on the vanishing days of employee loyalty and an ode to some John Cheever short story about an elevator operator at Christmastime, and a dog seemed to be barking the entire time he spoke. When he finally settled into throaty harrumphs and avuncular disappointment, she knew they were nearly done.

"Dammit, Ellery, why can't you just behave like a good writer?"

She almost laughed. She had never thought she'd live to see the day when she was chastised for misbehaving. Score one for the uptight, straitlaced company gal. Er, make that *former* company gal. She flopped on her back.

"I'm sorry to have it end this way, Mr. Black. I appreciate all you've done for me. I really do. But I can't write how you tell me to write. That's not how it works—at least, not for me."

He snorted. "You'll change."

I hope not, she thought, but said nothing.

"Is your erstwhile photographer with you?" he asked dryly.

Black was mad at Axel too. Kate was right. "No."

"Do you have any idea how I could reach him?"

"You might try his cell." She held Axel's phone at arm's length and wondered what Black would say if she answered that one too.

"Thank you. I would have never thought of that. Let me just put away my signal flags."

She swallowed.

"When you see him, tell him I want to talk to him."

"I will."

She desperately wanted to ask if the story of paying Axel to corral her was true, but it was likely that Kate and Axel were the only people other than Black who knew; while Ellery probably wouldn't have minded getting Axel in trouble for it, she definitely didn't want Kate to catch any flak.

"Good day, Ellery."

If this was good, she'd settle for below average. "Good day." She hung up.

Christ.

She lay in a formless heap, reimagining her life. No more *Vanity Place*. No certainty about Lark & Ives. Jill in trouble. And Axel a great big question mark. With any luck, this could turn into the worst day of her life.

She picked up the phone and dialed Carlton Purdy.

"Carlton," she said happily when he answered. "I'm glad you called. I was just going to call you. I have some good news."

"You do? And what might that be?"

"I have officially left *Vanity Place*. I'm a free agent and I'm raring to go."

The silence was, well, if not deafening, then certainly highly muffled.

"Glad to hear it, glad to hear it." Purdy cleared his throat significantly. "Ellery, I heard something about you that I simply can't believe."

Bingo. Worst day of her life.

"A little birdie told me that your swan song for *Vanity Place* is a piece extolling the joys of romance novels."

"'A little birdie'? Who might that have been?"

"I don't think it's important who told me—"

Of course not.

"—but the person *he* heard it from seems like she should have reason to know. Bettina Moore."

Well, it was no great mystery who told Moore, but

who was the missing link between Moore and Carlton Purdy? Kate? No. Axel? Unlikely. Black? Downright impossible. Then she remembered Barry effing Steinberg and the publishing conference in London. Would Moore have been at the conference? Of course, she would have. In fact, Ellery had a vague memory of seeing Bettina Moore's name in capital letters on the conference announcement in her e-mail. Would she have told Barry Steinberg? Hell, yes. She was probably telling everyone she knew Ellery Sharpe was writing an article on romance novels.

Barry Steinberg had just moved to the top of her hit list.

"Bettina Moore would have reason to know, you're right," Ellery said. "And I'm afraid that's part of the reason *Vanity Place* and I have parted ways. Look, let's cut the crap here, Carlton. The person who told you was Barry Steinberg, and I have the highest regard for his writing—I do—but let's face it: Steinberg is known for his blustery bullshit. I'm just saying you may have to ask yourself about his motivation."

"Then you're *not* writing a piece on romance novels?"

"It was my assignment, Carlton. I'm not writing it anymore."

"I see. Then that's not going to be the piece the board sees when the issue comes out?"

"Nope. But in disentangling myself from the romance story, I disentangled myself from my entire job."

"Do not fear. Uncle Purdy is here. First, you're my lead candidate. I'm sure the board will be encouraged to hear you're a candidate with principles. Second, let's not forget the DeLillo piece. That's going to win you points.

It's excellent. Hold on," he said, the sound of keys clicking in the background. "I'm pulling it up."

"Thank you," Ellery said. "I'm very proud of that one."

"Between you and me," Purdy said, speaking in a confidential tone, "a romance article would have been the shell that sunk the *Bismarck*."

"Yes," she said pointedly, "I am aware of that."

"I mean, my God, what would the world have come to?"

"Well, it's not as bad as, say, a hundred thousand people dying of cholera each year—I mean, right?"

Purdy made a nervous laugh. "Well, no. Of course not. But when you think of the literary world and books of real value . . ."

"The ones that capture the true essence of the human condition?"

"*Yes.* Thank you. When you think of them, you're simply looking at a much bigger canvas."

"You know, Carlton, I know you and I don't think of romance novels that way, but there're actually a lot of people out there who do."

"Don't I know it. The bib overall crowd."

She cringed. Is that how she sounded? "They're not like that. Honest to God."

"Bib overalls. Polyester pants. Cuddled up to their warehouse club-size tubs of Chips Ahoy."

Ellery thought of the lovely, sweet Rosemary Readers, the women cheering passionately at the Monkey Bar and Dr. Albrecht with her PhD.

"With all due respect, Carlton, you're wrong. It's young people, older people, the highly educated—even men. There's a whole host of romance readers out there, and they're pretty diverse."

"Yes," Carlton said, capitulating, "but they're not the sort of readers we want, really, are they?"

"Are there 'sorts' of readers?" His comments were moving from the offensive to the inane. "I mean, gee, with the number of book and magazine readers shrinking each year, I think we'd be happy for any sort of reader. I used to publish a local arts paper, and we had a saying: 'The best reader is the one who'll plunk down his fifty cents each week.'"

"Yes, Ellery, there are. Do you know what would happen if we started targeting people who read stuff like romance?"

Yeah, you'd probably sell about a gazillion more magazines.

She was growing uncomfortable with the arbitrary distinction between "literature" and "romance"—and ashamed that she had made the same distinctions herself.

"Romance novels explore important territory," she said. "The territory might not be of interest to every reader—no territory is—but that doesn't mean it's not important."

"For heaven's sake, Ellery, you sound like you might have liked to write that romance article. Sorry, I know it's not true. But, honestly, have you ever read some of that stuff?"

She frowned. "Have *you*?"

"God, no. It's deadly dull."

She stifled a giggle. This had gone from a heated debate to an *SNL* sketch. *Ah, Jemmie, what have you done to me?* She grinned at her surprising new role as defender of romance. A smart interviewee would hold her tongue, but she was starting to feel a streak of recklessness worthy of Axel Mackenzie. Come to think of it, maybe it was Axel who was having the real impact on her.

"Actually, Carlton," she said, breaking into a sly grin, "they can be quite page-turning."

"Are you serious?"

"They speak to an essential human condition. It's not surprising to me at all that so many readers enjoy them."

"That's hardly the purview of literary fiction," he said, sniffing.

"An essential human conditions is not the purview of literary fiction?"

"I can't believe you feel like this."

"It's not like I just suggested we burn the literary magazine industry to the ground. I'm pointing out that as good journalists and scholars we might want to cross-examine the data we're using to draw what appear to be some pretty arbitrary conclusions."

"Those conclusions are not arbitrary," he said, voice growing sharper.

"Carlton," she said gently, "you haven't read a single romance."

"I don't need to read a romance to know they're without value."

Ellery shook her head. She almost asked if his powers of deduction extended to the outcome of football games and *Dancing with the Stars,* but what was the point? If you couldn't see it, you couldn't see it. Besides, she was still hoping he'd be her boss.

"Well, we've certainly gotten a bit off track here," she said. "You're okay with the DeLillo piece, then?"

"Yes. Between that and your portfolio, we'll have what we need."

"Great. I'm looking forward to meeting your board."

"And they you. I'm glad we can put this romance misstep behind us."

Ellery hung up with his last words still sounding in her ear. "Misstep." She didn't feel like her foray into the world of romances had been a misstep. Despite the fact that she hadn't wanted to write the damned article, she had to admit the last few days had been kind of magical. She'd *liked* standing on the ledge, wearing that Monkey Bar T-shirt. She'd *liked* talking about Jemmie and his wedding night with the Rosemary Readers. She'd *liked* hearing Dr. Albrecht's construction of the case for romance novels. Reading a romance novel was like walking a dog in the park. It gave you an instant connection with almost every person you encountered. And she didn't need to ask Dr. Albrecht to know why. Romance novels allowed readers to live over and over that tsunami of human experience, falling in love.

It *was* a tsunami. She remembered the dizziness she'd felt those first few months with Axel, as if all the joy in the world were being pumped into her lungs. Nothing was feared. Anything was possible.

And the sex! Holy moly! She fell back on the bed and covered her head with a pillow at the memory.

Sex was the steam valve on the relentless engine of love and infatuation. God, she could feel the bubbling in her veins as if it were happening right now—

She stopped, startled, and ran an inquisitive finger over her lips.

I'll . . . be . . . damned. . . .

Immediately, a warning voice inside her head asked, *Axel? Again? Are you crazy? What's changed?*

A lot, she answered.

Maybe you have. He hasn't.

Maybe that's enough.

Maybe that's what you want to believe.

"Dammit, it *is* what I want to believe," Ellery said aloud. "So cork it, will ya?" She closed her eyes, trying to will away the doubt.

It was one thing to accept Axel's friendship, even a friendship with some knee-trembling benefits. It was another to feel like she could put her trust in him.

The band began their second set. She could hear the plaintive chords of the guitar and the beckoning notes of the tin whistle as the song's slow melody rolled across the yard. She closed her eyes and inhaled, letting the wonder of a warm Scottish night wash over her.

Carlton Purdy was wrong about romances. So wrong, she felt bad for him.

She felt the flames of creation begin to flicker at her fingertips. Perhaps it was just more of that Axel streak of recklessness, but if it was, she didn't care. Maybe she'd even thank him for it.

She flipped open her laptop and pressed ON.

CHAPTER FORTY-EIGHT

The faint beats of the bodhrán echoed across the yard, and Axel lifted his eye from the viewfinder. He felt the pull of the music, and since the moon had disappeared behind a cloud just as he'd finished setting up the tripod, he decided to go back in to listen for a few minutes.

He sauntered across the grass, stopping in the barn's darkened doorway to search for a certain green skirt and raven black hair, but found neither. The dancers on the floor had paired into those odd corporate twosomes marked by drunken disinhibition or halting discomfort. But it was the older couple turning in slow circles that inspired Axel to lift the camera once more to his eye. He clicked off a dozen shots, capturing the azure sweep of the man's kilt and the pink of the woman's cheeks.

A red-haired man in his midthirties made his way through the spectators and stopped not far from Axel. He, too, was kilted, though unlike Axel and Reggie he wore not only a kilt but a plaid looped over his shoulder, a homespun shirt, distinctly old-fashioned leather brogues and what looked to Axel's eye like real knives in both his belt and sock sheath. The red of the tartan was nearly the same brightness and hue of his hair. Axel thought of Jemmie and chuckled.

He sidled up to the man. "You a hiree for the evening as well?"

The man spotted Axel's kilt and grinned. "Aye. You're the Canuck, I see. I'm Duncan. Nice to meet you." He held out his hand.

Axel's shoulders relaxed. He'd had enough experience breaking up bar fights to know it was easier to escort potential brawlers out before they started swinging than after.

"What's with the knives?" Axel asked, shaking his hand. Axel was three inches taller and twenty pounds heavier than Duncan, and while they'd gotten off to a friendly start, Axel's tone made it clear the answer better be one he liked.

"What? Oh, these?" Duncan looked down. "Part of my kit. But I dressed in such a hurry tonight, I forgot to replace them with the dress ones."

"Kit?"

"There's quite a business around here in the portraying of a character from this book. Ye probably don't—"

"*Kiltlander?*"

The man's face split into a huge grin. "Ye do! Having hair the color of a persimmon has always been a bit of fash, but suddenly the women love it. There's a bookstore in town that hires me quite regularly for events. The book's become a nice little industry for Bathgate. We get tourists all the time, looking at Cairnpapple and the wee kirk where Jemmie and Cara renew their vows. We even have a tearoom in town called the Jem Stone. I'm not exactly right for Jemmie"—he gazed at Axel's greater height and sighed—"but the hair seems to make up for it."

"Interesting."

"It's just a hobby, but it's a well-paying one, and it fits with some other stuff I do."

The woman in the leather blazer caught Axel's eye and purposefully raked her gaze up his legs, finishing with a suggestive wink.

"Do you have any trouble with women because of the kilt?" Axel asked, adjusting his stance primly.

"Oh, aye."

"I'm finding it a little scary tonight."

Duncan snorted. "Tonight is nothing. You need to see the women at these bookstore events." He blew a quiet whistle and leaned in closer, lowering his voice. "Sometimes they ask me to sign their paps! And the things they offer to do . . ." He trailed off, but the deep crimson stain covering his cheeks gave Axel the general flavor of what he meant. "I'm as adventurous as the next man, believe me, and at the start I was more than happy to sample the wares a time or two, but now I feel like they need to get to know me first. Me, that is, not Jemmie."

Axel laughed. "It's a problem a lot of men would dream about having."

The song ended, and Dr. Albrecht said something to Reggie, whose skin flushed. Then she wandered in Axel's direction, nearly running into him as she turned to catch another glimpse of her dance partner.

"Whoa!" Axel caught her by the shoulders. "Eyes forward, always a good bet. You cut a fine rug, there, Frau Doktor."

"I haven't danced in years," she said, dimpling. "Archie vuzn't a dancer."

"It suits you. Have you seen Ellery? Is she still on the phone?"

"She vuz on a call when I left the house. Still vurking things out, I think."

Axel chewed his lip. If she was talking to Jill, he didn't want to interrupt.

"Go to her," Dr. Albrecht said. "You might be able to help."

He looked at his watch. "I'll give her a few more minutes."

"Oh, dear!" Dr. Albrecht said, throwing her hands up suddenly. "We've forgotten the bar. Axel, can you open it back up?"

He turned to Duncan. "Would you be able to catch the first fifteen minutes or so? I want to grab a few shots of the moon. Do you mind?"

Duncan didn't, and Axel returned to the tripod out in the yard.

The clouds had passed, and the moon was high enough to spill its silver light over the treetops and cast a layer of cool incandescence over the lawn and fields beyond. He thought of the assignment he was supposed to be on and felt a twinge of guilt. He wished he hadn't promised Black he'd try to persuade Ellery, not because it hadn't worked, but because it hadn't been exactly honorable to be maneuvering behind her back. He should have remembered that, with Ellery, it was much more fun to be maneuvering face-to-face, all cards on the table.

In the middle of reattaching the camera to the tripod, something in the distance caught his eye. It was Cairn-papple, aglow in the moonlight. His fingers slowed. He wondered what the countryside looked like from up there, with the gilded blanket of Scotland, spangled with lights, stretching out below him. God, what a shot that would be. He bet he could see for twenty miles in every direction on a night like this. He glanced at his watch. The mound was no more than a quarter mile away. If he hurried . . .

He unscrewed the camera, grabbed the tripod and walked quickly toward the mound.

While he navigated the shadowed path, his mind was sorting through the photographic prospects he might have at the top of the hill and considering the ideal aperture and shutter speed.

For an instant the world seemed to weave, and he nearly stumbled.

Odd, he thought, feeling suddenly dry-mouthed. The jet lag was finally catching up to him.

He ran up the long path leading from the visitors' hut to the level ground that surrounded the much higher rise in the mound's center. He could feel his blood begin to prickle, amazed at the vista across the Lowlands.

He climbed the steps to the top of the second mound two at a time and swung in a circle, taking in the spar-kling lights that streaked across the undulating hills. He wished Ellery were there to see it, then remembered how oddly she'd acted when they'd come here earlier. The view of fields in the afternoon light had been interesting, but low-lying clouds had obscured the prospect. Now the sky was as clear as glass, and the stars twinkled like fairy lights on an ink-black canvas.

There was a thickness in his chest when he thought of Ellery and Jill. Running into Jill again—and being able to partner with Ellery to help her—had made him remember what it was like to be a part of a family he had helped create.

He leaned down to set up the legs of the tripod and again felt another wave of dizziness. He reached for one of the legs to steady himself, but the effort seemed overwhelming. An instant later he was on his back, staring at the sky. The constellations morphed into pulsing neon creatures darting about like the view inside a kaleidoscope. He groaned, confused, and closed his eyes. When he opened them again he realized time had passed because he had kicked the tripod over, which struck him as oddly funny. He had a blurry, shifting idea in the back of his mind that this had something to do with his insulin shot and that he was in trouble.

Axel struggled to move, and the next thing he knew he could feel the cool earth under his knees and the view had changed from the sky to grass; but whatever it was he'd been trying to do, the effort was too much. He fell back to the ground and darkness overtook him.

CHAPTER FORTY-NINE

Ellery's fingers flew to the end of the sentence and clicked the period key decisively.

Beautiful.

The best times in a writer's life were when passion combined with craft. That had just happened with Ellery. It was only a draft, not even a whole one, but she still felt the addictive rush of creation.

The best twenty minutes I've ever spent.

Then she remembered yesterday afternoon in the hotel room with Axel.

Okay, maybe the second best. She reread the title: "Who's on Top? Romance Readers Teach the Literary World a Lesson."

Ha! She'd nailed it.

She clicked SAVE, and launched herself from the chair. She wanted to find Axel and tell him everything: about Jill, Black, Purdy and this. Oh, how he'd laugh.

The phone rang. This time it was hers. She didn't recognize the number. "Hello?"

"I don't appreciate you telling Purdy I'm a blowhard."

Barry Steinberg. And he sounded like he'd been drinking. Jesus.

"Oh, really?" she said. "Well, I don't appreciate you telling him I'd embarrass Lark & Ives."

"I didn't tell him that."

"And I didn't tell him you were a blowhard. Sometimes people can't help the conclusions they draw."

Barry snorted. "Nice little pick Axel threw for you back at the Rosemary, the prick."

It had been, she thought. Even if she'd nearly rung his neck over it. She was so overcome with the memory of Axel's Jemmie-like heroics, she didn't quite catch what Steinberg said next.

". . . hard-core for you."

"What?"

"I *said*, you should know Axel Mackenzie's probably a little hard-core for you. Certainly if you end up at Lark & Ives. They wouldn't want their lily-white reputation besmirched by a publisher who's screwing a smack freak."

She felt like she'd been slapped. Even in his down-and-dirty days, Axel's drugs of choice had been alcohol and pills. "Axel is not a smack freak. Jesus, Barry, do your research."

He hooted. "So you don't even know? Lemme tell you what: I walked into the men's room last night and saw him sticking the needle in."

"Barry, you're an asshole. And adding alcohol only makes you a drunken one."

She hung up, trembling. She carefully separated her fury at Steinberg from her uncertainty about Axel. What he'd said had been stupid, just stupid. There was no way Axel could hide something like that from her. They'd been together almost nonstop for the last four days. She scanned her memory for anything suspicious. Yes, there were the regular trips to the men's room, but for God's sake, even she knew that wasn't really evidence.

She took a hesitant step. It was as if she had lost the power to move forward or back. Without an answer, she was stuck.

She wondered how much she'd hate herself for what she was thinking of doing.

The phone rang again. She wished the damned thing would go dead. It was Kate.

"Sorry I had to rush off."

"Yeah, no problem." Ellery grabbed Axel's duffel and swung it onto the bed.

"What happened? Did you talk to Black?"

"Oh, yeah. Fired." The zipper made a quiet *whrrr* as she drew it along the length of the nylon.

"Oh, *El*!"

His jeans, shorts and T-shirt were rolled in a ball. She scooped out the mass of fabric and dropped it on the spread. "It's all right. I can make a living without *Vanity Place*."

"Lark & Ives?"

"Mmm, maybe. If Carlton Purdy surprises me by liking the article I'm about to send him." The brown leather of the Dopp kit was smooth with age. It had been his father's. She unzipped it, fingers shaking.

"What's it on?" Kate asked.

She didn't even need to look. There it was, on the top

of everything, a used syringe. She felt something large and dry in her throat, as if she'd swallowed a rock.

"Listen, I'm sorry, but I have to hang up."

And she did, right in the middle of Kate's response.

She sunk slowly onto the bed, the Dopp kit in her hands. She didn't know what to say or think. There was a roaring maelstrom in the room, sweeping around the tight, still space that contained only her, the Dopp kit and the syringe.

She couldn't touch it. Her hand wouldn't move. All she could see were the glistening drops that remained from whatever had been loaded into the barrel, and she stared at it, confused, as if the picture didn't match the words in her head.

She could sense a presence at the door, but couldn't lift her head.

"Ellery," Dr. Albrecht said, "are you all right?"

"Yep. What's up?"

"My friend with the car service is here. I think he vuz confused. He can still take you to the airport if you need to go."

Ellery stared at the syringe. Which Axel was he? The man who ran to her aid or the one who disappeared on her?

"Ellery? Should I tell him to go?"

She zipped the Dopp kit closed and folded her hands on top of it. "Give me a minute."

CHAPTER FIFTY

Ellery hurried down the porch stairs and toward the car.

The driver smiled when he saw her and rolled down the window. "Do ye not have a bag, lass?"

"I'm sorry for the confusion," she said, bending to talk. "I'm not going. Please let me give you this for your time." She pulled a ten-pound note from her purse and handed it to him.

"Och, keep your money. I live a quarter mile from here. Tell Gertrude we'll see her at the Historical Society meeting on Monday."

"Will do."

Ellery tucked her purse under her arm. She and Axel were going to settle this once and for all. And, dammit, if she found out he was using, she was going to kick his ass from here to New York.

She hurried to the barn and scanned the heads of the crowd for Axel's, always half a foot above everyone else's. She spotted the older man with the blue kilt who'd spoken to her earlier. But before she could make her own inquiry, he said, "Have you found Axel?"

"No. Is he here?"

"No." The man frowned. "Duncan's looking for him."

"Duncan?"

"The lad at the bar. He was spelling Axel for a bit while Axel shot the moon. But it was only supposed to be fifteen minutes, and it's well nigh on forty."

Shooting the moon. That's our Axel. "Don't worry. I'm sure he got lost in what he was doing. I'll find him."

She doubled back toward the house and found his camera bag sitting unattended in the middle of the yard. The hairs on her arm rose. Axel was not known for abandoning his über-expensive equipment. She looked around for his shooting spot. The open fields were unlikely because, as she'd heard him say many times, without a foreground, the sky has no impact. She ran a few paces to see if the rental car was still in the little lot beside the house. It was, which meant he hadn't left.

She reached in her purse for her phone to call him, then realized she had both phones. And he hadn't been in the house. The place had been completely empty except for her and Dr. Albrecht.

Maybe he's looking for me in the woods?

She hurried down the path they'd followed earlier that evening, swinging into the barn one more time to look for him, to no avail. The moonlight had turned the forest into a canvas of glimmering blacks and browns, and she moved as quickly as the uneven ground would allow.

In the distance she heard voices, and when she looked

she saw a light on in the distillery and two people talking outside the entrance.

If he's over there, I'm going to kill him.

But the light clicked off, and the people got into a truck and drove away.

Dammit, Axel, where are you?

She turned in a slow circle, trying to think like him. Then she saw Cairnpapple, a silvery hump against the purple sky. That was where he was. It had to be. She could almost feel the pull.

She began toward the cairn, breaking into a jog wherever the ground was clear enough for it.

When she reached the open field, she called, "Axel! Axel!" and though she received only the echo of her voice in reply, the pull she felt grew exponentially.

She couldn't explain why his disappearance worried her. Lord knew, he'd disappeared enough in their time together for it to seem as natural as rain. But tonight for some reason it didn't seem right.

She bounded past the visitors' center and up the long rise to the area of flattish land.

"Axel?" No answer. She ran up the steeper path to the top of the mound.

The moment she crested the hill, she saw him. Her heart jumped in her chest. He lay lifeless on his stomach on the grass, his tripod and camera on the ground beside him.

"Axel!"

She didn't care what he had taken—she just wanted him to be alive.

She ran to his side and fell to her knees. "Axel," she

cried, shaking him. He was warm, thank God, but his skin was sweaty and he moaned lightly when he moved. With effort, she rolled him onto his back.

Hands shaking, she shoved two fingers in his mouth to see if he had choked on something, and he immediately pushed them out with his tongue, gagging. He was breathing, but he looked dazed—in a stupor, far beyond drunk. She pulled her hand back and slapped him.

"Jesus." He rubbed his cheek.

Her fear, so forcibly funneled through the aperture of relief, turned to anger. "Dammit, Axel! Wake up! What have you taken?"

"'nsahin," he murmured, rubbing his cheek.

"What? What did you say?"

He squeezed his eyes shut as if the light of the moon was blinding. "In-su-lin."

One word. But enough to make her arms fall to her side.

"Axel, are you diabetic?"

He grunted.

She gazed wildly around for a bag of some kind. The only thing she saw was his sporran, which was hanging loosely to his side. She leaned past his bent knees to reach it and found nothing but cash. "Where's your syringe?" she demanded.

"No syringe. Food."

Food! She scrambled to her feet and was halfway down the mound when she remembered the carob soy bars in her purse. She found one and her fingers shook so hard, she nearly dropped it trying to tear the wrapper off. She prayed this was the right thing and that he'd be able to eat it.

"Here, Axel." She put it in his hand. *"Eat."*

He took a bite, chewed and swallowed, then gagged so violently she thought he might vomit.

"Not that nasty bar," he sputtered, and she laughed despite herself. "I think I'd rather die."

"Eat it."

He ate the rest and swallowed dryly.

"I'm sorry I don't have a bottle of water."

"I'm sorry you don't have a bottle of novocaine."

He lay back on his back, knees bent, rubbing his eyes with his palms. "Oh, God, this is bad."

"Probably not so great for the folks to the south, either," she said, gazing at the haphazardly puddled kilt.

He opened one eye. "I'm dying here and that's what you're worried about?"

"'Worried' is a bit strong. 'Mortified by,' perhaps."

He laughed, then winced, shuddering convulsively. She took his hand. "Oh, Axel, is this going to fix you?"

"It's going to take more than a carob bar for that. Do you have anything else?"

"Another carob bar."

"My lucky day." He took it and ate that one as well.

"When were you diagnosed?"

"Mmm. A few months ago. Quite a thrill, graduating to needles."

"Uh-huh. And does your doctor know about your other little foibles?"

"Yeah, I'm afraid she was a no-go on those. My only excitement these days is beer—well, that and accidental overdoses of insulin." He turned on his side and laid his head on her thigh.

"I can hear the sigh of relief from the south from here."

"Jesus, I feel like shit."

She stroked his head and he closed his eyes. "Should I call an ambulance?"

"Let's give this a few minutes."

After what seemed like forever to her, he made a sound close to a purr. "Thank you."

She smiled, so relieved not to be taking him to the hospital. "What were you doing out here, anyhow?" she said. "You're supposed to be bartending."

"Have you taken a look around?"

She did, and gasped. The dots of light scattered over miles of gentle hills, some huddled in galaxy-like clumps and others as random as fireflies.

"See," he said. "I think—can't remember—if I got any shots in."

"Shall I look?" He grunted and she reached for the camera, which had fallen on its side. She turned it on and pressed the ALBUM button. "Do mediocre ones count, or do I have to be blown away?" The last thumbnail was of a moon, not a landscape, but a title in the list of albums caught her eye—*Ellery Before*.

"Mediocre?" He pulled a haughty face—an impressive feat, given the pathetic state of his person.

She opened the file and looked at the pictures. They were of her, five years ago. All had been taken in the dead of winter, judging by her clothes, which meant all had been taken in the weeks leading up to their breakup. She flushed, feeling deep shame about her anger and abruptness then.

He laid his palm on her hand, which had come to a rest over his ear. "Did you find something?"

"Yes—I mean, no. Only the moon. You didn't shoot anything here."

The pictures were close-ups of her—mugging for the camera, looking in a mirror—and she wondered why these, of all the pictures he'd taken of her in their year together, had ended up here, saved on his camera's hard drive.

Ellery Before.

She felt a frisson of sorrow go down her spine.

"I don't need you to look at the moon shots," he said. "I know for a fact those are outstanding."

"You'd think an exalted artist like yourself wouldn't be leaving the business."

"Oh, you know, new challenges. How was Jill?"

It took Ellery a moment to draw her attention from the screen. "Ah, she's good. She's strong. She has the appointment on Monday. Her girlfriend's going to go with her. We won't know anything until then."

"You should be there."

"Oh, God, I want to be. But she told me she could handle it, and I want her to know I believe her."

He nodded. "Good sister."

She closed the file and powered down the camera. Perhaps someday there would be a new file—*Ellery After*. She slipped her hand free and laid it on top of his, squeezing it tightly. He let out a long sigh.

"Is it still getting better?" she asked.

"Yes. I can feel my head clearing."

"How did it happen?" She'd heard about the things

diabetics needed to worry about, but didn't really know the specifics.

"I dosed myself for eating, then didn't eat."

She patted his shoulder with a schoolteacher's sternness. "That doesn't sound very smart."

"I had the taste of you in my mouth. I didn't want to lose it."

Her breath caught. "Oh, Axel."

"Here," he said, rolling onto an elbow. "Help me sit."

"Are you sure?" she asked, steadying his arm as he maneuvered himself up.

"I want to taste you again."

He put his hand around her waist and brought his mouth down to hers. His kiss was a cocktail of affection and longing, and it sent a wave of sparks across her nerve endings.

"Can you feel it?" he whispered. "Here. This place."

She could. The hill seemed to buzz with the magic of the night, a fine hum that set her hairs on end. "Is it us or is it something else?"

"Does it matter?" He kissed her again, and she hugged him close, weaving her fingers into his fine, thick hair. He tasted of sugar and nuts with just a hint of whiskey, like one of her mother's pralines. The hem of his kilt lay warm on her knee.

"Yes," she said, answering his question. "It does matter."

"Why?" He laughed.

"I want it to be us."

The mirth left his face, replaced by a searching vulnerability. "Then you'll have your wish."

He pressed her firmly to the cool earth. The stars hung in a halo around his head.

"I want you," he said, drawing a thumb across her collarbone.

Her heart beat like a rabbit's, pounding hard enough to muffle her hearing. Surely he felt it. "Here?"

"Do you dare?"

"Yes. I want you so much."

He stroked her cheek. "And I want you. Here, pinned under me. And there as well." He made a gesture that seemed to encompass the rest of the world.

"What do you mean?"

"You know what I mean."

And she did. Bound together, one way or another. It had been so long since she'd thought of Axel that way. She could feel the wall toppling that had separated them for the last five years. The struggle to make it happen was all-consuming—forgetting had been a matter of survival—and the tremor in her voice was evidence of it.

"I want it, Axel. I do. But how? I mean, my God . . ."

So much hurt. So much to forgive. On his part as much as hers. They would be starting again wounded and wary. It was the worst possible position from which to try to salvage a relationship.

"Stop worrying about what comes next. Let's only think of now."

His hand had found her hip, and she could feel the primitive stirrings begin. It was this damned hill. The reverberations of a millennium's worth of midnight joinings hummed in the air. They shook her bones and loosened her desires. Whatever had happened here still carried its power. Axel's hand tightened slowly, and she arched without thinking.

Even in the dark, she could see the rise at the corner of his mouth.

He resettled his weight along her side and she turned to meet him, hip to hip. She let her hand run down his thigh, to the end of the kilt. His skin was warm and the hairs there brushed her palm. Then she followed the trail back, this time under the wool, to his smooth, flexing buttock, answering the question that had burned in her thoughts since the moment she'd seen him in that bathroom.

"A true Scot," she said, impressed.

"You should see my tip jar."

She laughed. She could feel her breaths coming faster and knew that, soon, the time for words would be over. She brushed a lock from his forehead. His hair smelled of apples. "I'm so sorry, Axel."

He caught her hand and kissed it. "I wish I had been there when you needed me."

Unspoken promises floated in the air like seeds from a dandelion. *Stop worrying about what comes next. Let's only think of now.*

Did Axel have it right? Could it be that she'd spent all this time fighting his philosophy of life, only to find out that he'd actually known what he was talking about? She let out an amused exhalation. It would be just one more thing she'd have learned from him.

He ran his thumb under her sweater, just skirting the edge of her aureole. The touch tightened both nipples and elicited a satisfied mewl of approval from their owner. Perhaps she'd taught him a thing or two as well.

She caught him by the neck brought his mouth to hers,

teasing him with her tongue. He opened her sweater, grinning when he saw what the demure angora had hidden.

He loosened the halter straps with a practiced hand.

"You know this isn't how I would dress on my own," she said.

"Do I?"

"Yes."

"Okay, I do. But I like it anyhow."

He brushed away the fabric and caught a nipple between his thumb and forefinger, drawing it into a rosy peak. "Don't get me wrong: I'm happy to undress you out of anything. But I have particularly fond memories of a pair of jeans and a button-down shirt that suited you very well."

She thought of that night in the Warhol. Oh, what a *good* night it had been.

"This dress, on the other hand, looks like it's for a woman who wants the boots put to her in plain sight of every Scot between Edinburgh and Glasgow."

She stretched her legs till her feet were touching his and was reminded he would, in fact, be putting actual boots to her. "It's night. No one can see," she said, and he laughed.

"And a good thing." He lifted the handfuls of tulle and disappeared under the skirt.

She swallowed a gasp as he twisted her panties out of the way and applied his mouth to her bud. He was world-class at this, and time had only polished his skills. She damned the years she'd let him waste this gift on others. She anchored herself in the grass and shifted her weight, trying to govern the fire that danced between her legs.

"Be still."

But the rising heat made that impossible. He grabbed her wrists and pulled them under her hips, rocking her open to him. The tulle sizzled like butter on a hot skillet.

"This isn't fair," she said.

The glorious ministrations halted. "Then answer."

"Answer? Answer what?"

"The question."

His question. "Say it again."

"I want you. Will you have me?"

"Yes."

"Here?"

"Yes."

"And there? Forever?"

"Yes."

The actions that followed set her legs to trembling. Her feet found purchase on his granite shoulders.

The heat was coming in waves, like blasts from a furnace, and the stars overhead seemed to pulse and twinkle. She could smell the loamy earth under them and the faint smoke of a fire in the distance. He released her hands and clasped her hips.

"Oh, oh, oh." The waves were growing stronger.

Suddenly, she wanted Axel beside her, to look in his eyes, to know his thoughts.

"No, come," she said, scrabbling to an elbow and tugging at his shirt. "Come here."

He rose obediently, wiping his mouth on his palm.

"Be with me," she said. "In my arms."

He rose to his knees. She could see the pulse beating in his throat. With the cool blue moonlight framing his dark locks and flooding over his considerable shoulders, he looked like an ancient Norse god.

She felt very small, and very underdressed.

The kilt was heavy, but it was no match for the object straining against it. He crawled over her, alternately kissing and tasting his way from her navel to her neck, settling himself at last on top of her.

He married his mouth to hers, and she tasted his smoky nectar.

"Mmm," she moaned.

"Mmm," he agreed.

He brought his palm between her legs and kneaded the mound there.

"Oh, Axel."

"We are going to have to improvise," he said, introducing his thumb slowly.

"Oh. Oh. Why?"

"I don't have a condom." The careful circles he was drawing grew smaller and faster. "And I suspect you don't have one, either."

She didn't, and the sultry movements of his hand quickened.

"No," she said. "No." She wanted him thick inside her.

"Don't worry, Pittsburgh," he said, his breath warm in her ear. "I know how to take care of you."

She shivered. Oh, God, he did.

"No," she said again. "No. In me."

"We can't—"

"We can."

He caught her chin and turned her toward him so he could search her face.

She thought about her fear and anger, and how useless it had all been in the end. But she had never not wanted him, and she had never not wanted a child of theirs.

"I want a child with you," she said. "Again."

He closed his eyes, face flushed with emotion, and she took his hand and held it against her cheek.

He rolled to his knees, gazing at her in fear and desire. In his eyes she saw every warrior, every berserker, who had fornicated on this hill, spilling his seed to strengthen the harvest or claim a battle's spoils. He dug under his kilt, grabbed his cock and bent over her. With a grunt he entered her, and she inhaled sharply.

He was large, as large a man as she had ever known, and he filled her so completely, she thought she might burst.

Abandoning finesse, he began to pound the sensitive flesh. The waves, which he had already risen to whitecaps, soared higher. She clutched his forearms, his tan, taut muscles flexing with each thrust. It was as if he were battering down the last vestige of concealment between them.

"Oh, oh, oh." She shook with the force of it, trying to catch a breath. But there was more to it than the physical pleasure: There was a lightness in her she hadn't felt in so long. She wrapped her arms around his like a seedling's roots, as if she could extract the nourishing joy and give it back to him.

He rocked back on his heels and hooked her knees. With a husky moan he slipped even deeper inside. He was pummeling her womb, planting a future for them with a life-or-death fervor, and every movement seesawed her on the edge of searing pleasure.

"Here," he said, willing her to respond.

"And there. And *there*. Damn you."

She fretted and squirmed, but he held her tight. Desperate, she wrapped her legs around his buttocks and arched, bringing her breasts against his chest and crying out softly.

A look of shock came over his face, as if the end was overtaking him. She brought herself in close and he reared back, riding her for half a dozen masterful strokes until the surge took her and smashed her into a thousand pieces against an endless, pleasuring shore. At the same moment he jerked, filling her with his seed. He groaned and shook until he collapsed beside her.

"It's this hill," he said, rubbing his cheek blindly. "I have never ravaged a woman like that. Forgive me."

"Forgive you?" She'd probably be numb for days, but an incomparable warmth suffused her, as if she'd been steeped in an ancient elixir. "Demand that you repeat it, perhaps. Not forgive you."

"Oh my God, my balls feel like they've been smacked with a cricket bat."

Laughing, she settled against his shoulder, tucking her head under his chin. She liked the feel of his strong, even breaths after sex and the earthy scent of his skin.

"I have some good news for you," she said. "I can go with you to Pittsburgh—at least for a few weeks."

He laughed, a short, ironic laugh and shook his head. "I have some bad news for you: There's no Pittsburgh to go to."

"What?"

"I lost the brewery. Outbid. Found out today."

"Oh, Axel." The only thing worse than the thought of him leaving New York was the thought of him leaving his dreams behind. "I'm so sorry."

"And how is it that you can go to Pittsburgh?" He raised himself up on an elbow and looked at her, curious.

"Fired. Black is furious about the story I sent him. I don't think he's too happy with you, either."

A look of shame crossed his face. "I have something I have to tell you—"

"I know."

"You *do*?"

"About the deal you cut with Black," she said. "I know. Kate found out." Ellery gave him a gimlet eye. "Not very gentlemanly."

"Sort of a theme this week."

"And definitely not a smart bet." She pushed his chin gently. "As if someone would know better than me what I should write."

"It was stupid. What can I say?"

"I know what works best on paper. No one should mess with that."

"Right. That would be like giving art direction to a photographer."

"It was better in landscape."

He laughed and drew her closer. "You're right about your writing. It's so damn good. You always surprise me."

"Oh, Axel," she said, giddy, "sometimes I even surprise myself."

"Please, don't say you mean that snoozefest I looked at earlier. There are some surprises that should be avoided."

"Nope," she said, grinning. "I rewrote it! I ended up writing a paean to romances, an abso-freakin' valentine—"

She clapped a hand over her mouth, realizing what she had just admitted to.

"Pardon me?" He cupped a hand behind his ear.

She shook her head, refusing to say another word.

"Ha!" he cried, pumping a fist in the air. "I did it!"

"After the interlude we just had, *that's* what you're going to crow about?"

"That?" he said with a deprecating wave. "That sort of sleight of hand I can whip up anytime. Reversing the direction of the USS *Ellery Sharpe*? Now, *that's* an accomplishment."

She laughed. It felt so good lying next to him. She ran a hand under his sweater, warming herself against the broad expanse of muscle.

"I've got a pocket full of money, Pittsburgh. Name your dream. I can definitely keep you entertained for a month, at least until the Lark & Ives thing starts."

"Well, I've always wanted to see the Highlands."

He moaned.

"I could always do a travel story."

"You can't sell a travel story without pic— Oh, boy, I really walked into that one. Would I get paid?"

"What's money to a guy like you?"

"Well, there's this little thing called rent. . . ."

"I'm not going to charge you rent. I mean, assuming the services-in-lieu-of-cash thing continues."

"A kept man?" He scratched his chin, considering. "I like it."

"Well, you wouldn't forever," she said, turning toward him. "I know that much about you. But I'm happy to take advantage of it as long as you do. Besides, we need to find you a brewery."

"Well, there's this thing I can set up in your spare bedroom—"

"Aaarrrgh." She covered her ears. "What have I started?"

"What *have* you started?"

He laid a hand on her cheek, and the warm green of his eyes told her that whatever it was, he loved it too.

"I don't know," she admitted, "but it feels wonderful. No one will believe it."

He snorted. "If they know me, they will."

"That confident of your abilities, eh?" She gave him a dubious look.

He shrugged. "I got the girl. I got the article."

"And the brewery?"

"Give me time. I'm on a streak."

CHAPTER FIFTY-ONE

Dining Room, Thistle Bed & Breakfast

Dr. Albrecht pulled up sharply, nearly spilling the contents of the breakfast tray onto the floor. "You're still vairing your kilt?"

Axel, pink from a just-completed shower, cleared his throat uncomfortably. "Um. Writer request."

Ellery, who had been allowed to sleep in after a long and rather glorious night and was now eyeing a crossword puzzle and eagerly awaiting the coffee on Dr. Albrecht's tray, flushed. "I need some local color."

"Mm-hm." Dr. Albrecht placed the tray on the table and poured the coffee for her guests.

"Nothing for you?" Ellery asked.

Dr. Albrecht shook her head, eyes sparkling. "I've been up for a vhile."

Another set of steps sounded on the stairs. Ellery turned and nearly dropped her cup. The white-haired gentleman from the night before ambled down, smiling happily and tucking his shirt into the top of his kilt.

"Ah," he said, spotting Axel and lunging for a piece of

toast. "I see we find ourselves in the same predicament, laddie."

"Not quite, Reggie," Dr. Albrecht said. "Axel has other clothes upstairs."

Reggie's brow rose puckishly. "I wasn't talking about the kilt."

This time both women flushed, and Axel and Reggie chuckled.

"Oh, my," Ellery said and took a fortifying sip of coffee. Dr. Albrecht hurried off to the kitchen.

Axel said, "Ellery, I'd like you to meet Reggie Sinclair. He owns the distillery next door. Reggie, this is Ellery Sharpe. She's a literary critic and writer."

Reggie shook her hand.

At that moment a man in a burnt-orange shirt that set off the singular color of his hair bounded through the front door. He gazed at the breakfasters, who were shifting in their seats and trying to keep from smiling. "What? What's going on?"

"Nothing important, Duncan," Axel said. "Just a crossword clue that got the best of us."

"Oh, what?"

Axel reached for the cream, momentarily stymied. "A seven letter word for unlicensed."

Duncan pursed his lips thoughtfully. "'Illicit'?"

Axel pointed at him gratefully. "That would be it. Thank you."

Ellery bit her lip to stifle laughter and stared deep into her cup.

"Care to join us?" Reggie asked, apparently already feeling host-like.

"Oh, no, thank you. I've already eaten. I'm here to help Dr. A. with her bathroom."

"Oh," Ellery said. "Are you a plumber?"

"A bond trader, actually. But I grew up in a house full of leaky toilets."

"A bond trader and a Jemmie Forster impersonator?" Axel said. "Interesting mix."

"A Jemmie Forster impersonator?" Ellery's head swung around hard enough to make her cup rattle in its saucer.

"Settle down, Pittsburgh," Axel said. "You're taken."

Ellery could definitely see the similarity to the image of Jemmie in her head, especially in the wide blue eyes and angled features.

"Och," Duncan said self-deprecatingly, "just a way to help out my hometown. But I'm afraid they're going to have to find another Jemmie soon."

"Oh?"

"My firm's transferring me to the New York office. Not as much call for a man in a kilt there, I should think."

"Oh, you'd be surprised," Ellery said, and Axel gave her a kick under the table.

"Who vants a fry-up?" Dr. Albrecht said, returning from the kitchen with an empty skillet in her hand. Reggie, Axel and Ellery all raised their hands eagerly.

"I see," the sociologist said, smiling. "Must be something in the air."

Duncan frowned again. "Reggie told me you two live in New York. I'm hoping for a local guide when I arrive. Perhaps someone who can introduce me to some people to do things with?"

While either she or Axel could easily serve as his guide,

Ellery supposed the latter part of the request was directed toward her, as she felt certain the "people" in question were to be of the female persuasion.

Axel, who clearly had understood Duncan's request, looked at Ellery.

"I'd be happy to show you around," she said, and immediately began to run through an inventory of single friends in her head. The harder job would be limiting the list to a manageable number. Who, after all, *wouldn't* be interested in a Scottish bond trader who doubled as a romance hero?

Duncan nodded his thanks and followed Dr. Albrecht through the swinging door into the kitchen.

Reggie snagged the pot of jam. "Axel, have you talked to the lass yet?"

"Um, no," he said significantly and fell into a deep observation of his toast.

Since flustered was an unusual state for Axel, Ellery turned her full attention to him.

"Oh, dear," Reggie said. "Sorry, lad."

"It's all right." Axel put his napkin on the table and said to her, "Let's go for a walk, okay?"

Ellery's stomach began to churn. "What? What is it?"

He led her from the table and out the front door, stopping to grab his coat from the rack in the hall. "It's good. I promise. Don't worry."

Good? Good for Axel could mean anything from a chance to ride with the Hell's Angels to a Pulitzer nomination. But the news Ellery most feared was the offer of a position in a distillery in Scotland.

He led her into a small garden behind the garage. The

annuals were mostly gone, but there were still dried blue mopheads on the hydrangeas and a patch of small sunflowers upon whose dark florets several orange-breasted birds stood to feed. A large black cat slumbered peacefully at one end of a weathered bench, warming in the sun, and rather than tip him out, Axel sat at the other end and pulled Ellery onto his lap.

"Oh, I don't like this," she said, burying her head against his neck, waiting.

"Even with the kilt? Well, that certainly doesn't do much for the old ego." He threw the jacket over her shoulders and hugged her close. The cat opened a green eye, observed the disturbers of his peace, then shut it again, burying his nose deeper into his tail.

"I mean the news," she said.

"I told you it was good—well, at least not bad. I ran into Reggie on my run this morning; he was quite an athlete in his day, it seems. He's offered me a job."

"Oh, I knew it."

"Hang on." He lifted her chin and looked into her eyes. "I haven't said yes."

"At his distillery, right? I knew you'd like that place."

"Actually, the job is partner. In Brendan's brewery."

She threw her arms around him. "Oh, Axel! That's wonderful! But how?"

"Reggie's an investor. And he loves beer. He's willing to take a share and let me run it. He's authorized me to call Brendan today and offer him more money."

"Oh my God! That's fantastic!"

"And he wants to invest—I mean, really invest. And not to go national but to give me the resources I need to do things right, to make a name for the beer. He said he wants a winner."

"Oh, Axel." She hugged him again, then stopped. "But why haven't you said yes?"

Axel took her hands in his. "I'm not sure it would make me as happy as I think."

"But your dream is to brew beer."

"Look, I'm old enough to know what will make me happy and what won't. That's part of what comes from having done all the stuff I've done. And while owning my own brewery would make me happy, I don't think I want to do it if it means leaving you."

"But—"

He held up a hand. "I can be happy anywhere, Pittsburgh. I don't need much. You're younger and ambitious. And, God, you're so smart. I'd die if I stood in the way of that."

She had thought the task would be insurmountable, like counting the grains of sand in a beach, and that it would literally destroy her to even try; but she was stunned to discover that imagining doing nothing more than living a life shared with Axel, Jill and a child filled her with a boundless joy.

Tears welled in her eyes.

"Now, come on, eh? I told you it's no big deal." He lifted the hem of his kilt to her cheek to dry it, and Ellery laughed while she was crying.

"Oh, Axel, it *is* a big deal. For me, at least." She started to cry harder. Could she even say it? She had to. It was the brass ring.

"Axel, I want us to be together—you and Jill and I. As

a family. At Christmas, for my birthday, sitting around the breakfast table."

"I know I can afford a table."

She laughed again and cried even harder. "And I would love, love, love to think of you running Brendan's brewery." She clung to his sweater like a child and daubed at her nose with her wrist.

"So, what are we saying here?" He leaned forward infinitesimally, buoyed, she thought, by a hope as overpowering as hers.

"I'm saying we could be a family in Pittsburgh."

He looked at her, eyes a clear green. "Really?"

"It's like you said. Sometimes you just have to let your heart write the epilogue."

"Yes!" he cried, jumping to his feet with her in his arms. "Yes!"

He swung her in a happy circle and sat back down. The cat, evidently tiring of the interruption, slipped off the bench and ambled away.

"Wait a second." Axel gave her a steely look. "What about a job?"

"You think I need to work?"

"I think I need to eat."

She laughed. "Well, we'll see what Carlton says about the new article I wrote."

"Do you think he'll let you live in Pittsburgh?"

"Nope. Not for the publisher's job. But maybe he'll have something else for me. Or maybe someone else will. And, if not, there's always freelancing."

"Yeah, maybe Barry Steinberg could toss something your way."

She whooped. "Yeah, like a bomb."

"Well, well, well," he said after a long moment, smiling happily, "Ellery Sharpe as my brew maid. Who knew what a change twenty-four hours could bring?"

"Hang on there," she said. "That wasn't part of the plan."

The corner of his mouth lifted. "Was part of mine. Low-cut top. Dirndl skirt. Mugs of beer. Just like the girl on the St. Pauli Girl label."

"Hm. Isn't she a blonde?"

"I'm flexible."

Indeed, you are, she thought, recalling a few of his moves from the night before.

Axel grinned, reading her mind as always, and slipped a hand between her knees.

"What I don't get," she said, "though I'm happy for, is why Reggie would want to invest in you. I mean, nothing personal, but he's only just met you, right?"

"Oh, that." Axel waved away the oddness. "I may have had a small hand in bringing him and Dr. Albrecht together."

Ellery shook her head, confused. "Do you mean to say last night was their first night together?"

"That's about the sum of it, yes."

She blinked. Axel as Cupid? What other surprises did he have up his kilt?

"What's that smile for?" he demanded.

"I, uh, didn't know you had matchmaker tendencies."

"Well, I don't, usually. But the way he was making cow eyes at her . . ." He shook his head. "It was worse than you at the Warhol that night."

She gasped and poked him while he tried to defend himself. "*You* were the one who couldn't stop looking."

"Uncle! Uncle!"

"Admit it!"

"Yes. I wanted you, Pittsburgh. Wanted you bad."

She settled back against him and made a happy sigh. "I always wanted a nickname, you know. They're the coolest things."

"Not always," he said. "Which reminds me. I texted my sister last night to tell her about us. Here's what she said." He reached into his sweater and pulled his phone out of his T-shirt pocket. " 'YOU'RE THE LUCKIEST MAN ON EARTH,' " he read.

"Let me see." She grabbed the phone excitedly from his hand.

"No!"

" 'YOU'RE THE LUCKIEST MAN ON EARTH, *BONER*'?" She squawked with delight.

Axel buried his face in his hand. "I had an unhappy childhood."

"I'll bet." Ellery's eyes caught the message from his sister that followed: *"Don't screw it up a second time."*

"Axel," she said softly, "you didn't screw it up."

"I helped," he said, retrieving the phone. "And let's have that be the end of looking backward, eh?"

She curled against him, and for a long moment neither said anything. She sighed. "Everything's perfect—except for Jill."

"She'll be okay. No matter what."

"They say a third of pregnancies this early just end with your period."

He squeezed her gently. "She'll be okay. We'll be there for her."

Ellery's phone buzzed with an incoming e-mail and she opened her in-box in case it was from Jill. "Oh my God."

"What?"

"Black sent me a note." She brushed at the screen. "And so did Carlton Purdy!" She laughed.

"About?"

"I sent them each the revised draft."

"You did?"

"Yeah, last night. I think I just wanted to knock the wind out of both of their sails."

"And?"

"Well, Black wants to publish it."

"Damn. Maybe I'll actually get paid."

"And," she said with a happy gleam in her eye, thumbing the keys with determination, "I am telling him to fuck off."

"Or maybe not."

"He did fire me, you know."

Axel gave her a look. "Okay, fine." She backspaced over what she'd typed. "I'll tell him I'll consider it."

"There you go. And Carlton Purdy?"

"He does *not* want to publish it. No surprise there. But he's still willing to present me to the board. He likes my chutzpah."

Axel hesitated. His eyes were greener than Dr. Albrecht's pea soup. "It's a hell of a place, Lark & Ives. You'd be fabulous."

"Are you withdrawing your proposal?"

"Proposal!" His brows shot up. "I remember a table."

"Table, ring, it's all the same thing. No, I am not taking Purdy's offer. I want the flexibility to be in Pittsburgh."

"Tell him that."

"I'm almost tempted to say 'Fuck you' to him too."

"You know, there's another way to get that message across. It's called a killer negotiation."

She laughed. "Fine." She began typing again. "How about 'Let's talk. I'm not really sure I belong at L&I.'"

"Bingo."

She hit SEND and leaned in closer. They kissed long and slow, and every instant made her want to drag Axel right back to Cairnpapple. Who knew what the vibes might be like in the first morning light?

He reached under her shirt and cupped her breasts.

"Axel."

"What?" he said innocently, and Ellery, mindful of the neighbors, brought the coat over her head as a shield.

"Yes, I believe I like your arms up like that." He slipped his hands over her breasts.

"You know, Dr. Albrecht said one of the first things you learn in sociology is that the only conclusions you can draw must be based on observable, measurable data."

"And?"

"And I'm feeling something pretty measurable at this point." She shifted on his lap.

He turned her so she was straddling him. "But it's the observable part I wonder about. Perhaps if you . . ." He brought his mouth to her ear and vividly described the scientific method he had in mind.

"Axel!" But the thought of that sun-drenched hill stuck

in her head. "Say, do you know what you've never pho-tographed?"

"Yes," he said definitively, and lifted the shirt up.

The sound of the garden gate squeaking jerked them apart. Axel pulled down her shirt and said, "Don't you dare get off my lap."

"Oh, Jesus!" Duncan said as he popped into view. "Sorry. I didn't—" He turned on his heel.

"It's all right," Ellery said.

"Don't get up," Axel repeated.

"We were just, um, talking."

"Kissing," Axel said honestly. "But we were done."

She poked him.

A red-faced Duncan said, "Dr. A. says your breakfasts are ready. God, sorry." He shook his head. "I always seem to be stepping in it. Two weeks ago I barged in on a cap-tain and a grieving widow at the Battle of Neville's Cross. Let me tell you, she went from grieving to pissed off in a bloody damned hurry."

Axel looked at Ellery.

" 'The Battle of Neville's Cross'?"

"Oh, aye. I'm a war reenactor. My second love—after bonds, of course. That's how I came to have the kit. Made the Jemmie thing a piece of cake."

Axel's look turned to astonishment, and Ellery's mouth fell open. "Well," she said, "have I got a guide for you when you get to New York."

"Och, I like the sound of that," he said. "But let me leave you to your . . . Oh, Christ, let me just leave, period. I'll tell Dr. A. you're coming. Ack! On your way." With that, he disappeared, the gate squeaking in his wake.

"That'll teach us," Axel said.

"Speak for yourself. I rather liked it."

He shook his head. "Women scare me."

"Really? After what you just whispered in my ear? It was as if Jemmie Forster himself had brought me out here."

"I don't need Jemmie Forster's inspiration." He gave her a blistering kiss.

"Wow."

"I hope we're done with Jemmie Forster now."

"Leaving him where he belongs, eh? Between the covers. Of a book! Of a book!" she added when he lunged at her.

"Hm. Well, at least I have the name of my first ale," he said, helping her to her feet.

"What?"

"Well, I was considering 'Musket Ball' in a series of beers commemorating the French and Indian War. But I think I prefer 'Ruby Muses.'"

"Really?" She gave him a long look.

"Oh, yeah. Perfect on the tongue."

"Axel."

"C'mon. Let's get into breakfast. I'm eager to get Cairnpapple and shoot that thing I've never shot before. God, what a beer label it would make."

She laughed and put her arm around him. "I'll never get tired of you."

"We'll see about that. Never is a long time."

She stretched on her toes and kissed him. "The longest, I hope."

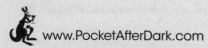